Th

Kevin Ashman lives in South Wales with his wife and dog and has been writing for eight years.

Mainly concentrating on historical fiction books, especially in the Roman and Medieval eras, he found significant success with the India Summers Mysteries, a series of books about a librarian and her Special Forces partner, who delve deep into history to solve modern-day problems.

Also by K. M. Ashman

The India Summers Mysteries

The Vestal Conspiracy
The Treasures of Suleiman
The Mummies of the Reich
The Tomb Builders

The Roman Chronicles

Roman – The Fall of Britannia
Roman II – The Rise of Caratacus
Roman III – The Wrath of Boudicca

The Medieval Sagas

Medieval – Blood of the Cross
Medieval II – In Shadows of Kings
Medieval III – Sword of Liberty
Medieval IV – Ring of Steel

The Road to Hastings

The Challenges of a King
The Promises of a King

The PROMISES of a KING

K. M. ASHMAN

CANELO

First published in the United Kingdom in 2022 by

Canelo
Unit 9, 5th Floor
Cargo Works, 1–2 Hatfields
London, SE1 9PG
United Kingdom

Print ISBN 978 1 80032 366 7
Ebook ISBN 978 1 80032 365 0

Look for more great books at www.canelo.co

Printed and bound in Great Britain by Clays Ltd, Elcograf S.p.A.

1

Character List

Anglo-Saxon

Edward the Confessor	King of England
Ealdgyth of Wessex	Queen consort

Nobles

Godwin	Earl of Wessex
Gytha Thorkelsdóttir	Godwin's wife
Harold Godwinson	Earl of East Anglia
Tostig Godwinson	Son of Godwin
Gyrth Godwinson	Son of Godwin
Leofwine Godwinson	Son of Godwin
Edyth Swanneck	Harold's wife
Aelfgar	Earl of Mercia
Edwin	Son of Aelfgar
Morcar	Son of Aelfgar
Alditha	Daughter of Aelfgar
Gruffydd ap Llewelyn	King of Gwynedd
Rhydderch of Gwent	King of Gwent and Deheubarth

Clergy

Archbishop Stigand   Archbishop of Canterbury

Robert of Jumièges   Norman bishop

Norman

William the Bastard   Duke of Normandy

Alan the Red   Lord of Richemont

Other characters

Guy of Ponthieu   Count of Ponthieu

Owen of Hereford   Harold's second-in-command

Thegn Dunstan   Instigator of the rebellion

Thegn Gamelbearn   Instigator of the rebellion

Prologue

Earl Godwin of Wessex and his wife, Gytha Thorkelsdóttir, sat in the main hall of King Edward's residence in Winchester, attending a feast to celebrate Bishop Stigand's elevation to the position of the Archbishop of Canterbury.

The winter had been hard for the Godwin family, for despite their full return to prominence, there had still been no news of Wulfnorth and Hakon, the two children that had been abducted by the Norman bishop, Robert of Jumièges the previous year, and the earl was keen for the weather to break, so he could continue his search in Normandy.

Despite this, the feast was a merry occasion with many prominent earls and lords in attendance, and, despite their worry, both Godwin and Gytha were starting to enjoy themselves.

The evening was drawing to a close when Godwin saw one of the royal servants whispering in Edward's ear and pointing towards him. The king glanced in his direction before dismissing the servant and summoning Godwin to approach.

'Ealdgyth,' said the king, turning to his queen, 'would you allow your father to sit beside me for a moment? I have important news he should hear.'

'Is it about my brother and nephew?' asked Ealdgyth, a look of fear on her face. 'Have they been hurt?'

'No, but the matter is no less grave. Let me speak to your father first, and then I will share the news with you.'

'Of course,' said Ealdgyth and stood up as her father approached.

'Your grace,' said Godwin, approaching the king, 'you summoned me?'

'I did,' said the king. 'Please sit.'

Godwin sat beside the king and stared at Edward with concern.

'Earl Godwin,' said Edward, 'I have just become aware of some very unpleasant news. Yesterday, a ship arrived from France. On that ship was a man called Owen of Hereford. I believe you know him?'

'I do,' said Godwin, 'he is one of my son's huscarls. He joined Sweyn on his pilgrimage to Jerusalem last year. How is he back so soon?'

'This man,' continued the king, 'is in a terrible state. Apparently, he and your son reached Jerusalem unharmed but were attacked by brigands in a place called Lycia on their return journey. There is no easy way to say this, but if what this man is saying is true, then your son did not make it. Earl Sweyn was murdered, Earl Godwin. Your son is dead.'

For a few moments, Godwin looked at the king, hardly able to take in the news. Slowly he turned away and stared across at his wife on one of the side tables. His heart raced, and he felt sick as the blood rushed to his head. Slowly he got to his feet, knowing he had to talk to her. He stumbled backwards, sending his chair crashing to the floor, and all heads turned to see the ashen look upon his face. He looked around desperately, realising something was not right. The room looked hazy, and he spun towards his wife, a look of fear etched upon his face. He tried to call out, but the words would not come, and he knew something was desperately wrong.

Gytha placed her goblet on the table and returned her husband's stare.

'Godwin?' she said, getting to her feet. 'What ails you?'

Those around her fell quiet as they realised what was happening.

'Godwin,' she said louder, 'what is the matter? Answer me.'

Godwin tried to respond, but again, the words would not come.

'Earl Godwin,' said the king at his side, 'what ails you? Do you need anything?'

Again there was no response, and as Gytha screamed his name from the other side of the hall, Godwin of Wessex collapsed against the table, sending food and utensils flying across the hall.

'Call the physicians,' roared the king, dragging away the chairs. 'Archbishop Stigand, attend me.'

As the room burst into frantic activity, the earl looked up and, moments later, saw his terrified wife staring back down at him. Her voice echoed dimly, as if a hundred paces away in a fog-filled forest, calling his name, yet strangely, he was in no pain. A calmness befell him, and for the first time, he realised he was probably dying. The awareness did not scare him, for he knew all men died, but the thought of leaving his wife alone filled him with sadness and regret, and with that thought swimming around his mind, Godwin of Wessex slipped into unconsciousness.

–

A few days later, in the king's bedchamber, Godwin lay in the bed, hardly able to move or communicate. Since the feast, he had been surrounded by physicians, but despite employing every remedy they knew, nothing had worked, and it was obvious he was dying.

Around the bed stood Gytha and their sons, Harold, Tostig, Gyrth and Leofwine, along with Queen Ealdgyth and Harold's wife, Edyth Swanneck. Archbishop Stigand stood beside the bed, administering the Last Rites, but just as they thought the end was nigh, Gytha gasped as she felt her husband squeeze her hand.

'Godwin,' she said quietly with tears rolling down her face. 'I am here, my love.'

'*Gytha*,' whispered Godwin, '*I have loved you more than life itself.*'

'And I have loved you,' whispered Gytha, smoothing her husband's hair from his eyes. 'God placed you here with a purpose, my lord, and you have served him and your family far better than even he could have imagined.'

'Is Harold here?' asked Godwin, his voice hardly audible.

'I am,' said Harold, pushing forward to his father's bedside. 'We all are.'

'There are things left undone,' whispered Godwin, 'and I leave them to you to finish.'

'Anything,' replied Harold, struggling to control his own emotions.

'You have to find them,' said Godwin, his voice fading away, 'promise me you will bring the boys home.'

'I swear I will do all that I can,' said Harold as his own tears started to flow. 'Goodbye, Father.'

Godwin's hand finally relaxed in his wife's grasp, and as Gytha Thorkelsdóttir let out a soul-destroying wail of grief, the light of life left Godwin's eyes.

Part One

Chapter One

London, March, AD 1055

Harold Godwinson and his brother, Tostig, sat in a small audience chamber deep in the heart of Westminster Palace. Both men had been summoned from their earldoms in Wessex and East Anglia respectively to attend a royal council with the king, but had taken the opportunity to speak to their sister in private before the meeting.

Ealdgyth was King Edward's wife and consequently the Queen of England, but when they were alone, all three siblings treated each other as just family with none of the trappings of royal protocol.

'Surely you must know something,' said Tostig.

'He shares very little with me when it comes to matters of court,' said Ealdgyth. 'I know as much as you.'

'The fact that he has summoned all the earls means it is a matter of utmost importance,' said Harold.

'Well, I for one, could do without this,' said Tostig. 'Doesn't he realise we have better things to do than ride back and forth from London?'

'He is the king, Tostig,' said Harold, 'and we are his subjects. He can do whatever he wants to do.'

'All I am saying,' continued Tostig, 'is that since Father died, it seems we are summoned here every month or so, and for what? To listen to his edicts and then ride back whence we came. He could achieve the same outcome by just sending us the documents outlining his decisions. At least that way, we would cut out all this travelling.'

'It sounds like you do not enjoy your position of influence in the king's court,' said Ealdgyth.

'What position of influence?' said Tostig. 'I am a minor earl at most and have never been invited to speak at these councils. What is more, when Aelfgar of Mercia receives the Earldom of Northumbria, as no doubt he will, I suspect my standing will be even more diminished.'

'You don't know that,' said Harold, 'so let us just see what happens before jumping to conclusions. Anyway, we have to go.'

The two men got to their feet and nodded towards their sister, a recognition of her station. 'Thank you, my queen,' said Harold, 'perhaps we can share some wine before we leave tonight.'

'That would be nice,' said Ealdgyth, 'now go and see what he wants.'

The two men left the room and joined the slow-moving row of clergy and nobles as they filed down the corridor and into the audience chamber.

The room was empty of chairs apart from the royal throne, so over a hundred men found a place to stand on either side of the aisle. Amongst them were many clergymen of various positions, including Bishop Ealdred of Worcester and, near the front, Stigand of Norwich, the Archbishop of Canterbury and close friend to the Godwin family.

Harold looked around and saw most of the other noble houses were also represented. Earl Leofric of Mercia and his son Aelfgar looked particularly enthusiastic and spent a lot of time talking quietly amongst themselves and other noblemen who had accompanied them on the journey.

Harold had no doubt about what enthused them. It was no secret that Aelfgar was one of the most senior nobles in the north of England and, as such, had a strong claim on the Earldom of Northumbria, currently vacant following the death of Earl Siward.

Once the last of the attendees entered the room, the giant doors closed, and everyone fell silent, anticipating the king's arrival.

Several minutes later, the far doors opened, and King Edward appeared, joined a few paces behind by Ealdgyth. They walked up to the dais and, after a quick acknowledgement of the large audience, took their seats.

'My lords,' started Edward, 'and honoured guests. I have summoned you here today to discuss matters of grave importance. As you are aware, a few weeks ago, Earl Siward of Northumbria was accepted into God's care after a long and distinguished life. His service to me and to the Crown of England has always been exemplary, particularly so these past few months against the Scots.'

A murmur of approval and agreement rippled around the room. Siward had been a powerful and popular man, and he was a great loss to England.

'His feats of bravery were second to none,' continued the king, 'and it is due to him and him alone that Macbeth was driven back on the day of the Seven Sleepers. Unfortunately, he lost many men that day, including his son, Osbjorn, and his nephew and namesake, Siward. They gave their lives in loyal service and for a great cause, but their untimely deaths, followed by the death of the earl himself, left me with a dilemma that has been difficult to resolve: who will take up his mantle. I make no apologies for my lengthy deliberations, for the decision has to be right, not just for Northumbria, but for England.' He paused and looked around the room, his eyes finally settling on Leofric of Mercia.

'Earl Leofric,' he said, 'you of all men knew Siward best. Not only was he an ally, but I know that you and he became close friends. Indeed, I also know that both houses were very close, and all concerned would have been affected by the deaths of the three men. My first thoughts were to award the earldom to Siward's one surviving son, Waltheof, but the thought fled as quickly as it came due to his age. We need a man of strength in the role, not a child. We need to keep the Scots under control along the northern borders, and for that, there is only one man.'

His gaze turned towards Aelfgar of Mercia, causing the young man to stand just a little bit taller in anticipation of the honour about to land upon him. The two men stared at each other for a few moments before Edward finally made the formal announcement they had gathered to hear.

'The man I have chosen to become the new Earl of Northumbria,' he began, turning his head to the other side of the room, 'is Tostig Godwinson.'

An audible gasp echoed around the room.

Tostig had been looking at the floor thinking about his lands in East Anglia, but at the mention of his name, he was snatched back to reality and slowly raised his head to see everyone staring at him.

'What?' he said quietly to Harold. 'I don't understand.'

'Stand up straight and face your king, Tostig,' Harold growled back. 'He has just granted you one of the most powerful earldoms in England.'

Tostig stared at his brother before turning to face the king, shocked at the sudden elevation in status.

'Your grace,' he stuttered, 'I know not what to say.'

'Perhaps a thank you would be a good start,' said the king, an amused smile upon his face.

'Of course,' said Tostig, 'please forgive me, your grace. I am both honoured and humbled by your award. The appointment was unexpected, but I humbly accept the trust placed upon me, and I swear I will serve you to the best of my ability in all things.'

The king nodded his acceptance of the response, and many of the men called out their congratulations. One of the nearby nobles walked across and slapped Tostig on the shoulders.

'Well done, young man,' he said, 'your father would have been very proud.' Others joined in, but as the noise increased, one family had only confusion and anger in their eyes.

'No,' shouted Aelfgar above the din, 'there has to be a mistake.' He faced the king and took a few steps towards the dais. 'Your grace,' he continued, causing everyone to fall silent once more, 'I believe you have been advised poorly. I am the most senior noble in the north, and that earldom is mine by right. Tostig Godwinson is already the Earl of East Anglia. He does not need further lands or titles.'

'Aelfgar of Mercia,' said the king, 'it is for that precise reason I have given him this title. He knows the north, is used to managing the responsibilities of an earldom and is part of one of the strongest families in England. He may not need the title, but the Crown has need of him and the stability he will bring to the north. My decision is made.'

'No,' shouted Aelfgar, again, 'you can't do this.' He stepped closer to the king, but two guards quickly blocked his way.

'Aelfgar,' shouted his father, 'hold still. The king has made his decision, and we will abide by it.'

'Why,' shouted Aelfgar, addressing the room, 'the choice is flawed, and the king has obviously been swayed by the influence of Archbishop Stigand. That earldom is mine and everyone here knows it.' He turned back to Edward. 'Your grace,' he said, 'I am your humble servant, but I beseech thee, do not do this. Grant me Northumbria, and I will protect the northern borders with my life. Give me what is due to me, and I swear that, within the year, I will bring you the head of Macbeth himself.'

The room was silent again, and everyone watched the king. Edward rose slowly to his feet and faced the angry young man.

'Aelfgar of Mercia,' he said. 'You have stood in this room, in the presence of your peers and heard my royal decree. You have spoken without invitation and raised your voice to challenge my decision. Out of respect for your father, I will take no issue with these insults but say this. First, nobody inherits earldoms by virtue of birth, they are mine to bestow upon whom I please. Never again make the mistake of claiming they are yours by right. Secondly, though I need not explain my decisions, I have done so and will not do it again. Tostig Godwinson is my choice as the new Earl of Northumbria, whether you like it or not. However, I am nothing if not fair. As compensation for your upset, I grant you the lands of East Anglia once they have been vacated by Tostig. This is my decision, take it or leave it.'

Aelfgar could feel his heart racing. To be denied Northumbria was one thing, but to be thrown some scraps as compensation was an insult he could not take. His father saw the ire rising in his son's face and hissed a warning.

'Aelfgar, accept the king's generosity.'

The silence stretched on, and the king started to turn away to conclude the audience.

'No,' said Aelfgar, to gasps of shock from all present. 'I am not some dog to be thrown scraps from his master's table. I am Aelfgar, son of Leofric, son of one of the noblest families in England. I have worked long and hard for this position, killed many men in service of my country, and I am willing to die for my king, but I will not be treated like a peasant. I demand that you retract your decision.'

'You *demand*?' asked the king, incredulously.

'I do,' said Aelfgar, 'for it is only right.'

One of the guards stepped forward towards the young man, but Edward held up his hand, stopping him in his tracks.

'Hold,' he said, 'for I would hear what he has to say.' He addressed Aelfgar. 'Tell me, for we are all waiting to hear. If I do not bow to your demands, what will be the consequences?'

Before Aelfgar could respond, his father stepped forward and punched his son across the face, sending him crashing to the ground. His men pounced on Aelfgar and dragged him from the room as Earl Leofric turned to face the king.

'Your grace,' he said urgently, 'please forgive my son his disrespectful outburst. He is young and knows not what he says. I speak on behalf of all in the House of Mercia when I say we welcome your choice of Earl of Northumbria and hereby swear before everyone present that we will offer all the support Earl Tostig needs in keeping our northern borders safe.'

The king looked up as Aelfgar was bundled from the room, before turning his attention back to Leofric.

'And what of your son?'

'He is rash, and he is foolish,' said Leofric, 'and the disappointment got to him, but he spoke in haste and is not a bad man. If you can forgive him this outburst, I will mete out a punishment he will never forget.'

'The axeman's blade is what he should get,' shouted a voice from the back of the room.

'No!' said Leofric quickly. 'He is foolhardy, yes, but he is young and strong and can wield a sword better than most men. His words were treasonous, on that we can agree, but if he is to lose his life, let it be in the service of the Crown in the front lines of our armies. Let him pay the price of his outburst with Scottish blood, not his own, and perhaps, if he survives, then one day you will see him for the man he is destined to be, not the foolish boy you saw before you today.'

The king stared at Leofric, seeing the desperation in the old man's face. Leofric was a good man and a loyal subject, but he could not stand back and allow anyone to threaten him without being punished.

'Earl Leofric,' he said eventually, 'I recognise your anguish, but it is my opinion that your son just threatened the Crown of England in front of many witnesses. That cannot go unpunished.' He paused for a few moments, and the room fell silent, waiting for his judgement. 'In recognition of your loyalty,' he continued eventually, 'I will not execute Aelfgar, for his death would punish you long after his pain has gone, so I say this. Tell your son that I hereby declare him outlaw, and he has until the sun sets on the last day of the month to leave the country. After that time, if anybody captures him and brings him to me, Aelfgar will feel the axeman's blade. More than that, I cannot do.'

'But your grace!' gasped Leofric.

'My mind is made up, Earl Leofric, and I suggest you thank God that my mood was good before coming here today. Tell your son to run, for there is no longer a place for him in England.'

Leofric stared, knowing he could do no more. Finally, after a quick bow of his head, he left the hall, followed by his entourage. Once they had gone, Edward turned back to the room.

'Unless anyone has anything to add, this council is over. Earls Harold and Tostig, attend me in my chambers; we have business to discuss.'

—

Half an hour later, Harold and Tostig waited outside the king's chambers, both men bewildered yet excited at the recent events.

'I still can't believe it,' said Tostig. 'Never in my life have I dreamed of such an elevation, at least, not so soon.'

'Think yourself fortunate,' said Harold, 'for you are indeed lucky to be in charge of such an earldom at such a young age. It seems that God cleared a path for you.'

'Him and Scottish steel,' said Tostig. 'The death of Osbjorn threw all sorts of complications into the succession.'

'Indeed,' said Harold, 'but whatever the reason, make sure you do not let the king down.'

'Since when have you become such a supporter?' asked Tostig, looking at his brother. 'Do not forget how he treated our father.'

'Our family has had its problems with Edward, that much is true,' said Harold, 'but those days are behind us, and Edward is still our king. If you can forget the past and embrace the reality of what lies all around us, I feel there are great things yet to come for the House of Godwin.'

Before Tostig could answer, the doors opened, and they were beckoned into a receiving chamber. Inside stood the two men Harold fully expected to be present, the king himself and the Archbishop of Canterbury, Stigand of Norwich, but as the two brothers bowed their heads in respect, Harold noticed a third man standing near the window, Bishop Ealdred of Worcester.

Ever since he had been a young monk in York, Ealdred had been a friend of the Godwin family, a relationship that had continued even after gaining the diocese of Worcester. He was a pious man, but was also known for his military prowess, especially against the ever-present threat of King Gruffydd's patrols along the Welsh border.

He had once been instrumental in getting a pardon for Harold's older brother, Sweyn Godwinson, after King Edward had exiled him. Not only that, when the Godwin family was forced to flee England four years earlier after a confrontation with the king, he had allowed them to escape despite having been ordered by Edward to take them prisoner. It was an act of friendship that Harold would never forget.

'Bishop Ealdred,' said Harold, walking over to embrace his friend, 'it is good to see you again.'

'I returned a few days ago,' said Ealdred, 'but the journey was arduous, and I am not the man I used to be. I have hardly left my cot since I got back, such was my exhaustion.'

'You are here now,' said Harold. 'So, how was Rome?'

'I did not go to Rome,' said the bishop, 'I was… elsewhere.'

Harold's brow creased with confusion.

'I do not understand,' said Harold. 'Whenever your name was mentioned, everyone said you were on a pilgrimage to the Holy City.'

'That's what we wanted them to believe,' said the king from behind Harold, 'and it looks like it worked.'

Harold turned to face Edward.

'Your grace,' he said, 'forgive me, I forget my place. You invited us here, and since I arrived, I have been fawning over Bishop Ealdred like a newly ordained acolyte.'

Edward waved the matter away, lowering himself into a chair and accepting a tankard of wine from a servant.

'It makes a change to see important men meeting as allies with no hidden agendas,' he said, 'please, join me. You too, Tostig.'

All four men walked over and took a seat before the king. The servant poured them all drinks and departed.

'So,' said Edward, when they were alone, 'there is much to discuss, but first, we should congratulate your brother on his new earldom.' He turned to Tostig and raised his tankard. 'It was a hard decision, Tostig Godwinson, and one that may yet cause me problems, but I am relying on you to keep the Scots at arm's length. Do not let me down.'

'I will not, your grace,' said Tostig. 'I will fight and, if necessary, die in your service.'

'Well, try not to die too soon,' said the king with a smile, 'at least not until we have someone strong enough to take your place.'

Everyone laughed at the jest and raised their tankards before falling quiet to wait for the king to explain the reason for his summons. Edward placed his tankard on the table before turning to the Bishop of Worcester.

'Bishop Ealdred, I think this may be a good time to enlighten our guests as to where you have been for the last year.'

'Of course, your grace,' said Ealdred. 'As you know,' he said, leaning back in his chair, 'the Lord has not yet blessed the king and queen with a child, and the longer the situation continues, the more at-risk England becomes. If, God forbid, something happened to the king, the country would be at the whim of every noble from here to Germany who thinks he has a claim to the throne. The king, in his wisdom, saw fit to put precautions in place that would prevent war should the worst happen.'

'What things?' asked Harold, intrigued.

'The reason the Bishop of Worcester has not been here these past few months,' interjected the king, 'is because he was arranging safe passage across Flanders, Germany and Hungary.'

'Safe passage for whom?' asked Harold.

'For King Edmund Ironside's son,' replied Edward. 'He is the only living descendant of any English king, and we thought it would be prudent to seek out his views on sitting upon the throne, should I die childless.'

Harold stared at the king. Edward the Exile was the son of Edmund Ironside, who had been dethroned by King Cnut many years earlier. By seeking his attendance, King Edward was making a strong statement of intent, one that he was not sure he agreed with, but those thoughts were not for this meeting. He turned to face the bishop.

'Your grace,' he said, 'I had no idea. To travel so far across territories that have no allegiance to us was a great risk. You have my admiration. Can I ask, were you successful in your quest?'

'To an extent,' said Ealdred. 'I managed to make strong contacts, but alas was forced to return without actually speaking to Edward myself. However, you can rest assured that he is well aware of the king's interest as he has since acknowledged my messengers, albeit without commitment either way.'

'Then that is a good start,' said Harold, turning back to the king. 'However, may I be allowed to offer some advice?'

'Proceed,' said the king.

'Your grace,' said Harold, 'the bloodline is unchallengeable, but can I remind you that the ultimate choice of who sits upon the throne lays in the hands of the Witan. If this is the path you want to pursue, it would be good to get their approval before taking such steps.'

'I am fully aware of the obligation to consult the Witan,' said the king, 'and have already done so with many of its members, albeit informally. The mood is one of support, and before I send the next messenger to Hungary to formalise the offer, I will, of course, get their full approval.'

'I received no such communication,' said Harold.

'An oversight,' said Edward, 'nothing more. Besides, I anticipated your full support.'

'Of course,' said Harold. 'So, what is the next step?'

'Now I know he is interested,' said the king, 'I will summon the Witan for their approval before sending another messenger to formalise the offer and escort Edward the Exile back to England.'

'And who is that messenger to be?' asked Harold.

'Why do you think I asked you to remain?' asked the king with a smile. 'It is you, Harold Godwinson. I want you to go to Hungary and bring me the next king of England.'

Chapter Two

A few days later, Harold and his bodyguards rode through the gates of the family home in Bosham. Since his father's death, he and his wife, Edyth Swanneck, had relocated to administer the huge Earldom of Wessex and be closer to his widowed mother, Gytha Thorkelsdóttir. As he dismounted, Edyth emerged from the manor and walked over to greet him.

'Harold,' she said, 'welcome back. We received your message about Tostig – it is indeed wonderful news. Is he not with you?'

Harold kissed his wife on the cheek before responding.

'He is not,' he said, handing the reins of his horse over to a groom. 'There is much to arrange before he takes his seat in Northumbria, so he has ridden back to Anglia to start the process.' He looked across at his mother, peering out of the doorway. Although it had been over two years since Godwin had died, she still grieved for him.

'Has she been all right?' he asked quietly.

'She is fine,' said Edyth gently. 'Just give her time.'

'I will go to her,' said Harold and started walking away.

'Harold, wait,' said Edyth, 'there is something you need to know. A man arrived yesterday asking to see you. I explained you would be back today, so he found lodgings in the village.'

'Did he give his name?'

'He did not, nor would he share his business. All he said was that he needed to speak to you, and you alone.'

'When is he coming back?'

'He is here now,' said Edyth, 'and has been since dawn. He is waiting in the chapel.'

Harold looked over at the small stone building.

'I had better go and see him,' he said and started walking across the courtyard.

'Harold,' said Edyth as he left, 'be careful. There is something about him that makes me uneasy.'

Her husband acknowledged with a nod and continued to the chapel, ducking under the lintel to step into the gloomy interior. The space was illuminated by several candles, and at the far end, a lone figure knelt on one of the red cushions before the altar. The chapel was silent save for the gentle guttering of the flames and the slow breathing of the visitor.

Harold stared at the riding cloak hanging from the man's shoulders. It was badly stained and worn through heavy and prolonged use, a clear indicator that the wearer was a frequent traveller or even a man of conflict. Harold took a few paces forward.

'Greetings, stranger,' he said, 'I hear you seek an audience with me.'

The man raised his head but focused on the crucifix upon the wall.

'I do, my lord.'

'Then state your business,' said Harold, 'for your presence causes worry in the hearts of my family.'

The man slowly got to his feet and turned to face him. His cloak was open, and Harold could see a sword hanging from his belt.

'We do not allow the bearing of weapons in God's house.'

The man looked down at the sword before drawing it from the scabbard and placing it on the table beside him.

'My apologies,' he said slowly, 'my heart is so full of shame and self-hate, I forget the niceties of common courtesy. I am surprised you do not recognise me, my lord, for we have met on several occasions.'

Harold's eyes narrowed as he stared at the man in the gloom. He certainly looked familiar, but his face was drawn and covered with the dirt of the road.

'It is my turn to apologise,' he said eventually, 'for though I recognise your features, your name escapes me.'

'My name, my lord,' replied the man, 'is Owen of Hereford, and I rode at your brother's side for many years.'

Recognition sparked in Harold's eyes. He hadn't seen Owen since well before the huscarl had joined Sweyn on the fateful pilgrimage to Rome several years earlier, and now he had been reminded, the memories came flooding back.

'Owen,' he said, taking a step forward, 'I'm sorry, I just did not...'

Owen held up his hand, stopping Harold in his tracks.

'Come no closer, my lord,' he said, 'there are things to say and actions to take.'

'I do not understand,' said Harold. 'You were a good friend to my brother and were with him when he died. There will always be a place at my hearth for you.'

'The time for such things is long gone,' said Owen, 'for there are truths to be told.'

Harold stared at the haggard man. The more he looked, the more he could see that he had suffered greatly. His clothes hung loose, and his hair was unkempt, matched by an untrimmed beard.

'Owen,' he said, 'perhaps we should get you cleaned up first. After that, you can say what you have come to say. Have you eaten recently?'

'Not for many days,' said Owen, 'but there is no need for food or fancy garments where I am going, and my journey is long overdue.'

'Owen,' said Harold, realising the man was in great distress, 'come inside, and we will discuss this.' He took another step forward, but Owen reached across and grabbed the sword. Harold stopped abruptly and stared at the man. His own sword was still in the scabbard attached to his saddle outside, so he was unarmed.

'What are you doing?' he asked. 'This is God's house. What sort of man are you?' He watched as tears welled up in Owen's eyes before cutting a path through the grime on his face.

'I'll tell you what sort of man I am,' he said. 'I am a thief, a drunk and a liar, but more than that, I am a common murderer, destined to burn in the fires of hell.'

'Owen,' said Harold, 'I know not what has happened to you, but this is not the place to have this discussion. Lower your sword and tell me what this is about.'

Owen looked at the weapon in his hand as if only just realising what it was. Slowly he turned it around and, holding it by the blade, handed it over to Harold.

'Do you recognise it, my lord? Look close, for it bears your family seal.'

Harold looked at the hilt and recognised the Godwin emblem before looking back up at Owen. 'This is Sweyn's sword,' he said eventually. 'We were told he had been buried with it at his side.'

'That was a lie,' said Owen, 'one of many that have since passed my lips.'

'I don't understand,' said Harold, 'how have you got it?'

'Because,' said Owen, 'I took it from his body… after I killed him.'

Harold stared at Owen as the implications sank in. When news of Sweyn's death had arrived a few years earlier at a banquet, the shock had given his father, Godwin of Wessex, a seizure, something he never recovered from, dying only a few days later. The messenger had said that Sweyn had been attacked by brigands in Turkey and only his huscarl had survived the attack, but before they could receive any confirmation in person, Owen had disappeared and hadn't been seen since. Now he stood in front of Harold, a broken man, apparently confessing to Sweyn's murder.

'I must have misheard you, Owen of Hereford,' said Harold, his tone lowering with menace, 'so I will ask you to repeat what you just said, but think carefully for your response may well dictate whether you live or die.' As he finished speaking, he raised Sweyn's sword towards Owen's chest.

'You heard me well enough,' said Owen quietly. 'I took that sword from his body before I buried him. I meant to return it to your father, I really did, but when I got back, the enormity of what I had done filled me with fear, and I ran. I have been running ever since.'

'I care not about the blade,' snarled Harold, taking a step closer. 'I want to know what happened to my brother.'

Another silence descended on the chapel, one so dense it seemed like even the flickering candles waited for a reply.

'I killed him,' whispered Owen. 'I murdered the man I had served for most of my life. And now I have come here to pay the price for my sins.'

Harold stared in silence, the sword still pointed at his brother's killer, fully aware that if what Owen had said was true, there was only one outcome that was just.

'You are telling me that you killed my brother,' he said eventually, through clenched teeth.

'I am,' replied Owen, his eyes closed.

'And you dare to come here today to beg for mercy?'

Owen's eyes opened sharply, and he stared at Harold.

'Mercy?' he said. 'You do not understand. I have not come here to ask for mercy.' He took a step towards Harold and grabbed the sword's blade with both hands before pressing the point against his chest. 'I seek no mercy,' he said. 'I seek release from my sins by paying the ultimate price.' He stared into Harold's eyes. 'I have come here to die, my lord, and to grant you the peace of knowing the truth.'

Both men stared at each other in the gloom, one filled with remorse, the other consumed with anger.

'Do it, my lord,' gasped Owen, leaning against the blade, 'take your retribution.'

Harold did not move, but his face contorted with rage.

'Do it,' shouted Owen, 'release me from this torment, I beseech thee.'

Harold flexed his sword arm, preparing for the killing thrust, but something was not right, and he knew that, whatever the truth, he could not kill a man in a chapel. Without warning, he withdrew his sword, causing Owen to stumble forward, landing on his knees at the earl's feet.

Harold looked down at the broken man sobbing on the floor. What he had just heard shocked him to the core, but he knew there was more to be learned. This man, the murderer of his brother, would probably still face the executioner for his deeds, but before he did, Harold wanted to know exactly what had happened.

'Get to your feet,' he snapped, 'and come with me.'

—

Further south, in the port of Bristol, Earl Leofric of Mercia and his son, Aelfgar, sat in a tavern alongside half a dozen of Aelfgar's huscarls. The mood was quiet, and outside, the crew of two of Earl Leofric's ships were making the final preparations to take the earl's son and his men to Flanders, thus fulfilling the sentence of King Edward.

'When you arrive,' said Leofric, 'you will be met by a close ally of mine. I have already sent word, and you will be well looked after until such time as you can return.'

'And when will that be?' said Aelfgar, nursing a jack of ale. 'You heard the king; he said my exile was for life.'

'He did,' said Leofric, 'but that may not always be the case. Just give me some time to petition on your behalf, and if God is with us, I reckon we can have you back here within a year or two, five at the most.'

'Five years,' sneered Aelfgar, 'and what am I supposed to do in that time?'

'You will serve whatever master takes you in and build a reputation for yourself,' replied his father. 'Do that, and the chances of a pardon grow stronger. In the meantime, I will rally support from our allies throughout England and press for a pardon.'

Aelfgar fell silent and stared into his drink.

'Aelfgar,' said Leofric, recognising the look on his son's face. 'What are you thinking?'

'I am thinking,' said Aelfgar slowly, 'that not so long ago, a man probably sat in this same tavern having been sentenced to a similar fate. Now he is probably the most powerful man in England, second only to the king.'

'You talk of Harold Godwinson,' said Leofric.

'Aye, I do. He and his whole family were outlawed, and look at them now. Almost untouchable in the eyes of the law.'

'That was different,' said Leofric, 'the sentence was unjust, and they garnered much support throughout the country.'

'That and a Viking army,' said Aelfgar.

'What do you mean?'

'Is it not true that Harold and Leofwine engaged a fleet of Irish mercenaries to head their fleet when they sailed up the Thames?'

'It is,' said Leofric, 'but that was just the vanguard. Godwin had his own huge army at his back, so do not make the mistake of thinking that you can copy his actions.'

'Why not?' asked Aelfgar. 'It is well known that there are many Viking ships moored in Ireland, just waiting for the next man to come who can pay the price. Why can it work for Harold but not for me? Are we not all equal under God's gaze?'

'We are,' said Leofric, 'but the circumstances are different. Everyone witnessed the extent of your outburst before the king, and you have lost a lot of allies. There is no way you will ever raise an army strong enough to challenge the king.'

'We have a strong army in Mercia, do we not?' asked Aelfgar, staring at his father. 'Surely you would support me if it came to a confrontation?'

Leofric stared in shock at his son. To even suggest that he would ever march against the king was absurd.

'Don't worry,' said Aelfgar, seeing the look on his father's face, 'your response is obvious. Loyalty to the king is far more important to you than loyalty to your son.' He stood up and drained his jack.

'Aelfgar,' said Leofric, getting to his feet, 'do not be stupid. Just go to Flanders and do what I said. Within a few years, I swear I will get you home. It may seem like an age, but it will pass on the wings of an eagle. To seek any other resolution is foolhardy, especially if it means confronting Edward.'

'You do not understand, Father,' said Aelfgar, 'I am only seeking what is mine by right and if that means bloodshed, then so be it.' He turned to his huscarls. 'Get the horses off the ships and get ready to ride.'

'Aelfgar!' said Leofric. 'If you return now, you will be captured and executed.'

'I am not going north, Father,' said Aelfgar. 'I am going to follow the path that Harold took when he was outlawed.'

'You are going to hire a fleet?'

'Aye, I am.'

'But without an army, they will be a drop in the ocean and will be destroyed in hours.'

'I may not have an army yet,' said Aelfgar, 'but I know where to get one. Stay well, Father, and I hope we never meet across a battlefield.' Without another word, he turned away to march out of the tavern.

Leofric's face creased with frustration, but he knew how hot-headed his son could be, and when he was in this frame of mind, there was just no stopping him.

Twenty minutes later, Aelfgar and his six huscarls mounted their horses and rode away from the docks. Outside the city, they headed along the eastern road towards London before coming to a junction. The rider in front stopped and looked back towards Aelfgar.

'Which way, my lord?' he asked. 'Onward to London?'

'No,' said Aelfgar, 'take the northern road to Hereford.'

'Why Hereford?' asked the huscarl. 'Earl Ralf is loyal to Edward, so we will find no succour there.'

'We do not head to Hereford,' said Aelfgar, 'it serves as a signpost only.'

'Where are we going?'

'We are going to Gwynedd,' said Aelfgar, 'to speak to the King of the Welsh.'

All the riders turned to stare at their lord. Although there was currently no war, there was certainly no love lost between the Welsh and the English.

'Are you sure?' asked the lead scout. 'We could have our heads on stakes before we get a league across the border.'

'Aye, we could,' said Aelfgar, 'but I would wager that King Gruffydd will want to hear what I have to offer. Lead on, my friend, for the path to a different future lies at our feet.'

With a reluctant sigh, the lead huscarl dug in his heels and turned his horse northward, knowing that whatever happened next was completely out of his control.

Chapter Three

Bosham, March, AD 1055

Harold stood bare-chested at a table in his quarters, washing the dust of the road from his body. As he wiped down, the door opened behind him, and his wife entered the room. Harold glanced over before throwing the cloth onto a chair and reaching for a clean undershirt.

'You look tired,' said Edyth, watching as her husband got dressed. 'Was it a worrisome visit?'

'On the contrary,' said Harold, 'it was very productive. It was not until I got back here and talked to that man did my mood worsen.'

'I understand your anger,' said Edyth. 'To hear that Sweyn was murdered by the man he trusted most is almost unbearable. Do you know what happened?'

'Not yet,' said Harold, pouring warmed ale from a pitcher into a tankard. 'But I will find out. Where is he now?'

'He is still in the stables being scrubbed by the grooms. I have also arranged some clothing and hot food. He is in a very bad state.'

'A man comes into my home and confesses to murdering my brother,' said Harold, staring at his wife incredulously, 'and you bathe, clothe and feed him?'

'We are not animals here,' said Edyth, 'we are a decent family, and until we find out what happened, I will not see any man, woman or child suffer under this roof. If what he says is true, then he will face the consequences, but he will not suffer before that for lack of compassion on my part.'

Harold shook his head but turned his attention to his ale. When Edyth had that look in her eye, he knew there was little point in argument.

'So be it,' he said, 'but let me know as soon as he is ready, for if there is a hanging to be done, it will be at dawn in front of the whole town.'

'I will send for you,' said Edyth, turning away.

'Edyth,' said Harold as she reached the door, 'make sure he is restrained before you get anywhere near him. Any man capable of overcoming Sweyn is more than capable of hurting a woman.'

'In his present state,' said Edyth, 'I doubt he would be a match for anyone.'

'Just be careful,' answered Harold and watched as his wife left the room.

—

Several hours later, Harold watched as one of the servants fed more logs into the dwindling fire. The evening was unusually cold, and the large hall needed a constant blaze in the hearth to keep it warm. Later, there would be a grand meal for the family and his huscarls to celebrate Tostig's good news, albeit in his absence. The family's name, reputation and power base was growing rapidly, and that was always something to celebrate.

'My lord,' said a voice behind him, 'he is here.'

Harold watched as two of his guards led the chained prisoner into the hall. Despite his undoubted misery, Owen of Hereford looked a lot different to the man who had broken down in the chapel earlier that day. His hair and beard had been shorn, his body scrubbed with a stiff broom, and he now wore clean leggings with a poorly fitting linen jerkin tied around the middle with a length of rope.

The two guards waited by the doorway as Harold slowly dragged two chairs from the table to the centre of the room, placing them so they faced each other just a few paces apart. He lowered himself into one before placing an unsheathed sword on the floor at his side and turning back to the guards.

'Bring him here.'

The huscarls dragged Owen over and pushed him down into the chair before producing a piece of rope to secure him in place.

'That will not be necessary,' said Harold.

'My lord,' said one of the guards, 'he may still present a threat.'

'Oh, he is a threat,' replied Harold, 'but it is one that can easily be dealt with.'

For a few moments, there was silence as the earl stared at his brother's killer, but his gaze was not met as the prisoner continued to stare at the floor.

'So,' said Harold, 'I hear you have been fed and watered.'

'I have,' mumbled Owen, without looking up.

'And the smell has been washed away,' continued Harold.

'I have been well looked after.'

'Why do you not look at me when I am talking to you?' asked Harold.

'Because the shame of what I have done weighs upon me like a sack of Judas silver,' said Owen.

'Shame you may have,' said Harold, 'guilt you may carry, and this day may be the last you walk upon this earth, but you are still a man and as such, should act like one. Look at me, Owen of Hereford, and meet your fate like a man, not a whimpering child.'

Owen slowly looked up to stare at the earl.

'And sit up straight,' snapped Harold. 'You were once a feared huscarl in my brother's house, and whatever the outcome of this day, you will honour his name by being the man you once were, not the wretch you have since become.'

Owen straightened up and stared Harold squarely in the eye.

'Better,' said Harold. 'Now, before we begin, let me make it clear that while you are in this room, you will speak nothing but the truth, no matter how hard that may be. Do you understand?'

'I have nothing left to hide,' said Owen, 'though my words will be my death sentence.'

'They may well be,' said Harold, 'but if so, you will go to the gallows with your conscience clear and your soul unburdened. Now, I want to know if what you said earlier is the truth. Did you kill my brother?'

Owen stared at Harold before breaking his gaze and turning as Edyth Swanneck led the rest of the family and all the household staff into the hall to witness the questioning. Each person took their place lining the walls as one of the servants carried over a chair for Edyth to sit next to her husband.

Harold stared, surprised by her actions, but he knew her well enough to know that she was her own woman and would have her reasons for joining him. Eventually, the noise died down, and Harold turned back to face Owen.

'I will ask again,' he said. 'Did you, or did you not kill my brother?'

Owen glanced at Edyth for a moment, but the look of concern that he had seen in her eyes earlier was long gone, replaced now with one of distaste. He turned back to Harold.

'Yes, my lord,' he said, 'I killed Sweyn Godwinson.'

Total silence fell throughout the hall. That admission alone was a death sentence, and all eyes turned to Harold to see his reaction.

'So be it,' said the earl eventually, 'and you have condemned yourself with your own words, but before I pass sentence, I want to know exactly what happened and why you felt compelled to commit murder.'

'No,' said Owen, 'you do not want to hear the truth, for by doing so, you will only sour the memories of your brother, and there has been enough damage done by my hand.'

'What are you saying?' asked Harold. 'That you acted in self-defence, for if that is the case, I will suspect the claim is to save your own skin.'

'I have no wish to save my own skin,' said Owen, 'and I know that whatever I say, my time here is done, but if you want

31

to hear the truth, then you must be prepared to hear things that will tarnish your family's name.'

Harold looked around the room, now populated by all the staff of the manor. To send them away would be an admission that he feared what was about to be said, but to leave them there risked exposing even more of his brother's wayward reputation. Making his decision, he turned back to face Owen.

'You are free to tell your tale, Owen of Hereford,' he said, 'but I swear that if I think you are lying at any point, I will cut your throat here in this very hall.'

'So be it,' said Owen. 'The journey to Rome was uneventful. Your brother was unusually quiet, and I believe it was because he knew the importance of his visit. Whilst there, we met the Holy Father, and Lord Sweyn received absolution for his sins. He was a very happy man.'

'So what happened to cause the confrontation on the way home?'

'His manner changed, my lord – it was as if he felt that now he had been forgiven, he was able to continue his life as he saw fit. The Sweyn I had known for so many years re-emerged, but worse than before.'

'In what way?'

'His drinking increased, and he was quick to violence with any man who crossed him, but that was not the worst. His lust for women grew ever greater, and he helped himself to whoever was available.' He paused and looked around the room. 'Whether they were willing or not.'

A whisper of distaste rippled around the room, but it was not a great revelation. Sweyn had always had a bad reputation but, as an earl, had rarely been admonished.

'So you killed him because he had a woman who may not have been fully engaged?' asked Harold.

'No, my lord. Whilst we were in Turkey, we came across a woman and child asking for food. At first, your brother demanded payment, but they had nothing of value. Eventually, he consented, but only on condition that one of them would lay with him.'

'Obviously, the older woman,' said Edyth at Harold's side.

'No, my lady,' said Owen, turning to face her, 'he insisted that it be the child, a girl hardly old enough to emerge from behind her mother's skirts.'

This time the mood in the hall took a definite turn for the worse, many whispering their disgust.

'No,' said Harold, 'you are lying. My brother was a lot of things, but to bed a child was too far, even for him.'

'You are wrong, my lord,' said Owen, 'for I had seen him do it on many occasions, especially when we fought in Wales alongside Gruffydd. His tastes were vile, but his power untouchable. When the lust came upon him, the age of the woman never mattered, only that his needs were fulfilled.'

'I do not believe you,' snarled Harold. 'Why would he do that when he could have any woman he wanted?'

'It matters not what you believe,' said Owen, 'for I am telling the truth. He tried forcing himself upon the child, but I talked him out of it. At least I thought I did. As soon as I turned my back, he attacked me with his knife, but I bettered him, and in the struggle, he was stabbed.'

The room fell silent again as the words sank in.

'Wait a moment,' said Edyth. 'Are you saying that the fight was a result of you defending the child?'

'It was, my lady, as God is my witness. It was never my intention to kill the earl, but in the heat of conflict, such things happen.'

'My brother was an excellent fighter,' said Harold, 'yet you say you bettered him. How did that happen?'

'Indeed, he was an excellent fighter,' said Owen, 'but it was I that taught him most of his skills. I say this not in pride but in repentance, for I should have held back.'

'If what you are saying is true,' said Harold, 'and the act was in defence of the girl, why were you so keen to die at the point of a blade this morning?'

33

'Despite his failings, Earl Sweyn was a good friend of mine,' said Owen. 'We fought alongside each other many times and saved each other's lives on more than one occasion. He was like my brother, and to be responsible for the death of such a man is a weight I cannot bear, especially when his family does not even know where lies his grave.'

'And you do?'

'I do because I dug it,' said Owen.

Harold turned to look at his wife.

'What are your thoughts on this matter?'

'My thoughts,' replied Edyth, 'are for your ears only. We should conclude this audience and talk in private.'

'I agree,' said Harold and turned back to face Owen. 'Is there anything else you wish to add to your testimony?'

'Only that it is the truth,' said Owen.

'In that case,' replied Harold, 'my decision is this. You have admitted before these witnesses that my brother was killed by your hand, and I am of a mind to hang you as a murderer, but there is something that does not sit well with me. So, until I make sense of the matter, you will be taken from here to a place of confinement. I suggest you use the time to make your peace with God.'

'As you wish, my lord,' said Owen.

The earl looked over to the guard at the door.

'Take him away and lock him up. He gets no favours, but neither will he be treated unfairly until such time as I pass judgement.'

'Yes, my lord,' said the guard and walked over to pull Owen to his feet.

'Thank you, my lord,' said Owen as he was led away. 'May the Almighty guide your path.'

Everyone in the hall watched as he was led out before turning back towards Harold and his wife. It was not often that they got to see such drama.

'Get back to work,' announced the steward quickly. 'There are many things still to do for tonight's celebrations.' He clapped his hands together, and all the household staff disappeared to their duties. Finally, only Harold and Edyth were left, and they both walked over to sit nearer the fire.

'So,' said Harold, 'your thoughts?'

'I believe him,' said Edyth. 'His testimony was brutally honest, even though he knew it could cost him his life, and not once did he ask for clemency.'

Harold breathed deeply and stared into the flames.

'I don't know,' he said, 'Sweyn was no angel, but I find it hard to believe he was such a godless man.'

'Do not forget,' said Edyth, 'he was the same man who kidnapped and raped an abbess, holding her prisoner for many months.'

'Many of those accusations were never proven,' said Harold.

'Nonsense,' said Edyth. 'The abbess refused to discuss the events for many reasons, not least amongst them the desire to put the whole situation behind her. But even if there is doubt about that, there is none that Sweyn murdered his own cousin in cold blood just to get his hands on his lands.'

'Lands that had been confiscated by the king,' said Harold. 'He was aggrieved at the injustice.'

'Harold,' said Edyth, her voice rising, 'listen to yourself. Every time I raise a valid point, you counter with a weak justification. There *is* no justification for kidnap, rape or murder and not only was Sweyn guilty of all three, everyone knows that he was responsible for far more equally vile acts. In my eyes, any man who can do that is more than capable of harming a child.'

Harold fell quiet, knowing his wife was correct. Sweyn had been a problem for the family for many years, and even now, long after he was dead, he caused complications.

'I need time to think,' he said. 'I want to hang that man with every fibre of my being, but if what he says is true, then perhaps there are grounds for clemency. Arrange for the steward to lock him in one of the basement rooms, and I will talk to him again in a few days.'

Edyth smiled and reached out to touch his arm.

'You look tired,' she said, 'and still haven't told me about what happened in London. Is Tostig happy?'

'Oh, he is more than happy,' said Harold, 'as you can imagine. I just don't think he is ready for this level of authority.'

'What do you mean?'

'I'm not sure. The way he was talking after the meeting gives me cause for concern.'

'In what way?'

'The tone of the conversation was very biased to wealth accumulation and the benefits of power. Indeed, when he talked, I could see shades of Sweyn's personality coming through, and that is the last thing we need.'

'Perhaps that is just his excitement,' replied Edyth. 'With time and your guidance, I'm sure he will become a good custodian. What about your intention to go to Normandy? Did you talk to the king about that?'

'I did not have a chance,' said Harold, 'and besides, he has a different quest in mind.'

'What quest?'

'He wants me to go to Hungary and bring back Edward Ætheling.'

'To what end?'

'To ensure there is a clear line of succession in the event of his death.'

'Why, is he ill?'

'Not that I am aware of. He is just painfully aware that if he dies without a clear heir, England could be torn apart by civil war.'

'When are you going?'

'Within a few weeks.'

Edyth stared at her husband. For the past few years, he had sent many messengers across the North Sea with the aim of finding out where his younger brother, Wulfnorth, and his nephew, Hakon, were being held hostage, but since they had been abducted by the Norman bishop, Robert de Jumièges, there had been no sightings. None until recently, when one of his men had returned with news that a boy similar in age and appearance to Hakon had been seen near the town of Rouen. It wasn't much, but with nothing else to go on, Harold had expressed an intention to go and find out for himself. Now, it seemed that the task was to be postponed yet again in favour of King Edward's wishes.

'So the boys will be kept in captivity even longer.'

'Not necessarily. Perhaps I can still go to Rouen on the way to Hungary, or even on the way back. We just have to be a little more patient.'

Edyth held her tongue. Harold was a good man, but his eagerness to serve the king and heal the rifts between the Crown and the Godwin family often clouded his thoughts.

'You must do what you think is right and just,' she said eventually. 'Now come, let us go to the chapel. It has been a while since we prayed together.'

'It has,' said Harold, but as they left the manor house to walk across to the chapel, his heart was full of torment. He was failing in the task his father had charged him with on his deathbed, and what was worse, the resolution seemed further away with every day that passed.

Chapter Four

East Anglia, April, AD 1055

Tostig walked back into his newly acquired manor house on the outskirts of York, encouraged by the smell of burning wood and roasting boar. The morning had gone well with his falconers, and the manor kitchens were now in receipt of a dozen game birds as well as a brace of rabbits. His face was ruddy from the attentions of the northern winds, but he was in good heart and enjoyed a healthy banter with his first huscarl, Copsi.

As the two men entered, a serving girl walked quickly over with a jug of warmed wine, knowing it was the new earl's favourite drink after a morning on the hills, and to loiter risked incurring his anger.

'My lord,' announced the huscarl, throwing his riding cloak towards another servant, 'you drive a hard bargain, but I really want that brown dog, so I will increase my offer to one hundred silver pennies, a princely sum for such an ugly beast.'

Tostig laughed as he removed his gloves.

'Ugly? Just this morning, you said you have never seen anything so beautiful.'

'I was referring to his hunting prowess, not his looks,' said Copsi. 'You have to admit he is the nastiest amongst your kennels. Let me take him off your hands before someone kills him out of pity.'

'Copsi,' said Tostig, taking two goblets of wine from the offered tray and handing one over to the huscarl, 'if ever I need to defend myself before the Witan, I want you to speak for me.'

'You do? Why?'

'For your mind is as sharp as a butcher's knife, and you can change your argument like the north changes its weather. That is a combination that would save the devil himself.'

'So you agree?' asked Copsi, excited at the possibility of owning such a fantastic hunting dog. 'You are going to sell him to me?'

'I am not,' said Tostig, before taking a sip of the wine.

Copsi shook his head in disappointment.

'You drive a hard bargain, my lord,' he said, 'but my purse is not bottomless. I may increase the amount, but alas, it will be my final offer. What will you take?'

'For the love of God, Copsi,' laughed Tostig, 'stop haggling and put away your purse. The reason I will not sell him to you is that I am going to give him to you for nothing.'

'My lord?' said Copsi, his brows raising with surprise. 'I do not understand.'

'It is a gift,' said Tostig, 'from me to you in recognition of your loyalty. In addition, I will also give you a breeding bitch so you can start your own kennel. That is, of course, as long as she doesn't find the beast too ugly.'

Both men laughed and clinked the goblets together before walking over towards the fire.

'My lord,' said a voice, 'there is someone here to see you.'

Tostig turned to see his steward standing at the door.

'Tell them to go away,' he said, 'I am busy.'

'My lord,' said the steward, 'Thegn Gamelbearn wishes to see you. He said he has urgent business.'

Tostig sighed and placed his wine on the table. Gamelbearn was an important man in Northumbria and was often the spokesperson of all the other men of power in the area. He turned to Copsi.

'Stay here and warm your bones,' he said, 'this should not take too long. And get someone to bring me an ale, that wine has soured.' He turned away and walked over to the steward. 'Where is he?'

'Outside the stables, my lord. Shall I bring him in?'

'No, I will talk to him there. To bring him inside would be to offer hospitality, and I do not like the man.'

'Of course, my lord,' said the steward and headed out of the door.

Outside, Tostig could see two men talking quietly next to their horses, both wrapped in their cloaks against the chilly northern wind.

'My lord Tostig,' said one of the men with the briefest of nods, 'thank you for receiving us at such short notice.'

'Gamelbearn,' said Tostig, acknowledging the thegn, 'it is good to see you again, albeit only a matter of a few weeks since last we met.' He turned to the other man. 'And this is?'

'Dunstan, son of Aethelnoth,' said Gamelbearn, 'a loyal man and true ally.'

'My lord,' said Dunstan with a nod. 'I have heard a lot about you and look forward to serving you.'

'Good,' said Tostig with a nod and turned his attention back to Gamelbearn. 'So, what is so urgent that brings you all this way?'

'Perhaps it would be better to talk inside,' said Gamelbearn.

'It would,' said Tostig, 'but alas, my household have been taken with an illness, and I would not want it spread to you. Will your business take long?'

Gamelbearn glanced at Dunstan, surprised at the response, but he had already learned that Tostig could be a rude man.

'It will not,' he said, turning back to the earl, 'and of course, I understand. I hope the ague clears up soon.'

Tostig nodded, pleased that the lie had been accepted so easily.

'So, what is this about?'

'My lord, the villages have received your recent edict about the tax increase on their lands and chattels. My fellows have asked me to come on their behalf to discuss the dictate.'

Tostig stared at the thegn with surprise. Of all the things to be discussed, he had not expected to be challenged so soon into his new role.

'What is there to discuss?' he asked. 'The proclamation was clear enough, was it not?'

'It was,' said Gamelbearn, 'but to double the tithe places untold pressure on each and every one of us.'

'Surely you can just pass it on to your land-workers?'

'We can, but they are already taxed up to their necks and to demand more risks even more dissent.'

'Then deal with it appropriately,' said Tostig. 'You are thegns, are you not? Use your power to make sure the common people pay their dues or face the consequences.'

'We will, my lord, and often do, but this level of increase will be hard to justify. I respectfully request that we pause it, at least until the end of next year's harvest.'

'Gamelbearn,' said Tostig. 'In the south, Northumbria is considered a wild and dangerous place, where men are forced to travel in groups of twenty and more to deter the many brigands dominating the land. I often dismissed such rumours as unlikely but, since arriving, have found them to be true. This earldom is essential in protecting our borders against the Scots, but how can we do that when our own land is in disarray? Before we can even begin to think about Scotland we need to bring our own house in order and to do that, we need funds. The tithe stands.'

'But my lord!'

'You heard what I said,' replied Tostig. 'Tell the rest of the thegns that I expect prompt payment, as well as an extra fifty silver pennies per village.'

'Fifty pennies per village?' said Gamelbearn. 'That was not in the proclamation.'

'It was not,' said Tostig, 'but it is now. I will have the edicts drawn up and distributed over the next few days.'

'My lord,' said Dunstan, 'surely this is a mistake—' but before he could continue, Gamelbearn held up his hand, cutting him short.

'In my opinion,' he said, 'and in the opinion of my fellows, the increased tax is excessive, but if your mind is set, my lord, and your intention is to rid these lands of brigands, then, so be it.'

'Good,' said Tostig. 'Now, if there is no other business, I suggest that you leave before the evening draws in. Thank you for bringing your concerns to me, and have a safe journey home.'

Without waiting for a response, Tostig turned away with a slight smile on his face. It was the first time he had needed to deal with dissent since becoming the new Earl of Northumbria, and he thought he had handled it rather well. Inside the hall, he walked over to join Copsi near the fire and poured himself a tankard of warm ale from the newly arrived jug.

'All sorted?' asked Copsi from his chair.

'Aye,' said Tostig, 'nothing to worry about. Now, where were we?'

'We were talking about ugly dogs,' said Copsi.

'Aye, we were,' said Tostig, 'and I believe I have just unloaded the ugliest of them all.'

—

Outside, the two thegns mounted their already tired horses.

'Well,' said Gamelbearn, 'what did you think of him?'

'I think your initial description of him was as accurate as it could be,' said Dunstan. 'He is a dangerous, self-serving arse with ideas of his own grandeur.'

'That's him,' said Gamelbearn, turning his horse to face the manor gates. 'Welcome to the future of Northumbria.' He dug in his heels and, followed by his comrade, headed back through the gates towards Bossall.

A few days later, Gamelbearn watched as a mounted messenger rode away, having delivered the latest edict from Tostig Godwinson. As the rider disappeared, Dunstan appeared from the tavern and looked at the sealed roll of parchment in Gamelbearn's hand.

'Who is that from?' he asked.

'Who do you think?' said Gamelbearn. 'Our new lord and master, Tostig Godwinson.'

'Another?' asked Dunstan. 'It seems that hardly a day goes by without him making some new law. What is it this time? Please don't say even more taxes.'

Gamelbearn broke the seal and unfurled the scroll.

'Well,' asked Dunstan, 'is he trying to squeeze even more pennies from our already threadbare purses?'

'Not this time,' said Gamelbearn. 'He has declared that every town or village in Northumbria erects at least one set of permanent gallows in a prominent place where they can be seen by all. In addition, he has ordered gallows set up at every crossroads throughout the north.'

'Why?' asked Dunstan, shocked.

'He goes on to say,' continued Gamelbearn, 'that any man, woman or child found guilty of brigandry by a group of twelve or more citizens, irrespective of standing, will be immediately hanged without mercy or right to appeal. In addition, in the absence of such people, any lord responsible to Tostig or any other earl can impose the same punishment, should evidence suggest the accused parties are guilty of that or similar offences.'

'So,' said Dunstan, 'he is actually carrying out his promise to rid Northumbria of all brigands. That is a good thing, right?'

'In essence, yes, but the powers bestowed on the nobles are overly strong. What this dictate says is that almost any man above a thegn can summarily accuse, judge and execute a man at his whim, without risk of condemnation.'

'I do not share your concern,' said Dunstan. 'That is what happens anyway.'

'Perhaps so,' said Gamelbearn, 'but now it is written into law, I fear the more unscrupulous men will use it to their own advantage.'

'Put your worries away, my friend,' said Dunstan, 'for there is nought to be done. Tostig is flexing his muscles, and with an army such as his at his back, we dare not challenge him. Now come, let us finish our ale and set about the task.'

Chapter Five

West Wales, April, AD 1055

In the west of Powys in Wales, Aelfgar dismounted from his horse and handed the reins to a squire before heading across a courtyard to the main manor house. Gerald Ericson, his lead huscarl, joined him, painfully aware that they were the focus of dozens of Welsh arbalists up on the surrounding palisades. Each was fully armed, and Aelfgar had no doubt that they would gladly cut them down given the slightest opportunity.

It had been several weeks since they had entered Welsh territory to reach the kingdom of Gwynedd, only to find that King Gruffydd was on campaign against his rival for the throne of Wales, King Rhydderch. At first, their presence had been treated with suspicion, but when he had outlined his plans to one of Gruffydd's officers, he had arranged to bring Aelfgar south to meet Gruffydd, but only on the condition the rest of the huscarls stayed behind in Gwynedd. With little other option, Aelfgar had agreed and at last, they had arrived at this hidden manor near the border between Powys and Deheubarth without major incident.

'They do not look friendly,' said Gerald as they walked. 'You'd think they would be more grateful to someone coming to help them win a war.'

'I feel just as uneasy,' said Aelfgar, looking around the battlements, 'but let us not forget why we are here. If we can help Gruffydd to achieve his aim of becoming the king of a united Wales, imagine how strong the alliance between us would be.'

'I am more concerned with how much of a risk a united Wales would prove to the Crown of England,' said Gerald. 'At the moment, they are too focused on killing each other, and that's just the way I like it.'

The guards led them through the manor and out into a smaller courtyard where a giant of a man, bedecked in well-worn chainmail, fought a smaller warrior wearing only a studded leather jerkin for protection. For a few moments, both Englishmen watched the seemingly one-sided fight, and the sound of clashing swords echoed off the walls of the enclosed courtyard.

Suddenly the bigger man knocked the smaller man's sword from his hands and lunged forward to administer the killing blow, but the unarmed warrior dodged the blade and threw himself onto his opponent, knocking him to the floor. Winded, the armoured man fought desperately, but his opponent produced a knife and pressed it up under his foe's throat.

'Do you yield, Macsen,' he asked, 'or shall I gut you like a fish?'

'I yield, your grace,' gasped the man, 'though you have to admit that I had you bettered in the fight.'

The smaller man got up and helped his training partner to his feet.

'No advantage can be counted until the fight is over, my friend,' said the victor. 'Was it not you who taught me that?'

'Aye, I did,' said Macsen, 'and I would do well to remember my own words.'

Both men sheathed their weapons before turning to face their visitors.

'Ah,' said the smaller man, 'you have arrived. I assume you are Aelfgar?'

'I am,' said Aelfgar, 'and I assume I am speaking to the great King Gruffydd?'

'Indeed, you are,' said the king. 'Who is this?'

'This is Gerald Ericson,' said Aelfgar, 'my right-hand man. I trust him with my life.'

'It is good to have such a man at your side,' said the king and introduced his training partner. 'This is Macsen, and I enjoy the same loyalty from him. Welcome to Powys, my friends, come; I have a thirst about me and would celebrate your arrival with mead.'

Across the border to the south, deep in the heart of Deheubarth, another group of men met with a king, though this time in the keep of one of the strongest fortresses in the area, Dinefwr Castle.

Summoned by King Rhydderch of Gwent, the Lords of Ystrad Tywi, the lands bordering the river running through the kingdom of Deheubarth, had met at the sacred castle built by Rhodri Mawr, the man who was called King of the Britons over two hundred years earlier, to discuss what they were going to do about the impending invasion from Gruffydd ap Llewelyn in the north.

'I fail to see what we can do,' said one of the lords, sat at the enormous table in the main hall. 'Even if we combine our forces, our numbers fall well short of those needed to defeat his army. There is also talk of him bringing English forces to strengthen his arm.'

'I know,' said Rhydderch, 'and that is why I am not advocating a full-scale battle with Gruffydd, but a more targeted response, aimed at disruption rather than conquest. I have it on good faith that Gruffydd himself currently resides just the other side of the Powys border, and I reckon that if we move fast, with a small enough force, we can catch him unawares.'

'Does he not have his army with him?' asked one of the other lords.

'He does not. He is protected by his teulu, about a hundred and fifty well-trained men pledged to protect his person. Make no mistake, they will be a formidable foe, but my spies tell me his main forces are still crushing a rebellion in Builth.'

'Builth is only a day's ride away.'

'Perhaps so, but if we attack Gruffydd's camp with all haste and then escape as quickly as we ride in, we can be back behind the walls of Dinefwr before they have time to react.'

'And after that?'

'Oh, I have no doubt he will wreak his revenge as soon as he can,' said Rhydderch, 'but that, of course, depends on whether he survives our attack.'

The Lords of Tywi looked around each other before one stood up, an older man with white hair and a long matching beard.

'Your grace,' he said, 'may I speak?'

'Please do, Gwion of Pembroke,' said Rhydderch, 'for when you speak, men listen.'

The old man looked around the table. All were younger than him, and many untried in warfare, but between them, they held great power.

'Members of the council,' he said, 'I have listened to all arguments these past two hours, and few have been without merit, but the fact remains that since Gruffydd laid claim to these lands three years ago, the peace he promised has failed to materialise. Not a month goes by without a family member or a comrade falling at the point of a blade, either in battle or at the hands of brigands. I, for one, have had enough of mourning those I loved, and though I may not be long for this world, I would welcome the opportunity to go to my grave knowing my grandchildren have a chance of living in peace. With only his teulu to guard him, Gruffydd is vulnerable, and if what King Rhydderch is saying is true, it is an opportunity too good to miss. We have heard all arguments, so the time for talking must come to an end. With the king's permission, I now call the council to a vote. The proposal is that each of us provides a hundred men at arms to immediately attack Gruffydd while he is isolated from his army. All those in favour, show your vote.'

The room fell silent before one man stood, drew his sword and placed it on the table.

'I agree, Lord Gwion,' he said, 'and I pledge my blade.'

'As do I,' said a second, getting up to stand beside the first.

Over the next few moments, all the lords stood up until all twelve had vowed their support. With twelve blades on the table, the white-haired man turned to face the king.

'Your grace,' he said, 'as you can see, you have your army. What would you have us do?'

--

Two days later, twelve hundred heavily armed men gathered outside the town of Llandeilo on the River Tywi. A rolling mist played between the horses' legs, and grey clouds hid the first of the morning sun. At their head sat Lord Gwion, the orchestrator of the makeshift force, waiting for the king to make his appearance.

'Where is he?' asked Robert of Gwent at his side. 'He should be here by now.'

Before Gwion could answer, a rider appeared from the gloom and rode up beside them.

'My lord,' he said, 'I have a message from the king.' He handed over a sealed parchment and waited as Gwion broke the seal and handed it to Robert.

'You read it,' he said, 'my eyes are not as good as they were.'

Robert took the letter and read silently before looking over to his comrade.

'Well?' said Gwion.

'It seems the king is not joining us,' he said. 'He has been struck down by a fever but urges that we continue with the plan.'

'I bet he does,' said Gwion. 'Truth be told, I fully expected his withdrawal.'

'What do you want to do?'

'When I spoke at Dinefwr,' said Gwion, 'I did so on behalf of all those who suffered and continue to suffer at the hands of Gruffydd – it was not in support of a king who has oft failed to support his own men. The situation has not changed: Gruffydd is vulnerable, and if we manage to get rid of him, at least we will have only one king to worry about.'

'So, we continue?'

'Aye, we do,' said Gwion. 'Tell the men to mount up, Robert; we are riding to Powys.'

—

Two days later, in King Gruffydd's fortified manor house in Powys, Aelfgar stumbled from the doorway and headed over towards the stables where Gerald was waiting with their two horses. In one hand, he carried his sword belt and in the other, his quilted jerkin.

'The morning has half gone,' said Gerald, a hint of frustration in his voice. 'Our men will be wondering what is happening.'

'You sound like a peasant's wife,' groaned Aelfgar, his head pounding from the night's heavy drinking session. 'Curb your manner and hold these.' He threw the sword belt and jerkin towards Gerald and retrieved a wooden cup tied to the edge of the water barrel.

'My lord,' said Gerald, as Aelfgar filled the cup, 'we need to remember what is happening here.'

'And what exactly is that?' asked Aelfgar. 'For as far as I am concerned, I am building relationships with a man who may help me with my own ambitions, and if that means partaking of his unrivalled hospitality, then so be it.' He paused and looked over at the manor as several young women exited the building to return to their village half a league away. 'See what I mean?' he said, before drinking the cold water down in one go.

'All I am saying, my lord,' continued Gerald, 'is the rest of our men are still at risk in Gwynedd. I know Gruffydd has assured their safety, but I wonder if that message has filtered out to the towns and villages. Any minor lord worth his salt may see our presence as an opportunity to kill some Englishmen and thus make a name for himself. If nothing else, we should at least be amongst them to lead should that happen.'

Aelfgar refilled the cup and again drained it in one before grasping the sides of the barrel and submerging his head in the water. Seconds later, he stood upright and threw his head backwards, his shoulder-length hair dripping. He rubbed his hands over his face and squeezed the excess water from his hair before holding his hand out for the jerkin.

'You worry too much,' he said, pulling the garment over his head, 'and do not understand how politics works. What happened in there last night is just as important as any formal agreement committed to parchment. Suffice to say, the King of Gwynedd and I now have an understanding, and once we rid Deheubarth of Rhydderch, we will create an alliance second to none across Britannia.'

'And how do we do that? We have only ten men.'

'Ten at the moment,' said Aelfgar, 'but Gruffydd has provided us with a ship to get to Ireland. There we can recruit a fleet to lead the vanguard should it come to conflict with Edward.'

'I am still uncomfortable with that outcome,' said Gerald. 'Even the thought is treasonous.'

'It is not something I seek or desire,' said Aelfgar, 'but it would be remiss of me not to prepare for such an outcome. This way, we will have ships and an army at our back when I approach Edward to claim my birthright. Hopefully, it can all be sorted out with parley between like-minded men, but until that day comes, we have work to do. Come, we should be going.'

The two men mounted their horses and, watched by the arbalists high on the palisades, headed out of the gates.

–

A few hundred paces away, amongst the trees at the edge of the forest, Robert of Gwent watched them depart.

'Who are they?' he whispered. 'They do not look like they are from around here.'

'I know not,' replied Gwion, 'but at least that is twelve less we have to worry about.'

'Are you sure about this?' asked Robert. 'Perhaps we should wait until dark.'

'We can't wait any longer,' said Gwion. 'Gruffydd's army could be here any moment. We must strike while we can. Ready the men.'

Robert sank back into the forest as Gwion briefed the other men at his side. Once everyone was ready, he gave a signal, and a covered cart emerged from the trees a few hundred paces away. As it approached the gates, some of the men on the palisades looked down at the two scantily clad women leading the horses, both unaware that there were several arrows aimed at their backs in case of treachery.

'Hold there, my lovely,' shouted one of the guards as the cart neared, 'for if you have come to entertain the king and his guests, you are too late; the festivities were last night.'

'Though you can entertain me any time you want,' added his comrade with a sneer. 'What business do you have here?'

'We have brought fresh fish from the seaport,' said one of the girls, 'as requested by your master.'

'I have no knowledge of this,' said one of the guards to his comrade. 'I will bring the steward; you go down and check their load.' Both men disappeared from the palisade but were immediately replaced with two more.

'Keep going,' whispered a voice from the cart behind the women, 'and stop between the gates.'

Both women were terrified, knowing that there were at least a dozen warriors hidden in the back, and whatever happened in the next few minutes, they were unlikely to survive. They urged the horses onward, and moments later, reined them in between the gate posts. Before them, the second guard blocked their way, his hand resting on the hilt of his sword.

'That's far enough,' he said. 'The steward will be here soon enough, but in the meantime, I need to see your load.' He walked around to the back of the cart and pulled down the tailgate, only to stare into the face of an armed man holding a sword. Before he could react, the hidden warrior drove his blade through his throat, severing his spine and sending him falling backwards into the mud.

Up above, one of his comrades saw the killing and, as the attackers jumped from the cart, turned to sound the alarm.

'*To arms,*' he roared. '*We are under attack!*'

The defending men at arms reacted almost instantly, but by the time they realised what was happening, the hidden attackers had already spread out either side of the gates, determined to keep them open as long as they could. They were heavily outnumbered but knew they only had to last until their comrades arrived from the forest.

Across the clearing, Gwion heard the alarm and turned to the rest of his makeshift army.

'To your feet!' he roared. 'Follow me.'

Within seconds, over five hundred men broke their cover and raced across the clearing towards the open gates. Up on the palisades, the arbalists sent their arrows scything through the air into the attackers, striking many down before they had gotten even halfway, but the numbers were too many, and by the time they had reloaded their crossbows, Gwion and his men had reached the gate and poured into the courtyard.

Across the compound, more guards raced from their barracks, unprepared for such an audacious attack, but, they fought with a fury hardly matched across Wales.

Within moments, the battle spread out, and even more men poured out of the manor, including the king and his right-hand man, Macsen. Both held no fear of death and, with a roar of anger, waded into the fight with their own weapons, cutting a swathe through the men of Deheubarth.

Up on the palisade, the attack had taken its toll, and though the arbalists were also armed with swords, they fell back desperately. One of the commanders looked over the wall to see even more men racing from the woods and knew there was no way they could possibly win the fight. Fiercely loyal to the king, he shouted down into the courtyard.

'My lord Macsen,' he roared, 'there is no end to their numbers. You have to save the king.'

Macsen heard the warning and turned to see the king fighting two men, his back against the stable wall. He raced over and plunged his blade into the back of one, and as Gruffydd bettered the second, he grabbed the king's tunic and dragged him through the doorway into the stable.

'What are you doing?' shouted the king. 'Are you mad?'

'We have to get you out of here,' shouted Macsen, 'this fight is lost.'

'Not yet it isn't,' said the king, heading back towards the door.

Macsen reached out and grabbed Gruffydd, throwing him against the wall.

'Listen to me!' he roared. 'We have to get you out of here, right now.'

'Unhand me, Macsen,' hissed the king, 'or I swear I will have your head.'

'My head is yours to take,' said Macsen, 'but for now, I need you to listen to me. We are heavily outnumbered again, and the walls have been breached. The only reason they are here must be to kill you, and if that happens, Gwynedd itself is at risk. Our men can hold them for a few more minutes, but once we are overrun, there is nothing more we can do to protect you. Let me get you out of here, your grace, and keep you alive to fight another day.'

Gruffydd hesitated, knowing that Macsen was right. As much as it disgusted him to run from a fight, his life was more important, not just for him, but for the whole of Wales.

'So be it,' he said. 'What do you want me to do?'

Macsen looked around at the line of unsaddled horses tied to the rails.

'Remember the time we raced bareback along the shore at Ynys Mon?'

'Aye, the loss cost me a hundred silver pennies.'

'It did,' replied Macsen, 'so this is your chance to win them back. Mount up, your grace, and prepare to ride harder than you ever have ridden before.'

Moments later, both men rode out of the stable and headed for the rear of the compound. Two dozen of their own men stood behind a shield wall and formed a gap as they approached.

'Open the gate,' shouted Macsen, and turned to the guard commander. 'Hold them off as long as you can, then try to make your escape.'

'Aye, my lord,' said the soldier, and watched as the king and his bodyguard kicked their horses into a gallop. Behind them was a scene of carnage as the men of Deheubarth rallied, and within a few minutes, overwhelmed the last of the king's personal teulu.

–

Ten minutes later, Gruffydd and Macsen caught up with Aelfgar and Gerald on the road north. Hearing their frantic approach, both men drew their swords and turned to see who was following.

'Lower your arms,' shouted Macsen. 'This is King Gruffydd of Gwynedd.'

'What is going on?' said Aelfgar as the men neared, and his eyes widened at the sight of the blood-spattered monarch with whom he had been sharing wine and women only hours earlier. 'Your grace!' he gasped. 'What happened? Are you hurt?'

'Only my pride,' said Gruffydd. 'That pig of a man, Rhydderch of Gwent, sent an army of assassins against me. I was lucky to escape with my life.'

'Your grace,' said Aelfgar, 'if I had known you were in the slightest danger, I would have stayed at your side.'

'It would have been a futile gesture,' said the king, 'and besides, I need to get back to Gwynedd. I suspect that by now, all my teulu in the manor are either dead or captured, and I need to take revenge.'

'We will fight alongside you,' said Aelfgar.

'No,' said Gruffydd, 'you continue to Ireland and raise your fleet. Once done, return to Gwynedd, and we will discuss what happens next. Agreed?'

'Aye,' said Aelfgar. 'Though I humbly request that you wait for my return before embarking on any campaign.'

'Curb your enthusiasm, my friend,' said Gruffydd, 'for I promise you, these next few weeks will be filled with more blood than you can imagine.'

Chapter Six

Bosham, August, AD 1055

Harold Godwinson was sitting at the table in the main hall, breaking his fast with his wife, when he heard a commotion outside in the courtyard. He lifted his head and listened but did not worry unduly. Bosham was well guarded, and at the moment, he had no enemies of note willing or indeed able to present his house with any sort of threat. He continued eating his oatmeal and eggs before looking up again as his steward entered through the main doors, followed by two men who were familiar to him.

'My lord,' announced the steward, 'these men have ridden from London. They have a message from the king.'

Harold put down his spoon and wiped his mouth on a cloth before rising and walking over to the men.

'So,' he said, seeing the exhaustion in the men's eyes, 'spit it out. What is so important that required you to ride through the night?'

One of the men delved into a satchel and retrieved a parchment.

'I know not the detail, my lord,' he said, handing over the parchment, 'only that you are required to raise your army forthwith.'

Harold's eyes narrowed with concern. A sealed message from the king was always worrisome, but coming with a call to arms meant there was a threat to the throne. He broke the seal and read in silence. Once done, he rolled up the parchment and turned to the messengers.

'You look exhausted,' he said. 'Get yourselves some hot food from the kitchens and go to the barracks. Tell them to give you a couple of cots to get some rest. We will look after your horses.'

'Thank you, my lord,' said the first messenger, and followed the steward from the room.

At the table, Harold's wife had been watching the events unfold with concern.

'Well?' she said as he sat back down to finish his meal. 'What is so important that the king needs our men?'

'It seems that Aelfgar has sailed to Ireland to raise a fleet,' said Harold. 'If the message is correct, then he wants to negotiate with the king to award him the Earldom of Northumbria, but cannot do so without an army.'

'Leofric would never turn against the king,' said Edyth.

'He would not,' said Harold, 'but his idiot son has acted alone and now nurtures support from the Welsh.'

'Is he mad?' gasped Edyth. 'Gruffydd is nothing short of a madman and is just as likely to kill Aelfgar as any of his many other enemies.'

'Gruffydd knows what he wants,' said Harold, 'the undisputed kingship of all Wales. By joining with Aelfgar, especially if he has a fleet under his command, it will make defeating Rhydderch that much easier.'

'So what does Edward want you to do?'

'He wants me to make ready the men of Wessex, just in case Aelfgar does something stupid.'

'Like what?'

'Like attacking Hereford. The city has always been at risk from the Welsh, and Gruffydd has already attacked it once but withdrew after a few weeks. It is the gateway to southern England, and Edward wants me to ensure it is kept closed.'

'Is Hereford not already protected by Earl Ralf of Mantes?'

'It is, but the nickname he has been given by his own men explains why the king wants me to raise an army.'

'And that nickname is?'

'Ralf the Timid,' said Harold. 'An accurate description of the man if ever there was one.'

'So, what are you going to do?'

'First of all, I will finish my meal. Once done, I will send messages to my thegns to raise the army.'

'What about your journey to Hungary?'

'I will have to put it aside for the moment,' said Harold. 'This is too important.'

'It seems there is always something else to do,' said Edyth. 'I look forward to the day when your destiny lies solely within your own hands.'

'As do I,' said Harold, 'but until that day comes, we all must do whatever we can to survive.'

-

In Wales, Aelfgar was once more on dry land, having returned from Ireland, a place renowned for being a meeting place for Vikings and mercenaries, with more than enough men at arms to fight under his banner, and a fleet of eighteen ships now lay at anchor off the coast of Anglesey.

Each ship was capable of holding up to fifty men, making over nine hundred warriors, and while he was away, he had sent word back to the north-east, summoning all those still loyal to his name to muster on the Welsh border, giving him an army of over two thousand men at arms. Gruffydd was suitably impressed and arranged a feast to celebrate the arrival of his unlikely allies.

Present were Aelfgar's closest huscarls as well as King Gruffydd's bodyguards and nobles. In the centre of the table lay the remains of a roasted boar, surrounded by game birds and platters of onions with dozens of jugs of ale and wine filling the side tables.

'This feast would do justice to any at the court of Edward,' said Aelfgar, leaning forward to stab his knife into another slab of pork. 'I am impressed.'

'Why would my hospitality surprise you,' asked Gruffydd, 'am I a lesser king than Edward just by virtue of location?'

'Of course not,' said Aelfgar, 'I meant no disrespect. In fact, my remarks were intended as a compliment rather than a slight, pointing out that he holds no advantage over you. My apologies if they gave you offence.'

'No apologies needed,' said Gruffydd. 'Have some more wine.' He sent one of the serving girls scurrying away for a full jug.

Aelfgar sighed inwardly. His remarks had been made without thought, and though he had put the Welsh king's mind at rest, it had been through untruths. Edward's banquets were far more elegant affairs with all sorts of exotic items dressing the tables along with spices, vegetables and fruit, all items that were conspicuously absent from Gruffydd's hall.

'So,' said Gruffydd, turning back to face Aelfgar, 'tell me about these Vikings.'

'They are all Ireland born,' said Aelfgar, 'but are from Norse ancestors. They have kept their fathers' ways and ply their trade by fighting for whoever has the bigger purse.'

'And I assume that you had enough money to pay the price?'

'Actually, I do not,' said Aelfgar, 'but they have taken my word on trust that they will be paid.'

'And how do you intend to do that if you have no coin?'

'By giving them a free hand to plunder what they can from anywhere we attack.'

Gruffydd stared at Aelfgar for a moment, a leg of rabbit grasped firmly in his fist.

'Now that may be a problem,' he said.

'Why,' asked Aelfgar, 'is not Deheubarth a rich kingdom?'

'Indeed it is,' said Gruffydd, 'but any plunder has already been promised to my men. If they were to find out it was to be shared with nine hundred Irishmen, then I fear their numbers will dwindle by nightfall tomorrow.'

Aelfgar thought furiously. This was a situation he had not anticipated, and there was no way he could pay the price of the

Irish fleet, at least not without the support of his father, and that was not likely to be forthcoming anytime soon.

'You look concerned,' said Gruffydd. 'I hope you haven't committed to a situation you are unable to manage.'

'Not in the slightest,' lied Aelfgar, 'but there is an agreement to be made here that will suit both our needs.'

'And that is?'

'If I help you get rid of Rhydderch, in return, you will help me send a message to Edward that I am playing no games and must be taken seriously.'

'And how do I do that?'

'By supporting an attack on Hereford. Do this, and not only do I declare my intentions to the king, but my men get the opportunity to fill their purses.'

Gruffydd chewed on a piece of rabbit for a few moments while still staring at Aelfgar. Finally, he swallowed the meat and picked up his tankard of wine.

'I think we have ourselves an agreement, Aelfgar of Mercia,' he said. 'Let us drink to kingship and warfare.'

Aelfgar picked up his own tankard to join the toast. It had been a risky ploy, but at last, he knew he could make it work. If everything went well against Rhydderch of Gwent, he would send King Edward a message that he could not ignore.

'To kingship and warfare,' he said and, following Gruffydd's example, downed the drink in one.

Chapter Seven

Gwent, Wales, October, AD 1055

King Rhydderch of Gwent sat in a wooden tub before a roaring fire in one of his manor houses. The day had been long, and a fall from his horse meant he stank of pig filth and sweat, a combination that had forced him to take a hot bath, for his wife's sake, if nothing else. For the first time in months, he felt safe and content. His kingdom was growing, having taken control of all Deheubarth in the southern third of Wales, and his recent attack on Gruffydd in Powys had come within inches of killing his main adversary, Gruffydd of Gwynedd, sending him scurrying northwards like a scared dog. There was a lot to be thankful for, and he had ordered a special service of thanksgiving to be carried out in all the churches throughout the kingdom on the following Sunday.

He lifted his ornate goblet of wine to his lips before handing it back to the young serving girl and sinking further beneath the hot water. He stared at the servant as she busied herself picking up his dirty clothes and smoothing the covers on his bed. As he relaxed, his mind turned from warfare to other things, almost equally important in his mind: the pleasures of the flesh.

'What is your name?' he asked eventually, as she glanced over and caught his gaze.

'Elspeth, my lord,' she said.

'I have not seen you before, Elspeth,' he said. 'Where is my usual girl?'

'She has been taken ill, my lord. The housekeeper asked me to take her place for a few days. I'm sure she will be back soon.'

'There is no rush,' said the king, 'for in truth, you are fairer to the eye than she. Where are you from?'

'From Caerphilly, my lord. My family worked a farm there, but alas, it earns not much money, so I sought work here in Caerleon. I hope my standards are to your liking.'

'You are doing a fine job,' said Rhydderch, 'and if this is the standard you provide, then I see no reason not to keep you as my maid on a permanent basis. Of course, there would be other expectations of you, but that is only to be expected.'

Elspeth swallowed hard as her fears were confirmed.

'I do not understand, your grace,' she said. 'Are you saying that you also wish me to share your bed?'

'On occasion,' said the king, as if the requirement was simply a formality, 'but only when the queen is absent.'

'Your grace,' said the girl, 'I am truly honoured by the offer, I really am, but I must regretfully decline. Please forgive me.'

'Why?' asked the king. 'Is it not a generous gift?'

'It truly is,' said the girl, 'but I cannot lay with you, for I am yet unwed and hope to marry in the near future. To go to the church unchaste would be a sin before God.'

'So you have never lain with a man?'

'I have not, your grace.'

'You do realise I could just take you anyway,' said the king.

'Yes, your grace,' said the girl, 'but I beseech thee not to do so, or I cannot wed the man who has asked to marry me.'

'Then do not tell him,' said Rhydderch.

'To carry such a lie into a marriage would surely condemn my soul to hell,' said the girl miserably, her head held down so as not to meet his stare.

'Look at me,' said the king.

Elspeth lifted her head and stared as Rhydderch raised himself out of the bathwater to stand naked before her.

'Elspeth of Caerphilly,' he said. 'I am your king, and though I will never force you to do anything you do not want to do, it would be a terrible shame if your family were to lose their farm. Do you not agree?'

Elspeth's hand flew to her mouth to stifle the cry of fear, but she knew the king was well capable of such an act. Tears rolled down the servant's face as she realised the situation was hopeless. She was about to beg him for leniency when a knock came on the door.

'Your grace,' cried a voice, 'I need to speak to you urgently.'

'Go away,' shouted Rhydderch, 'I am busy.'

'Your grace,' shouted the voice, 'this will not wait. Open the door.'

Rhydderch cursed and turned to the girl.

'Consider your thoughts,' he said, 'and we will resolve this matter when I return.' He walked across the room and unbolted the door to see the constable of Caerleon standing outside.

'I swear,' said the king, 'that if this is not important, I will have you flogged in your own stocks. State your business.'

'Your grace,' said the constable, 'you have to come now, you and your army.'

'Why?' asked the king. 'What has happened?'

'It's Port Skewett, your grace. It is under threat of attack.'

'Attack from whom?' asked the king, any thoughts of passion already forgotten.

'I'm not sure, your grace, but reports say that a fleet of longships lies offshore, each laden with many fighting men.'

'If they intend to attack, why have they not done so?'

'I think they were caught out by the tide,' said the constable. 'The river is low, but the tide has turned, and it will be a few hours before they can sail right into the port.'

'How many ships?'

'No more than twenty, your grace.'

'About a thousand men,' said the king. 'Alert my huscarls, and send word to the army. Tell them to muster on the northern edge of Port Skewett as soon as they can. If we act now, we may just get there before the tide is at its fullest.'

'I have already raised the alarm, your grace,' said the constable, 'and we will have many men ready to march within the hour.'

'Good. Now go and spread the word, we need as many men as possible.'

'Yes, your grace,' said the constable.

Rhydderch slammed the door behind him and strode over to the other side of the room, where a clean set of robes lay hanging from a peg in the wall.

'Your grace,' said the girl from across the room, 'what's happening?'

'It is men's business,' said the king, 'not yours.' He finished getting dressed, and Rhydderch marched across to the door before pausing and looking back at the girl.

'Do not think this is over, Elspeth of Caerphilly,' he said, 'for when I am done, we will resume this discussion, understood?'

'Yes, your grace,' whimpered the girl and watched as the king stormed off to battle, slamming the door behind him.

–

A few hours later, several leagues away, King Gruffydd lay hidden deep in a forest just a few leagues north of Caerleon in Gwent. Alongside him were almost two thousand men at arms, each having travelled south from Powys using the harder routes through the mountains and forests, moving only at night to avoid the eyes of anyone loyal to Rhydderch. Now they were only a few hours' march away from their target and waited impatiently for nightfall to come. A crouched figure came from within the forest and dropped to his knees beside him: Macsen, his second-in-command.

'Are the men ready?' asked the king as Macsen retrieved his water bottle.

'As ready as they can be,' said Macsen. 'They are well-rested and well-fed, just impatient for the fighting to start.'

'It will be here soon enough,' said the king. 'I just hope that Aelfgar keeps his part of the bargain. Our men are as good as any, but without his army and the Irish mercenaries, I fear that we could be taking on more than we can handle.'

'He seems like a good man,' said Macsen, 'so I do not think he will let us down. If he does, I swear there will be an assassin's blade across his throat before the next full moon.'

'Let us hope it doesn't come to that,' said Gruffydd. 'Have the scouts returned?'

'One has. He says that there is a lot of activity around Caerleon, with many men marching towards Skewett. It seems they have taken the bait and are rallying to oppose the Irish fleet.'

'Excellent,' said Gruffydd. 'I have agreed with Aelfgar that they will not land until first light tomorrow, so we have time to get down there. Make sure the men are ready to move by dark.'

'Are you sure, your grace?' asked Macsen. 'For the journey is still quite long, and we may not get there by dawn.'

'We will be there in time,' said Gruffydd, 'for once it is dark, we can use the main roads and force the march. Anyone seeing us will have no time to reach Rhydderch in time to warn him.'

'So be it,' said Macsen.

–

Back in Bosham, Harold paced the floor of his hall, deep in thought. The army had been mustered and waited several leagues inland, but he had returned to his manor, realising there was one thing left to do before he marched to Hereford.

'Your grace,' said a voice, 'he is here.'

Harold turned to see the steward standing alongside Owen of Hereford. Owen was no longer in chains but had his hands tied together for safety. His demeanour was a little stronger, and the regular meals he had been fed over the past few weeks had added life to his features. Harold walked over to stand before the prisoner.

'Leave us,' he said, and the steward reversed out of the door, leaving the two men alone in the hall.

'You have caused me many sleepless nights, Owen of Hereford,' said Harold.

'I, on the contrary,' replied the huscarl, 'have slept better than I have for over two years. A straw mattress and the smell of horses is strangely comforting. I strongly recommend it.'

'Keep your remarks to yourself,' said Harold, 'as I am still in two minds whether to set you free or kill you where you stand.'

'You must do what you have to do,' said Owen. 'I have made my peace with God.'

'But not to me.'

'I do not answer to you,' said Owen, 'only to my own conscience and to the Lord.'

'Yet you answered to Sweyn for many years.'

'I was sworn to him,' said Owen. 'That is different.'

'But still, you murdered him in cold blood.'

'The Lord guided my hand that day,' said Owen, 'I know that now. He acted to save the innocents.'

'So you are blaming God for your sins.'

'The sin was mine,' said Owen. 'God just opened my eyes.'

'You almost sound like a priest,' said Harold, 'such is your newly found piety. Perhaps that is the path you should take.'

'Perhaps I will,' said Owen, 'if I should survive this day.'

Harold stared at the Welshman, his feelings swinging between mercy and hatred.

'I am going to ask you one more thing,' said Harold, 'so think carefully before you answer.'

'Ask your question, Earl Harold,' said Owen. 'There will be only truth from this mouth.'

'Do you regret it?'

'Regret what?'

'Killing my brother,' said Harold, his eyes not leaving Owen's.

Owen paused and stared at the earl. He knew that one way or another, his answer would decide his fate.

'From the day I came here begging to be killed,' he replied eventually, 'I have spoken nothing but the truth. My words have only grown the anger in your heart, but I had made an oath to God to speak truthfully, a vow that I have not broken, nor will I break.' He paused for a moment before continuing. 'I regret that Sweyn put us in that situation in the first place. I regret being forced to confront the man I had fought alongside for many years. I regret killing my lord and master, a crime against the laws of this country, and I regret not coming to you sooner with this information. However, if the point of your question is, do I regret killing Sweyn Godwinson, the murderer, the kidnapper, the rapist, the child molester, then my answer is no. I only wish I had done it sooner.'

Harold grimaced and drew a blade from his belt before forcing Owen up against the wall with the point pressing against his chest.

'This is your last chance, Owen of Hereford,' he said, putting pressure on the handle of his knife. 'Give me one good reason why I shouldn't cut your lying heart in half.'

A silence fell in the hall, and under Owen's jerkin, a tiny droplet of blood appeared at the tip of Harold's blade.

'I will give you your answer,' said Owen, 'for despite my imminent death, I know I have spoken the truth. My reason is this. Your brother had a shadow of evil about him, and I ignored it for too long, but you, on the other hand, are a godly man, and I know that whatever you decide, it will be done with good conscience, whether that decision is right or wrong in the eyes of the Lord. Now, do what you have to do.'

Harold continued to stare into the prisoner's eyes and regripped the hilt of the knife, his face contorted with anger. Yet despite wanting to thrust his knife home, something stayed his hand – a nagging fear that as much as he wanted to believe his brother had not been capable of such things, deep down inside, he knew that there had been a dark side to Sweyn that he had kept hidden from the family. His mind raced. The man needed to be punished, yet he had been a valuable asset to the Godwin family over the years, and if his story was in the slightest way truthful, then justice would not be served by killing him in cold blood. Slowly he eased the pressure and, without breaking his gaze, took half a pace backwards.

'You can thank God that you still breathe,' he said eventually, 'for there is a flicker of doubt in my mind, but I will not stand in summary judgement until I am sure. When that day comes, you may still feel my blade between your ribs.'

'I am grateful,' said Owen, 'and will gladly face a trial.'

'There will be no trial,' said Harold, moving the blade down to cut the rope tying Owen's hands together. 'You are coming with me.'

'I do not understand,' said Owen, confused. 'Where are we going?'

'To Hereford,' said Harold. 'If I am not mistaken, you know the county better than anyone else.'

'I was born and bred there,' said Owen. 'What do you want me to do?'

'Whatever I ask you to do,' said Harold, 'and if you survive what is to come, perhaps I will let you live. Now go to the stables and tell them to furnish you with a horse, a weapon and a satchel of food. I will join you within the hour.'

'Yes, my lord,' said Owen and, still shocked at the outcome, made his way from the hall.

Once the door closed, Harold turned slowly around to face his wife, the red flush of rage slowly draining from his features.

'If it is any consolation,' said Edyth, 'I think you made the right decision.'

'I may yet kill him,' said Harold, 'but today is not the day.'

'And if you do so, and return to tell the tale, be assured there will be no judgement from me,' said his wife. 'Come, we still have time to eat before you leave.' She took his hand and led her husband over to the table where the servants had laid out a platter of cold meats, bread and cheese. 'Eat heartily, Harold Godwinson,' she said, taking a seat beside him, 'for today is a good day, and may God bless this house.'

Harold lifted his tankard and downed the ale, fully aware that the meal could be the last he and his wife ever shared.

Chapter Eight

Gwent, Wales, October, AD 1055

King Rhydderch rode along the road towards Skewett. Behind him came over five hundred mounted lancers, each heavily armed and well used to the ways of war. Less experienced men at arms walked on either side of the road, heading for the same destination, encouraged by the more battle-hardened sergeants. Each had been rounded up from the local villages over the past few hours, and whilst it was by no means the strongest army available, Rhydderch was comfortable that the numbers were more than enough to thwart any attempt at landing by the longships.

'How is the tide?' he asked one of his officers, riding at his side.

'It will peak in about two hours, your grace,' came the reply. 'We should be there in plenty of time.'

'Good,' said Rhydderch, 'I want them to see our strength before it gets dark. If we can cause them to doubt their ability to succeed until at least the morning, the rest of the army will be here to strengthen our defences.'

The column rode onward and, within the hour, reached the port of Skewett. Rhydderch looked out over the river and could see the longships waiting just out of range of his arbalists.

'Your grace,' said a man running over and taking a knee, 'thank God you are here. I thought we were done for.'

'Get to your feet,' said the king. 'Who are you?'

'My name is Gibson, your grace, the port master. Those ships have been here since dawn but caught the retreating tide,

71

so left it too late to attack. I suspect these waters were unknown to them.'

'Their colours look Irish,' said Rhydderch. 'Have they sent any messages?'

'None, my lord. I think they are waiting for high tide.'

'And what have you been doing in the meantime?'

'We have moved all the items of value from the stores to further inland as well as all the women and children. The men have been busy building barricades against any attack, though they are in no way sufficient. At least with you here, we can provide worthy opposition.'

'This place will be swarming with my men within hours,' said the king. 'Until then, make sure those ships are watched. I want to know the moment they move.'

'Of course, your grace,' said the man and ran back towards the temporary palisade erected atop the port walls.

'Lord Dafydd,' said Rhydderch to his second-in-command. 'Secure the horses to the rear and deploy our men along the foreshore. Get them to light torches, so those ships can see how strong we are.'

'Yes, your grace,' said the officer and relayed the order to one of the junior officers before walking over to stand beside the king.

'What are you thinking?' asked Rhydderch, still staring out at the silent longboats.

'I am thinking that I have no idea what their strategy is,' said Dafydd. 'Surely they must know that even when the river is at its highest, the port will be well defended and hard to subdue. They must know that there is a high chance of defeat.'

'These sort of men relish such odds,' said Rhydderch, 'and will take some beating, but beat them we will, as long as the rest of our men get here in time.'

'There is another way,' said Dafydd. 'We could wait until high tide and send out a messenger.'

'To what end?'

'To negotiate a withdrawal. Perhaps if we fill their boats with supplies and a few sacks of silver, they will go on their way.'

'Aye, that will work,' said Rhydderch, 'at least until they decide to come back for more. No, we will make a stand here, and if it comes to a fight, then we will be ready.'

'So be it,' said Dafydd and turned away to brief his men.

—

The following morning, at dawn, Rhydderch was shaken awake by one of the guards.

'Your grace,' he said, 'the ships are moving.'

The king jumped to his feet and ran out of the storehouse where he had rested to stare out over the river. The tide was high, but the ships were retreating further out into mid-channel.

'The signs are good,' said Dafydd, appearing at his side. 'It looks like they have had second thoughts.'

'We shall see,' said the king, fastening his sword belt around his waist. 'Stand to the men, just in case this is a ploy of some kind.'

'Yes, your grace,' said the officer. Within ten minutes, every armed man in Skewett lined up along the harbour walls and along the shoreline to either side. It was an impressive sight and one that would have to be taken seriously by any potential attacker.

'They have stopped,' said the king a few minutes later. 'Why do they not just attack or sail away?'

'I think we should send a boat to find out their intentions,' said Dafydd. 'At the very least, we will know what to expect.'

'It is worth a try,' said the king. 'Do it.'

Dafydd moved off to find a boat owner, but hadn't gone a few paces before stopping in his tracks and staring up the hill in shock. As far as he could see, row after row of heavily armed men raced down through the dying bracken. For a few seconds, he was confused, but as others around him also realised the danger, he knew it had been a trap, and the main threat was almost upon them.

'*To arms!*' he roared. 'We are under attack!'

Moments later, King Gruffydd's men burst onto the docks like a storm wave, but Rhydderch's army were no strangers to battle and frantically rallied to face the threat. The fight quickly spread out over a wide area, and with no time to form defensive lines, men fought alone or with just one or two comrades at their side.

The brutal impetus of the attack meant Rhydderch himself was forced to fight, but he was accustomed to violence and gave as good as he got. His bodyguards stayed close, repelling the worst of those desperate to claim the life of a king, but Rhydderch's sword was no less busy. He fought desperately, sword in one hand, dagger in the other, sending man after man crashing to the ground before finishing them off with a thrust through the heart or face.

The sound of steel on steel competed with the screams of wounded and dying men as the two armies cut each other apart, but within minutes, the advantage swung back to the men of Gwent. Step by step, and led by their fearless king, they started to force the northerners back towards the hill, but just as Rhydderch thought the day would be his, one of his men shouted from a nearby rooftop.

'Your grace,' he shouted, 'look upstream.'

Rhydderch stared along the riverbank to see the Irish mercenaries, leaping from their beached ships and forming up to open a second line of attack. He cursed and turned to Dafydd, already covered in the blood of his many victims.

'Take the foot-soldiers and hold them back,' he shouted. 'I will lead the rest of our men downstream and form a new position. Hold them as long as you can.'

'No,' said Dafydd, his face drawn in fear, 'I cannot.'

'*Do as you are ordered*,' roared Rhydderch, 'or I swear I will kill you myself.'

'I cannot,' retorted the officer, 'for there is nowhere for you to go. *Look!*'

Rhydderch followed Dafydd's stare and, to his horror, saw another army racing along the path from downstream, this time mounted and with lances drawn.

'We are doomed,' he gasped, turning to his second-in-command. 'Lord Dafydd, get me out of here.'

'How?' shouted Dafydd. 'There is nowhere to go. All we can do now is fight like men and, when it comes to an end, hope that they will show mercy.'

'No,' shouted the king, 'we cannot just stay here and die. Look to the hill, they are retreating. Let us follow them up and press home the advantage. If we can get to the treeline, we have a chance.'

Dafydd looked up and watched in horror as yet another line of men emerged from the treeline, this time forming two straight lines. His heart sank as he realised they were archers and there was nowhere left for them to run.

'It is too late,' he said, 'we have been tricked. May God have mercy on our souls.'

–

Up on the hill, King Gruffydd and Macsen watched with growing satisfaction as a storm of arrows rained down on Rhydderch's panicking army. Many of the defenders tried to escape upstream, but the waiting Irish mercenaries cut them down without mercy before heading in amongst the buildings to seek those who tried to hide.

Further downstream, Aelfgar's lancers thundered into the adjacent village, cutting down anyone trying to flee and torching the houses. The air was thick with smoke, and the screams of the innocent, as Gruffydd's army took out their frustration after so many years of war. Men and women alike

75

pleaded for quarter, but their cries were ignored, and all the remaining resistance crumbled before the brutal onslaught.

Eventually, the sounds of battle died away, replaced with the whimpers of the wounded and the prayers of those who waited to die. Seeing the battle was won, Gruffydd descended from the hill and walked between his cheering warriors. The battle had lasted less than an hour, but never in his wildest dreams had he expected such an overwhelming victory. Hundreds of men had been taken prisoner and now stood surrounded by Aelfgar's lancers.

'Where is Rhydderch?' shouted Gruffydd, looking around the hundreds of corpses. 'Someone show me his body.'

'We are still looking for him,' replied Macsen, wiping blood from his face with the sleeve of his gambeson. 'Nobody has yet claimed the kill.'

'We need to find him,' said Gruffydd, 'for if he is not dead, he may yet block my path to unite Wales.'

'He cannot be far,' said Macsen. 'Aelfgar and the Irish have blocked all the roads out – there is no escape.'

'I have no intention of escaping,' said a voice, and everyone turned to see the King of Gwent emerge from a small building.

'King Rhydderch,' said Gruffydd as his adversary approached, 'you are still alive. How unfortunate.'

'King Gruffydd,' said Rhydderch, 'congratulations on your victory. I have to say, albeit grudgingly, that your tactics fooled me completely, and I stand before a worthy victor.'

'Empty praise from a king who hid like a frightened child as his men died around him,' said Gruffydd.

'It is not a king's place to die in war,' said Rhydderch, 'but to deal with the aftermath, as the victor or the vanquished. On this day, for me, it is the latter, but my men fought well, and there is no shame in defeat. We will lick our wounds and, in time, will emerge from this stronger.'

'What do you mean?' asked Gruffydd. 'Your army is nothing but a pile of corpses waiting to feed the crows. You have no more time.'

'My army may be gone,' said Rhydderch, 'but I still have a kingdom to rule in the west. Name your price, and I will cede both Gwent and Morgannwg to you, a huge prize for a battle well fought. Not only this, but I will rule the rest of Deheubarth as a vassal king, serving you and Wales for the rest of my days. We are great kings, you and I, and are both feared by the English. But for too long, we have fought each other. So let us now become allies and send shivers of fear into the heart of the Palace of Westminster. Imagine it, one Wales ruled by two kings, equal in stature and feared by all.'

Gruffydd stared at Rhydderch for an age before slowly drawing his sword and resting the tip of the blade against his adversary's stomach.

'Do you really think that I will share anything with you,' he said, 'a man who has killed thousands of his own countrymen for no other reason than filling his own treasury?'

'That is not true,' said Rhydderch. 'At all times I acted with the good of Wales my only thought.'

'Tell that to all the people you raped, tortured and killed,' said Gruffydd. 'Your time here is over, Rhydderch, and I am going to send you to hell where you belong.'

'Wait,' said Rhydderch, his eyes widening with fear, but before he could continue, Gruffydd thrust his sword forward, sending it straight through his victim's gut.

For the briefest of moments Rhydderch's hands clasped around the blade, but as the pain kicked in, he collapsed to his knees. Gruffydd withdrew his sword and kicked the defeated king in the face with the heel of his boot, sending him crashing backwards to the ground. Throwing his sword to one side, Gruffydd dropped onto his victim's chest and drew his knife before leaning over to stare into Rhydderch's eyes, pausing to savour the moment.

'This country will be a better place without you, Rhydderch,' he said eventually, 'and few will mourn your passing. But as a fellow king, I grant you the privilege of a quick death,' and as the Gwent king looked up in terror, Gruffydd plunged his blade through the dying man's heart.

The surrounding men fell deathly silent as they watched Rhydderch die. Despite the enmity between the two camps, it was still a sobering moment to witness the demise of a powerful monarch. When the body finally stopped convulsing, Gruffydd got to his feet and cast away the blade before facing the prisoners.

'Do not spend any time on this man's memory,' he announced, 'for he was a weak king hiding behind brutality to scare his people into servitude. Today, we have rid this country of the one obstacle to a united Wales. Rhydderch is dead, and by right, I claim kingship over all his lands and chattels. Those of you who wish to move on from the past and help me achieve that goal, step forward and declare your allegiance. You will be welcomed into our ranks with no question. Those who cannot make that step will die here today alongside your king. Choose now.'

For a few moments, nobody moved until gradually, one by one, the prisoners realised they had little choice and stepped forward to join Gruffydd. Eventually, only a dozen or so remained, each brandishing a sword to sell their lives dearly.

Gruffydd stared at the men and realised there was no point in trying to change their minds.

'So be it,' he said and turned to Macsen. 'Cut them down.'

Seconds later, dozens of arrows flew through the air and as the last of Rhydderch's loyalists died, Gruffydd realised the war with Gwent was finally over.

'Make no mistake,' he shouted, turning to face his own men. 'There are still battles to be won and dissent to be put down, but that is for the morrow. Today, as promised, we will celebrate our victory, and I bid you all to seek whatever recompense you can from the town and surrounding villages. Take what is due, but harm no more innocents.'

The men roared their support, and the king raised his hand for silence.

'Enjoy what is yours by right,' he said, 'but be back here by dawn, for tomorrow, as was my vow, we march on Hereford.'

This time there was no stopping the excitement, and as the men dispersed to seek whatever they could find, the king looked across to see Aelfgar staring at him.

'Well,' said the king, walking over, 'does the day sit well with you?'

'It is indeed a great day,' said Aelfgar, 'for never did I expect such a victory.'

'God was with us,' said Gruffydd, 'and your men played their part to the full.'

'So tomorrow we march on Hereford?'

'That is what I promised,' said Gruffydd, 'and I am a man of my word. Get your men rested, Aelfgar of Mercia, because, within a few days, we will send a message to Edward that he will never forget.'

Chapter Nine

Archenfield, Late October, AD 1055

Several days after the victory in Skewett, Aelfgar of Mercia once again found himself surrounded by hundreds of dead and dying men. The place was Archenfield, just outside Hereford, and though Earl Ralf had amassed a sizeable army in defence of the city, they had been no match for the combined forces of Gruffydd, Aelfgar and the Irish mercenaries.

At first, the mobility of Ralf's cavalry had gained the advantage, but it was soon clear that they were not experienced in such warfare and made the crucial mistake of allowing their ranks to break, a devastating error that allowed the heavily armed infantry to get amongst them. The attack from Ralf's men quickly fell apart, and they became victims to the fury of a freshly bloodied army, desperate for more victory and more spoils. The slaughter had been unrelenting, with men and horses dying in their hundreds.

Again the cries of men facing their own death echoed across a blood-stained battlefield, and the killing continued long after Earl Ralf's signallers sounded the retreat. Wounded men, unable to run and with little chance of surviving their wounds, were quickly despatched by spear and sword, while hundreds of others were taken prisoner to work as slaves back in the kingdom of Gwynedd.

Eventually, Gruffydd's own signaller summoned his scattered army to reform, and having dealt with the only force between them and the city, turned towards Hereford.

'This day is not yet done!' roared Gruffydd from his horse. 'The greater prize still lies before us. Savour the taste of victory, my friends, for this day will send arrows of fear right into the heart of the English king himself.'

With an almighty roar, the combined armies turned northward towards Hereford. For the next two days, the city was devastated by the rampant Welsh. Buildings were burned to the ground, common people slaughtered, and even the city's motte-and-bailey castle totally destroyed. Aelfgar was shocked, for though this had been his plan all along, he had never realised just how devastating the outcome would be.

At last, the fury eased, and as the exhausted warriors wandered back to their camps outside the destroyed city walls, Aelfgar walked towards the one building dominating the skyline, the magnificent stone cathedral built under the auspices of the current bishop, Athelstan.

As he arrived, his face fell as he saw dozens of Gruffydd's men standing before the entrance, each holding a burning torch. Laid out in a straight line were the bodies of several canons who had fought to the last to defend the cathedral from the marauding Welsh. In front of the bodies stood three men, King Gruffydd, Macsen and Bishop Athelstan, the last bound with his hands behind his back.

'Your grace,' shouted Aelfgar, pushing his way to the front of a crowd of onlookers, 'wait, what are you doing?'

Gruffydd turned and saw Aelfgar being restrained by two of his guards.

'Let him through,' he said, 'he should witness this.'

Aelfgar ran forward and stood before Gruffydd.

'Your grace,' he said, 'what is going on? Surely you don't mean to burn down the cathedral?'

'Why not?' asked Gruffydd. 'It is the one thing that makes this city stand out amongst so many others. Hereford now belongs to me, and it is up to me to do with it as I wish.'

'But why?' gasped Aelfgar. 'The battle is won. Let the killing and destruction now stop.'

Gruffydd's eyes hardened, and he stared at Aelfgar.

'When you asked for my help,' he said, 'there was no talk of quarter or mercy. All you were interested in was sending a message to the king about some petty argument. Well, you have your message, Aelfgar of Mercia, and Edward cannot fail to see the implications.'

'But this is too much,' said Aelfgar, 'this is a house of God. We will all surely burn in hell for such an act.'

'What about the hundreds of houses burned along the border by Ralf and his men over the past few years?' interjected Macsen. 'They may have been of willow and mud, but those who lost their homes, or were killed for no more reason than being born on the wrong side of a river were just as godly as any man who set foot inside this monstrosity, no matter how gaudy their clothing.'

Aelfgar stared at the bound bishop as he realised what was about to happen.

'Stop your whimpering,' said Gruffydd to the bishop, 'and start praying we do not place you inside when we put it to the torch.'

'Your grace,' said Aelfgar, 'I beg of you. Yes, I needed your help, but if I had known this would be the result, I swear I would never have pressed my request. Please don't do this, it is a step too far.'

'Save your pleas, Aelfgar,' said the king, 'the decision is made.' With a nod to one of the nearby sergeants, he sent the row of men into the cathedral to set their fires. As they did, the bishop dropped to his knees and wailed in torment.

'Shut him up,' said the king.

Macsen walked over and punched the bishop hard across the jaw, sending him sprawling onto the ground.

'Do you want him carried inside?' asked Macsen, looking at the king.

'No,' sighed Gruffydd, 'let him live to report what he has seen here today. They need to know exactly what they are dealing with.'

Macsen nodded and, as two of his men at arms dragged the bishop away, returned to stand alongside the king and Aelfgar. A few moments later, the men tasked with setting the fires came back and watched as smoke started billowing from the doorways and windows.

Aelfgar's heart sank as he realised there was nothing more he could do and, as Gruffydd and his men walked away to start their victory celebrations outside the city, he fell to his knees, watching with despair as Hereford Cathedral was destroyed.

–

Several leagues away, Harold and his army marched towards Hereford, painfully aware that the whole mobilisation process had taken far longer than expected. At first, the recruitment had gone well, but when it became clear that Gruffydd was allied with Aelfgar of Mercia, the situation had become complicated. Aelfgar's father, Leofric, despite being a loyal servant to the king and in command of a strong standing army, refused to muster any of his men against his own son. Similarly, other nobles, friendly with Leofric, also refused to offer any military support, especially as they knew that the king himself was not at risk.

Consequently, Harold had found that recruiting an army strong enough to face the Welsh took far longer than anticipated, and by the time they neared the city, his scouts had already reported back that it was too late. Hereford had been razed to the ground.

Worried about what he was marching into, he stopped the army two leagues east of the city before joining his scouts to ride forward to see the devastation for himself.

Although all the fires were out, the smell of burning still filled the air, and a haze of smoke hung above the city as if lingering to enjoy the result of its efforts. Hundreds of people camped outside the ruins, using whatever they could as shelter against the elements, while others walked through the ash, trying to salvage anything that had survived the flames. But above all else, what caused him the most despair was the sight of what remained of the cathedral. What had once been an extraordinary building was now blackened with smoke, every window devoid of the wonderful glass that had graced them. The magnificent wooden spire that had for so long reached upwards as if towards God's heaven was now no more than a pile of burnt timber and rubble heaped at the base of the building.

Harold stared in horror. He had prepared for war; indeed, he had actually been looking forward to making his name in battle at the behest of the king, but his thoughts had been focused on the fighting, the combination of strategy and bravery that separated victor from vanquished. Never had he given thought to scenes such as this.

'Where is Lord Ralf and his men?' he asked quietly, realising that there was no sign of any military personnel.

'We do not know,' said one of the scouts, 'but I have been told by one of the survivors that they were last seen fleeing eastward.'

'They did not fight?'

'Oh, they fought, my lord, and what remains of Ralf's army now lies rotting just two leagues from here. My men counted over a thousand bodies, most of them ours.'

'It sounds like a slaughter,' said Harold.

'It was,' said the scout. 'But what is strange is that there are so many dead horses. Lord Ralf was not known as having any significant cavalry, but it looks like he tried to fight the Welsh with mounted men.'

'That man is dangerous,' said Harold, 'and has caused the unnecessary death of many in his time.'

'Does the king know of his incompetence?'

'Aye, he does, but Ralf is the king's nephew, so Edward brushes away any criticism. Is there any sign of Aelfgar?'

'We think he is in Archenfield. The town also fell to the Welsh, and though there was a lot of damage, it was not burned.

We saw hundreds of men fortifying the defences, so it looks like they are going to make a stand there.'

Harold nodded and stared down at what remained of Hereford city. It had once been a strong outpost on the edge of Wales, a base from which the king's men could control marauding Welsh patrols. Now it was no more than a pile of burning wood and collapsed stone buildings.

'What do you want to do, my lord?' said the scout. 'Do we march on Archenfield?'

'No,' said Harold eventually. 'Send men to bury the dead to the south. The rest of us will go to the city to see what we can do to help. I want patrols sent to collect food from any nearby towns and villages. These people will be hungry, and we do not carry enough supplies to feed them all.'

'As you wish, my lord,' said the scout.

'We are being watched,' said Owen of Hereford, at Harold's side, and nodded towards a group of mounted riders about half a league away.

Harold stared at the watchers. He could not make out much detail but had no doubt they would be scouts from Gruffydd's army.

'Do you want us to run them down?' asked one of his officers.

'No,' said Harold. 'Tell our men to set up camp here, on the slopes above Hereford. I want our strength to be seen by friend and foe alike. Let Gruffydd see exactly what he is up against.'

–

Over the next few days, Harold's men did what they could to help the people of Hereford. Any buildings able to be repaired were prioritised, and the people brought back into the city, tempted by the cauldrons of hot soup provided by the army of cooks brought along to feed Harold's men. Many of the foot-soldiers, as well as any healthy civilians who had survived the attack, set about building fortifications around the city, a mixture of hastily erected palisades and piles of rubble joining together to form protection against any further attack.

Within two weeks, despite the obvious devastation, the city gained a semblance of normality, carefully governed by Harold's officers. Outlying farms and villages brought what they could spare, and gradually, an air of stubbornness filtered throughout all those that had survived.

Things were going well, but Harold knew that this was not why he had assembled such an army. Gruffydd had to be dealt with, and winter was coming fast. Finally, after clearing all the burnt contents of what remained of the stone cathedral, the people of Hereford gathered in the clearing to say a prayer for all those that had died in the attack. Outside the city, dozens of carts lay waiting to enter, each piled high with timber and stone, all intended to rebuild the damaged cathedral.

Harold watched the service from the top of one of the few remaining buildings, along with Owen of Hereford and one of his officers, John Greenway.

'They should rebuild the houses first,' said Owen, 'not waste all that time and effort on a status symbol.'

'The people need somewhere to pray,' said Harold.

'Aye, they do,' said Owen, 'but a humble church would serve just as well. They should get the population fed and sheltered first.'

'The city is theirs, not ours,' said Harold, 'and this is what they want. We have other things to consider.'

'I agree,' said John. 'We have wasted enough time here and should march on Archenfield.'

'Gruffydd will not be in Archenfield,' said Owen quietly, 'he will be back in Wales, celebrating his victory.'

'You do not know that,' said John, 'and until we are sure, we need to assume he is still a threat.'

'I know him,' said Owen. 'He is not the sort of man to enclose himself behind a palisade. He prefers to fight out in the open, preferably with mountains and forests at his back.'

'How do you know him?' asked Harold.

'I have met him,' said Owen, 'on two occasions as your brother's second. We fought alongside him against Rhydderch many years ago, an unsuccessful campaign, but now the Gwent king is dead, there will be no stopping him.'

'What do you mean?'

'Wales has always been a powerful nation,' said Owen, 'but they have been far too busy killing each other to cause England a serious problem. Now, with Rhydderch dead, Gruffydd will seek to unite the country under one banner, and if that happens, Edward will have a serious problem, especially in Mercia where his men can strike and withdraw to the safety of Wales before anyone has a chance to respond.'

'So you think he is unlikely to be in Archenfield?'

'I am certain of it. He may have ambassadors there, but he will know it is a risk.'

'So who is fortifying it?' asked John.

'It can only be one man,' said Harold, 'Aelfgar of Mercia, and if that is the case, we have a chance to bring this war to a quick conclusion.'

'By attacking the town?' asked John.

'No,' said Harold, 'by appealing to Aelfgar's sense of decency. He may be an arrogant man, but even he will know that this sort of destruction is not acceptable.' He turned back to Owen. 'I brought you with me,' he said, 'as I was aware that you know the ways of the Welsh. If you serve me well, then I will consider freeing you from your obligations to my family. To that end, I am going to put my trust in you and treat you as one of my own men. Fail me, or run from your obligations, and I will hunt you down and kill you myself. Do we have an agreement?'

'I will not let you down,' said Owen, 'and will gladly do your bidding until you decree otherwise.'

'Then do we have an agreement?' repeated Harold.

'We do, my lord,' said Owen and held out his hand.

Harold stared at Owen's hand before looking up to meet Owen's gaze.

'I will not shake the hand of the man who bore the blade that pierced my brother's heart,' he said. 'But I will take your word if freely given.'

'Then you have my word before God,' said Owen, lowering his hand. 'What do you want me to do?'

Chapter Ten

Archenfield, November, AD 1055

Two days later, one of Aelfgar's men walked into the town hall in the centre of Archenfield, the temporary headquarters of Aelfgar and his huscarls.

'My lord,' he said, 'you should come. Harold Godwinson has sent a messenger; he seeks parley.'

'How many men does he have with him?' asked Aelfgar.

'Just one,' said the messenger.

'Then disarm them and bring them to me. I will meet them here.'

'As you wish, my lord,' said the messenger, and he left the room.

'Everyone out,' announced Aelfgar, turning around, 'except Gerald Ericson, you will act as my second.'

The room emptied, and Aelfgar dragged a table to the centre of the hall while his head huscarl placed two chairs to either side.

'Bring ale,' ordered Aelfgar to one of the servants.

'They are coming to negotiate, not drink,' said Ericson. 'Let them thirst.'

'Hospitality costs nothing,' said Aelfgar. 'We are nobles, not commoners.' They both took their seats on one side of the table and waited for the messengers. A few moments later, two men were ushered in and led to the table.

'Please,' said Aelfgar, not recognising either of the men, 'remove your cloaks and be seated.'

Both men did as requested and waited as the servant filled their tankards before leaving the room.

'To those who have died,' said Aelfgar, raising his tankard, 'may they rest well in heaven.'

'And to those who are still alive,' replied Owen, joining the toast, 'may they live to see their grandchildren.' All men drank from the tankards before placing them on the table.

'My name is Aelfgar of Mercia,' announced Aelfgar, 'and this is Gerald Ericson, my second. Whom do I have the pleasure of meeting?'

'My name is Owen of Hereford,' said Owen, and this is John Greenway, huscarl of the House of Godwin. We have been sent here to negotiate on behalf of the earl.'

'Welcome,' said Aelfgar. 'We acknowledge your intent and assure you of your safety while within the walls of Archenfield. What can I do for you?'

'My lord,' said Owen, 'I have been made aware of what happened at King Edward's court, and my master, Harold Godwinson, has sent me here to inform you that he understands why you were so upset. The decision was unexpected, yet it was the will of the king and, as such, could not be challenged.'

'That is easy for him to say because it was his family that benefitted, but that is not the point. What is done is done, and now the king must reap what he has sown.'

'My lord,' said Owen, 'there is no doubt that you have shown what you are capable of doing, though it has to be said that the entire destruction of Hereford was, in our eyes, unnecessary, as were the deaths of so many men, women and children. However, Earl Harold has instructed me to tell you that even at this late hour, it is not too late to stop this war. All you have to do is end your alliance with the Welsh and declare loyalty to the king, and he will do all that he can to get the banishment lifted as well as returning you to a position of power.'

Aelfgar stared with shock. He had expected a demand to surrender or face destruction, but here he was on the receiving end of an offer to be reinstated.

'I don't understand,' said Aelfgar. 'Why would he do that after all this?'

'Because we are more concerned about Gruffydd,' said Owen. 'Since that audience with the king, the political landscape has changed drastically, especially as Rhydderch is now dead. With a united Wales behind him, Gruffydd could threaten London itself, so we need every English man of noble birth standing fully behind the Crown. All you have to do is admit that you were wrong, and all that has happened will be forgotten. You can once again take your place at court.'

'And Edward has agreed to this?'

'Not yet, but messengers are on their way there to seek approval for Harold's suggestions. They should be back in three days, giving you a chance to consider the proposals.'

'So, what are the terms?'

'Only those that I have already told you. We want your allegiance, not your death. Besides, if it comes to battle between your men and ours, that will only result in the demise of even more good men, warriors we may need to stand against Gruffydd.'

'You do know that Gruffydd and I have an alliance?' said Aelfgar.

'We do,' said Owen, 'but agreements can be broken. You will be far better off standing in our lines than his.'

'I am a man of my word,' said Aelfgar, 'and will not betray an ally.'

'Then negotiate a break,' said Owen. 'I know Gruffydd, and he is a proud man, but he will quickly grasp the situation and act accordingly. If he thinks the move is inevitable anyway, he will do one of two things: either negotiate for something in his favour or kill you. There is an equal chance of either.'

'Not a very good option,' said Aelfgar.

'Then just shelve your pride and ride away from him,' said Owen, 'the choice is yours.'

Aelfgar stared at Owen. The offer had taken him by surprise, but he did not want to allow Harold Godwinson the satisfaction of knowing how welcome the proposals were.

'Tell your master,' he said, 'that I will consider his offer, but until there is something solid to negotiate, my stance remains the same. Edward must bestow the earldom of Northumbria upon me, or my allegiance with Gruffydd, and all the war and destruction that entails, remains in place.'

'I will relay your message,' said Owen, 'but please be aware that if Harold leads his army against this place, there can be only one outcome.'

'I disagree,' said Aelfgar, 'for Gruffydd and his army are just a horn blast away. Combined with my own men, I believe we would emerge the victor of such an encounter.'

'We will see,' said Owen, standing up. 'Thank you for the ale. I will return here in three days' time to receive your reply.' He nodded his head slightly before leaving the hall and heading back out through the fortified town's gates.

'How do you think that went?' asked the huscarl as he and Owen rode away from Archenfield.

'Better than could have been expected,' said Owen. 'He is desperate to agree terms but just as keen to save any shred of honour he may have left.'

'How do you know that?'

'Because I could see the relief in his eyes,' said Owen, 'a look I have seen many times in the eyes of men who thought they were about to die.'

–

Later that evening, Owen of Hereford reported back to Harold in the house next to the ruins of the cathedral. Harold listened intently and, when Owen finished, sat back to consider his options.

'When are the messengers due back from the king?' asked John Greenway.

'There are no messengers,' said Harold, 'it was an untruth to make Aelfgar feel more comfortable with the negotiations. It is important he thinks that I have the full support of the king.'

'Is that not a given?' asked Owen.

'Not necessarily. His pride has been hurt, and a pardon for Aelfgar may complicate the bigger picture.'

'Which is?'

'Dealing with Gruffydd. Aelfgar's arrogance is nought but a thorn in the side compared to the threat of the Welsh.'

'So you are just using Aelfgar to get to Gruffydd?' asked Owen.

'Aye I am,' replied Harold, 'and from what you just told me, it seems he may have taken the bait.'

--

A few days later, Owen and John Greenway once again rode towards the gates of Archenfield, but this time they were accompanied by Harold himself, honouring a request received directly from Aelfgar himself. At first, Harold's officers had urged him not to attend, but Harold was determined, keen to bring the whole campaign to an end as soon as possible.

'Are you sure about this?' asked John Greenway as they neared the gates.

'Aelfgar is not going to kill me in cold blood,' said Harold as they neared the town, 'it would invite terrible retribution upon Mercia from the king and the other earldoms. He may be arrogant, but he is not stupid.'

'I'm still not sure what you expect from him,' said Owen.

'As I told you, it is not him that interests me.'

'If nothing else,' said Owen with a sigh, 'at least the meeting is going to be interesting.'

Twenty minutes later, they sat at the same table within the town hall, though this time, there was a third man sitting alongside Aelfgar.

'Earl Harold,' said Aelfgar, 'thank you for attending. The reason for my request is that if all goes well, we can resolve this situation today with no need for further parley.'

'I am encouraged by your optimism,' said Harold, looking at the silent third man, 'but first, please introduce your friend here.'

'My apologies,' said Aelfgar, 'this man is Macsen of Gwynedd, the representative of King Gruffydd ap Llewelyn.'

Harold nodded to the Welshman before turning back to Aelfgar.

'Have you talked to the king?'

'I have, and he is willing to sign a treaty, assuming you meet his demands.'

'He is in no position to make demands,' said Harold, 'but I am always willing to listen. What are they?'

'You first,' interrupted Macsen, speaking for the first time. 'Tell me what is on the table.'

'It is very simple,' said Harold. 'There have been far too many deaths already, but we recognise that Gruffydd is riding a wave of triumph from his defeat of King Rhydderch. Sometimes, a victorious army is hungry for more and while I think he went too far, I understand why he did what he did.'

'You know nothing of our reasons,' said Macsen, 'so just tell me what you want.'

'So be it,' said Harold. 'If Gruffydd immediately takes his men back across the border, we will withdraw our army to Gloucester while we arrange further talks. In addition, Aelfgar must stand down his army and dismiss the mercenaries.'

'Is that it?' asked Macsen.

'It is a generous offer,' said Harold, 'and one that will save many lives.'

'Which lives, English or Welsh?'

'Both,' said Harold, 'as well you know.'

'We are not afraid to fight you, Harold Godwinson,' said Macsen. 'Yes, men will die, but you have much more to lose than us.'

'If you think you can march on London,' said Harold, 'you are truly mad. Even if you defeat me, there are many more men like me ready to defend the king to the death, more than you can imagine. The rivers of England will run red with your blood, and after you have been defeated, we will march on Gwynedd to kill your families and burn your villages.' He paused to let the threat sink in. 'Make no mistake, Macsen,' he continued, 'this is no idle threat. Up until now, we have allowed your kings to rule your own lands with little interference but threaten our own sovereignty, and we will sweep through Wales like a storm of fire. However, if you take this opportunity to negotiate, all that can be avoided.'

It was Macsen's turn to fall silent, meeting Harold's stare with one of his own, trying to judge if the threat was a bluff. Finally, he lifted his tankard of ale and downed it in one before slamming it back onto the table.

'Your threats do not scare us, Harold Godwinson,' he said, 'but Gruffydd is a merciful king, and he has instructed me to negotiate on his behalf. You can have your peace, but it will come at a cost.'

'Which is?'

'We want to keep Hereford,' said Macsen.

Everyone stared at the Welshman, shocked at the audacity of the demand.

'That is not going to happen,' said Harold eventually.

'Then we are done here,' said Macsen and got to his feet.

'Wait,' said Harold, 'sit down. I have not finished. You must have come here knowing that we would never give up Hereford. It puts our inland cities at too much risk, but that does not mean we cannot offer you something else in its place.'

'Continue,' said Macsen, sitting back down. 'I am listening.'

'I believe you have taken many farms and villages from here to Chester,' said Harold. 'What if I was to say you can keep possession of everything you have gained these past few days without threat of retribution.'

'It is a good start,' said Macsen, 'but it is not enough.'

Harold thought furiously. He wanted peace more than anything, but there was not much more to give.

'What about Archenfield?' said Owen, and all heads turned to face him.

'You do not speak for me,' said Harold. 'Hold your tongue.'

'It was a suggestion only,' said Owen. 'This town is of little value to Edward and has already been taken. Why not just leave it to the Welsh?'

Harold looked towards Macsen to see his reaction.

'Well?' he said. 'What do you think?'

'I think that if you add one hundred horses and a cart of silver, then we have a deal,' said Macsen.

The room once again fell silent as everyone waited for Harold's response.

'It is a heavy price,' said Harold eventually, 'but if I agree, will your king sign a truce guaranteeing he will not attack any more of our lands?'

'He will,' said Macsen.

'And what about Aelfgar and his men?'

'Take him, leave him, we care not,' said Macsen. 'We have no more need for him.'

Aelfgar bit his tongue. He was being talked about as if he was not present, but he also knew that the negotiations were on a knife-edge, and he wanted no more to do with the Welsh king.

Harold felt the stares of everyone present burning into him. Peace was within his grasp, but he was negotiating on behalf of the Crown without the knowledge of the king. Finally, he downed his own drink before looking again at Macsen.

'I agree to your terms,' he said. 'Tell your king to withdraw from Hereford, Macsen, we have just saved the lives of thousands of men.'

After Macsen had left to take the news back to the Welsh king, Harold walked over to stand beside Aelfgar, who was filling his tankard from a jug on a nearby table.

'I take it you are not happy with the agreement,' he said, filling his own tankard.

'It is not the agreement I found distasteful,' said Aelfgar, 'but the way I was treated as if I was not there.'

'It was nothing personal,' said Harold, 'it was just important that we stopped Gruffydd without resorting to warfare.'

'Why, did you not say there would be rivers of blood?'

'I said what needed to be said,' replied Harold. 'All I need to do now is convince the king.'

Aelfgar turned to stare at Harold.

'The king does not know?'

'How could he? I acted in the moment, but when I tell him what we gained, I am sure he will be agreeable. It also allows us to reunite our earls in preparation for what Gruffydd does next.'

'So what about me?'

'You have to remember that it was you that caused all this in the first place,' said Harold, 'but nevertheless, I think I can get your banishment overturned.'

'How?'

'By telling the king you were instrumental in negotiating this peace.'

'You would do that?'

'I would. Your father is not in the best of health, and when he dies, you will be the next Earl of Mercia. We need you back in England.'

'And what about in the meantime? Am I to be locked away like a forgotten blade?'

'On the contrary, I am confident I can get you reinstated as the Earl of East Anglia. I know it is not what you want, but I think that if you want to come back into the fold, it is the best you can expect.'

'I have no other choice, do I?' said Aelfgar.

'You do not,' said Harold. 'Take the offer and come home, Aelfgar. England needs you.'

Aelfgar downed the contents of his tankard once again before regarding Harold.

'You drive a hard bargain, Harold Godwinson,' he said, 'but I have seen enough killing to last a lifetime. You have a deal.'

Chapter Eleven

Bosham Harbour, 11 Months Later

Edyth Swanneck stood on the wharf, watching as her husband walked down the gangplank. He had been away for many months, but, at last, her prayers had been answered, and he had arrived safely home. Despite wanting to run and embrace him as soon as his feet hit the boards of the quay, she held herself back, knowing that with so many eyes watching, she risked admonishment. Impatiently, she watched as Harold greeted the harbour master and his waiting officers, exchanging pleasantries and sharing the relief of getting home after such a long journey.

It had been almost a year since Harold had brokered peace between King Edward and Gruffydd of Wales, and though there had been a few incidents, notably when the new Bishop of Hereford had gotten himself killed at Glastonbury by thinking he could lead a holy crusade against Gruffydd, the peace had largely held.

When Harold had returned from Hereford, she had hoped to spend some time with him, but those hopes were quickly dashed when King Edward resurrected his command for Harold to travel to Hungary with the aim of bringing back Edward Ætheling, the proposed new heir to the throne. Now, after many months away, Harold was finally back, and Edyth knew that at last, her family would once again be together.

Harold finished talking, and when he turned to walk towards her, Edyth could contain herself no longer, running forward to embrace her husband.

'Whoa,' laughed Harold, as she threw herself into the embrace, 'hold yourself, woman, I have not risked death in foreign lands only to be crushed by my wife upon my return.'

Edyth lifted her hands to hold his head still while she kissed him full on the lips.

'Oh Harold,' she said, 'I have missed you so much.'

'And I, you,' said Harold. 'Where are the children?'

'They are waiting at the house.'

'Why did you not bring them with you?'

'Because I wanted just a few moments of peace between us before the mayhem the children will undoubtedly bring.'

'Aye, that they will,' laughed Harold. 'How have you fared these past few months?'

'We have been fine,' said Edyth. 'Little Ulf was ill for a while with the ague, but he is well now. What about you, how went the journey?'

'It was good,' said Harold. 'I have seen some interesting places and dealt with even stranger people, but overall it was very successful.'

'So you found the Ætheling?'

'Aye, we did. It took some persuading for him to come with us, but in the end, I think the Crown of England was too much a temptation.'

'Is he with you?' asked Edyth, looking over his shoulder.

'He is,' said Harold, 'but in truth, we saw little of him on the return journey. He spent most of the time hidden away in his wagon on the land journey and, when it came time to board the ship in Flanders, insisted on one that had a cabin on deck.'

'How very strange,' said Edyth. 'I wonder why he did that?'

'Who knows?' said Harold. 'But you can judge for yourself tonight.'

'Is he coming to our house?'

'He is. I invited him to stay the night before he goes to London in the morning. Is that a problem?'

'Of course not,' said Edyth, 'I will make the arrangements. Anyway, enough talk of weird foreigners, let me look at you. You have gotten thin these past few months – I need to fatten you up.'

'In truth, I have missed the simpleness of our fare,' said Harold, 'and look forward to sharing a table with our family.'

'Then lucky for you, I have arranged just such an evening. Come, let me take you home. It has been far too long a wait.'

Later that evening, Harold walked into the hall to be met with a chorus of shouts and greetings from his huscarls and staff. At the far end, his children gleefully chased each other with hand-carved wooden swords and maces, a gift from their father after his journey to Hungary.

Edyth followed him in, having spent the entire afternoon with her husband in their chambers. The table in the hall was laden with all sorts of game birds and vegetables, as well as a roast swan as a centrepiece.

Harold walked around the room, greeting each one of his huscarls individually before returning to sit at the head of the table alongside his wife. On his left, an empty chair indicated someone was still missing.

'We need to wait until Edward arrives,' said Edyth. 'I have sent the steward with a gentle reminder – I hope that is acceptable.'

'It is,' said Harold. 'What do you think of him?'

'I only met him for a few moments,' said Edyth, 'but in truth, I am not impressed. He lacks the basic skills of social interaction, and his skin is as yellow as parchment. I believe he is sickening from something.'

'Perhaps,' said Harold, 'but do not judge him on his manners, his country is far different from ours, and they do things differently there.'

'That may be the case,' said Edyth, 'but there is no need for rudeness.'

'Just be patient,' said Harold. 'I am sure he will soon adjust to our ways.'

'My lord,' said a voice, and Harold turned to see the steward standing beside him. 'The gentleman sends his apologies,' continued the steward, 'and has requested that he dines alone in his quarters.'

'Did he say why?' asked Edyth.

'He proclaims illness,' said the steward, 'but assures me that he will be fine after a good night's rest.'

Edyth turned back to face her husband.

'See what I mean?'

'Let it go, Edyth,' said Harold. 'The man has travelled far, and anyway, after tomorrow, he will no longer be our problem.' He picked up his goblet and got to his feet. 'My lords,' he announced, 'my ladies, loyal friends. It is good to see you all again. The journey was long, with no little danger, but God has watched over my men and me, and saw fit to return us home. There will be plenty of time for reflection, but tonight there is only one thing on my mind. And that is that this feast is long overdue. Let the celebrations begin.'

With the room echoing to the sounds of cheering, Harold drained his goblet before leaning down to kiss his wife. It was good to be home.

–

Several days later, Harold walked along a corridor in Westminster Palace to the king's chambers, having brought Edward Ætheling to London. The new heir to the throne was currently being escorted to his newly furnished quarters, and Harold had continued without him, keen to give an account of the journey to the king. As he neared, he saw a familiar figure walking towards him, and his face broke into a grin.

'Archbishop Stigand,' he said, recognising his old friend, 'well met.' The two men embraced before standing apart and looking at each other.

'It has been a while,' said Stigand. 'Are you well?'

'I am,' said Harold, 'and glad to be home. It seems life as an archbishop is agreeable to you – never have I seen you look so healthy.'

'The role has its benefits,' said the bishop, tapping his stomach, 'and the sin of gluttony is hard to resist, but God helps me in my struggles.'

'He is obviously not helping you enough,' laughed Harold, looking at the bishop's stomach, 'but I am sure he has a purpose. Have you come to escort me to the king?'

'Alas, I have not,' said Stigand, 'in fact, I have come to tell you he is indisposed and cannot grant you audience, at least not today.'

'Why not?'

'He is gravely ill,' said the archbishop, 'and nobody is allowed inside his chambers except his physicians.'

'Is it serious?' asked Harold.

'For a while, we thought so,' said Stigand, 'but he seems to be pulling through. Give him a few days, and I'm sure he will want to speak to you. What about the Ætheling, is he with you?'

'He is and has been taken to his quarters.'

'His family?'

'They have also arrived,' said Harold, 'though the Ætheling insisted they sailed on a different ship in case of disaster.'

'A sensible decision,' said Stigand. 'What is he like?'

'I will leave you to make your own judgements,' said Harold. 'Suffice to say, he is not what I expected.'

'A damning statement in itself,' said Stigand, 'but we waste time. Come, we have much to talk about.'

He turned away and walked down the corridor towards one of the antechambers.

Harold's brow creased slightly as the bishop's manner seemed to suggest that he had something on his mind. Once inside, Stigand closed the door behind them and bid Harold sit at a table.

'I have taken the liberty of assuming that you haven't eaten yet,' he said, indicating the tray of cheese and sweetmeats on the table. 'Please, help yourself.'

Harold wandered over and sat on one side of the table before staring at his old friend.

'Bishop Stigand,' he said, 'is everything well with you? You look burdened with worry.'

Stigand locked the door before walking over and sitting opposite Harold.

'Something has happened,' he said eventually, 'something that could have grave consequences for England.'

'Go on,' said Harold.

'When the king was at his worst a few days ago,' continued Stigand, 'he flitted in and out of consciousness. For much of the time, I sat with him even though he often did not recognise me, such was his fever.'

'And?'

'During one of these occasions, he mistook me for Archbishop Robert of Jumièges and spoke to me as such. During that conversation, he asked me something that made my blood run cold.'

'Which was?' asked Harold, picking up a piece of cheese.

'He asked me if William of Normandy had accepted his invitation to become his heir.'

Harold's hand stopped halfway to his mouth, and he stared at the archbishop in shock.

'Are you sure?' he asked.

'Certain,' replied Stigand, 'he spoke as clearly as you do now.'

'What does it mean?'

'I'm not sure,' said Stigand, 'but if we take it at face value, it can only mean that when the king was heavily influenced by Robert of Jumièges, there was an offer made to William of Normandy to become Edward's heir.'

'Surely it was the ramblings of a sick man?'

'I thought so,' said Stigand, 'but to make sure, I engaged with him in the conversation and got the impression that the offer was actually made sometime when your father was in exile.'

'How can you be so sure about the date?'

'Because he also referred to the fact that the country was well rid of the Godwin family.'

'But if this is true,' said Harold, 'why would he send me all the way to Hungary to bring back the Ætheling?'

'I'm not sure,' said Stigand. 'I can only assume he has had a change of heart and is looking for a way out from his offer.'

'If this did indeed happen,' replied Harold, 'and he is now reneging on his promise, he risks invoking the wrath of William, and that man is rapidly gaining power and influence in Normandy.'

'I agree, but if the Witan supports Edward in his choice of successor, namely the Ætheling, then William would be foolish to take any action to force his claim.'

Harold fell quiet as the news sank in. He did not know much about William, only that he was growing a reputation in Normandy as a powerful man with ambitions far exceeding those around him.

'It is a worry,' he said eventually, 'but at the moment, it is nought but the ramblings of a sick man. Perhaps we should wait and see what Edward says when he is well.'

'I agree,' said Stigand, 'but I thought I should mention it, for if Edward dies without a declared heir, then who knows how William will react.'

'Even if it is true,' said Harold, 'will his claim be considered by the Witan?'

'Possibly,' said Stigand, 'especially if the conversation was witnessed by Robert of Jumièges.'

'But he has been exiled.'

'Even so, he is still a man of God and was respected by many. If Edward dies and William presses his claim before the Witan can agree the Ætheling as a successor, then the throne of England could be decided based on little more than the promises of a king.'

–

Several weeks later, Harold was once again in London, though this time on much more pleasant business. The king had made a complete recovery and had managed to get the full approval of the Witan for his newly proclaimed heir, Edward the Ætheling.

Many of the nobles had hesitated at the choice, but with nobody else available, the feeling had been that at least he had the royal bloodline and that with the support of the Church, he alone could avoid a potentially devastating civil war. In addition, Edward Ætheling's own son, Edgar, was now in England, a fall-back option in case anything untoward happened to the king or his father.

With the succession plans settled, Harold could concentrate and indeed celebrate the latest good news to come out of the palace: that his brother, Leofwine Godwinson, had been awarded the Earldom of Kent, an important award that added strength to the House of Godwin. Consequently, the whole family had taken up residence at their manor in Southwark, ready for the celebrations.

'Are you ready?' Godwinson asked his wife.

'Aye,' she replied. 'Tell the grooms to bring around the carriages.'

One of the servants ran from the room as everyone gathered their cloaks against the chill of the evening.

'Yet another earldom for the House of Godwin,' said Harold to Leofwine. 'Father would be proud. Make sure you lead with strength and respect.'

'I will,' said Leofwine, 'it is just a shame that Tostig will not be present.'

'You know he would if he could,' said Harold, 'but he has things to take care of in Northumbria.'

'I hear the people are unhappy with the way he rules,' said Leofwine. 'Is that true?'

'He has issues, that much is true,' said Harold, 'but he is a good man and will soon come to his senses.'

'He has to,' said Leofwine, 'otherwise the Scots could take advantage and just march straight into England.'

'That will probably never happen,' said Harold, 'but it is a point well made. Now come, this is going to be a good night.'

Before Leofwine could respond, the door opened, and one of Harold's huscarls burst into the room. Everyone turned to see what was happening and listened in horror as he shouted across the hall.

'My lord, I have terrible news. Edward Ætheling is dead!'

Part Two

Chapter Twelve

Harold sat in one of the king's audience chambers along with Edward and Archbishop Stigand, picking on sweetmeats and a high-quality wine that had been brought back from Rome by one of his brothers. The mood was relaxed, more like comrades than monarch and subjects. Over the past few years, Edward had grown to trust Harold far more than he had ever trusted his father, Godwin of Wessex. In fact, the relationship between the throne of England and the Godwin family was so good that when Leofric of Mercia had died a few years earlier and his son, Aelfgar, had taken over his earldom, the king had lost no time in offering East Anglia to the one remaining Godwin brother without such a title, Gyrth Godwinson. This hugely important decision meant that apart from Mercia, the Godwin family were now in control of all England and second in power only to the king.

Not everyone was happy with the situation, but with Harold enjoying such a close relationship with the king, there was little anyone could do about it. Aelfgar of Mercia in particular still held a grudge and, despite being warned yet again about liaising with the Welsh, rekindled his relationship with Gruffydd of Wales, becoming a close ally and trading partner. So strong was their affiliation that, in order to foster an unbreakable alliance, he arranged the marriage of his daughter, Alditha, to the Welsh king, confirming their bond.

This alliance worried Edward and, yet again, Aelfgar had been banished, only to be reinstated soon after by the diplomatic skills of Harold Godwinson, painfully aware that they had to keep Mercia as close as possible due to the growing threat of the Welsh.

Gruffydd was growing ever stronger, and now that he had managed to unite Wales under one banner, he had started to look outward yet again, coveting the fertile lands well within reach of his mounted warriors. It was a worry constantly on the minds of the king and Harold, but one which they could do little about, especially while Aelfgar nurtured his traitorous alliance.

'How goes it on the northern borders, your grace?' asked Harold, reaching for his wine. 'Is King Malcolm behaving?'

'He is,' said Edward. 'He flexed his muscles after defeating Macbeth at Lumphanan a few years ago, but it was not ever a serious situation.'

'Forgive me, your grace,' said Stigand, 'but I beg to differ. When he raided Lindisfarne, his men caused great damage to some of the holiest relics in England as well as causing the deaths of many souls who had dedicated their lives to God.'

'My apologies,' replied the king, 'I had forgotten the events on the holy island, and of course, it was a terrible situation. Regrettably, Earl Tostig was on a pilgrimage to Rome, and by the time we found out about the attack, it was too late. Malcolm's men had retreated across the border.'

'I accept the circumstances were beyond your control, your grace,' said Stigand, 'but even so, I cannot help but think that perhaps we could have done more to retrieve the artefacts stolen at the time.'

'Archbishop Stigand,' interjected Harold, 'the pain felt by you and the Church after such an outrage was shared by all, but sometimes we have to accept the pain to heal a wound, especially when it comes to making England a stronger and safer place.'

'What do you mean?' asked Stigand. 'What possible benefit could the loss of so many religious items be to England? I see nought but loss.'

'When Malcolm defeated Macbeth,' said Harold, 'it was an unexpected victory, so much so he found himself in the precarious position of being the next King of Scotland with little finance and a weak army. He had to send a statement to the Scottish people that he was worthy of that crown, and Lindisfarne was the easiest way to do it. Combine that with the value of the plunder, and the result was he answered all his doubters.'

'I can see that,' said the archbishop, 'but I still fail to see why it was any of our concern.'

'Before he was crowned,' said the king, 'Malcolm spent many years under the protective wing of Earl Siward in Northumbria. Their friendship was so strong that the chance of Malcolm now attacking England for no reason is unlikely.'

'If we enjoy such a good relationship,' said Stigand, 'perhaps it is a good time to broach the subject of the return of the artefacts?'

'I cannot risk it,' said Edward. 'With the threat from the Welsh growing on almost a daily basis, I cannot afford another war in the north.' He looked towards Harold. 'And as much as I hate to malign your family, Earl Harold, it has to be said that your brother is not engendering much confidence in running Northumbria. If there were a war, I am not sure that he is capable of holding the Scots back.'

'I do not think that will be a problem,' said Harold. 'In fact, Tostig and Malcolm also enjoy a close friendship.'

'Nevertheless,' said the king, 'it is still a great concern, although secondary to the one we face with Wales.'

'Has Aelfgar cut off his alliance with Gruffydd?' asked Stigand.

'He has not,' said Harold, 'nor is he likely to. He feels threatened by the House of Godwin and thinks of Gruffydd as insurance against any move on Mercia by my brothers or me.'

'Is that something you have considered?'

'Of course not,' said Harold. 'We have more than enough on our plate, and besides, we need a strong Mercia to protect the west coast from the attentions of the pirates.'

'So, what are you going to do about Gruffydd?'

'There is nothing we can do,' said Harold, 'at least not while Aelfgar and Gruffydd maintain their alliance. All we can do is wait.'

For the rest of the evening, all three men discussed the politics of the day, and by the time Harold rode through the streets of London back to his house in Southwark, he was ready for his bed. Finally, he rode through the gates and, after handing the reins to a groom, walked through the hall to his quarters.

'My lord,' said a voice, 'you have a visitor.'

Harold turned to see the steward standing next to a man he hadn't seen for almost a year.

'Tostig!' he exclaimed and strode over to embrace his younger brother.

'Hello Harold,' said Tostig, 'where have you been? I have been here since noon and, despite his hospitality, grow bored of your steward's company.'

Both men glanced at the steward and burst out laughing at his mock expression of offence.

'Nonsense,' replied the steward, 'I am the most interesting man in London. Now let me take your cloak, my lord, and I will arrange some food and drink. I take it you will want mead?'

'On the contrary,' said Harold, 'since he returned from Rome, my brother here has acquired a taste for fine wine. Is that not so, Tostig?'

'It is,' said Tostig, 'but in truth, a good mead sounds appealing right now.'

'Then mead it shall be,' said the steward. 'Please take a seat, my lords; I will send in the servants to bank up the fires.'

The two brothers sat near the dying flames while the steward left the room.

'So,' said Tostig, 'I know that Lady Edyth is not with you, so why are you in London?'

'Every two weeks, I meet with the king,' said Harold, 'to discuss matters of security and other such things. It sounds grand, but the meetings sometimes get monotonous.'

'It sounds fascinating,' said Tostig, 'and I would love to be honoured thus. It has to be said that your rise to importance has been as fast as an arrow these past few years, while my influence remains stuck in the quagmire of Northumbrian politics.'

'You have a difficult task in the north,' said Harold, 'though it didn't help that you undertook a pilgrimage to Rome just as the war between Malcolm and Macbeth was coming to a head.'

'The timing was unfortunate,' said Tostig, 'but everything is now fine. Malcolm is a friend of mine.'

'Nevertheless, you should be on your guard,' said Harold. 'The man is Scottish and subject to the whims of his own nobles. Should they demand a march south, he may not be able to contain them.'

'Unlikely,' said Tostig, 'but I take your point. So, how are you?'

'I am fine,' said Harold, 'but find myself spending most of my days either at court or attending functions with high-ranking officials and guests. A tedious but necessary responsibility.'

'I hear you have built a church to hold the many artefacts you brought back with you from Hungary.'

'Aye, I have,' said Harold. 'It was far too big a collection to be housed in Bosham, so I commissioned a collegiate church in Waltham. Anyway, what brings you to London?'

'Nothing in particular,' said Tostig, 'I just needed a break from the constant infighting of the Northumbrian thegns.'

'Is it that bad?'

'It is. If it is not one thing, it is another, and I find myself handing out punishment on a daily basis.'

'To your thegns?'

'Aye. For it is they who often stir up the trouble.'

'Is that wise?'

'What else can I do? I have virtually wiped out all brigandry across Northumbria, but still, they complain.'

'About what?'

'Taxes, laws, land allocation, the usual things, but they do not understand, it costs a lot of money to run an earldom, and I can't just cut their taxes on demand. Besides, I am the earl, and they should do what I say.'

'I have heard much of your money goes on a large standing army,' said Harold.

'That is true, but what else can I do? My life is under constant threat, so I have to take precautions.'

'Perhaps you should stay down here for a while,' said Harold, 'and we can discuss the situation in greater depth.'

'That would be good,' said Tostig.

'Then so be it. Now, where is that mead?'

–

The two brothers talked long into the night, and it was almost dawn before they retired to their beds, much to the relief of the steward and the servants who had stayed awake to keep them supplied in food and mead. It was almost noon the following day when Tostig emerged from his quarters to find Harold already sitting at the table alongside one of his men.

'Ah,' said Harold, looking up, 'you have emerged. I was just about to leave.'

'Where are you going?'

'I cannot say,' said Harold, 'at least not yet.'

'But you said we would talk about Northumbria.'

'I know,' said Harold, 'and we will, but something has come to my attention, a situation that I cannot allow to go unattended.'

'Who is this?' asked Tostig, grabbing a slice of hot pork from a side table before joining the two men.

'This,' said Harold, after a pause, 'is Owen of Hereford, the man I told you about last year.'

'The man who killed Sweyn,' said Tostig, putting the meat back down onto the table. 'What is he doing here?'

'Curb your manner, Tostig,' said Harold. 'Owen is a good man. These past few years, he has proved his worth to the family and to me many times over. It is time to move on.'

'No,' said Tostig, maintaining his cold stare, 'it will never be time to move on. This man killed our brother, and he should be made to pay.'

Harold looked up at Tostig.

'Don't you think I have had that very same thought many times over?' he asked. 'I too wanted revenge, but after hearing his story, I decided to give him one last chance. He has since repaid that trust many times over and is now one of my most dependable men. While you are in this house, you will be courteous. Understood?'

'Worry not, brother,' said Tostig, still staring, 'he is under no threat from me, at least while he is in your company, but if I meet him alone in a dark alleyway, then who knows what the outcome will be.'

'Enough,' said Harold, 'and listen to me. You said you wanted distraction from your troubles in Northumbria? Well, I may have an answer. How soon can you muster that army of yours?'

'What?' asked Tostig, turning his attention to Harold. 'Why would you want my army?'

'I cannot say yet,' said Harold, 'but something is afoot, and if it comes to fruition, I will need every man you can muster at a moment's notice. Are you interested?'

'Of course,' said Tostig, 'but I need to know our foe.'

'Forgive me, brother,' said Harold, 'for I cannot tell you yet. If even one word of this were to be known outside this room, then many men could die needlessly. Suffice to say, this campaign could be the saving of England.'

'Does he know?' asked Tostig, nodding towards Owen.

'It was Owen that came to me with the information, so yes, he knows.'

'This is so wrong, brother,' said Tostig. 'You favour Sweyn's murderer over me. How can that be so?'

'I know it is not good,' said Harold, 'but at the moment, it is the way it has to be. Now, are you interested or not?'

'Yes,' said Tostig eventually, 'what do you need?'

'Two thousand mounted men,' said Harold, 'and another thousand foot-soldiers along with enough wagons and supplies for a month's campaign. Can you do that?'

'I can,' said Tostig, 'but I will need time.'

'Time may be limited,' said Harold, 'so do the best that you can.'

'So be it,' said Tostig, but as he passed Owen, he paused and looked the Welshman up and down. 'You and I have unfinished business,' he said, 'and when this is done, there will be a reckoning.'

Before Owen could reply, Tostig left the hall and slammed the door behind him.

'He seems upset,' said Owen to Harold.

'Tostig is a hothead,' said Harold, 'but if this situation is what I think it may be, we will need every man we can muster. Now, get the horses; we need to get out of here.'

Chapter Thirteen

Harold rode his horse slowly towards Aelfgar's manor house a few leagues north of Chester. Alongside him rode Owen and six of his trusted huscarls, and they all stopped atop a hill to look down at the earl's manor in the valley below.

'There it is,' said Harold. 'I came here a few years ago to meet his father. Earl Leofric was a good man.'

'Aye, he was,' said Owen. 'It is a shame his son did not turn out the same way.'

'It is the way of the world,' said Harold. 'Come, let us find out what is going on.'

The men kicked their horses and rode down to the manor gates to be met by several armed guards.

'State your business,' said one as they approached.

'I am Earl Harold of Wessex,' replied Harold, 'and these are my men. We have come to pay our respects to your master, Earl Aelfgar of Mercia.'

The sergeant glanced at his comrade before turning back to Harold.

'You are welcome to come in, my lord,' he said, 'but I cannot guarantee an audience. Earl Aelfgar is very sick, and the physicians are with him constantly.'

'I understand,' said Harold, 'and if they decide that he cannot be seen, we will leave as soon as we have rested the horses.'

The sergeant nodded and stepped aside, allowing the riders to enter the grounds.

'The stables are on the north wall,' he said, following them through.

'I have been here before,' said Harold, 'thank you.' They rode to the stables and dismounted before handing the horses over to the grooms.

'Look after them well,' said Owen, 'and there will be a generous purse for your efforts.'

The grooms led the horses away, and the men of Mercia followed the sergeant into the manor house.

'The kitchens are that way,' said the sergeant, pointing along a corridor. 'Your men can wait there.'

Owen led the huscarls away while Harold followed the sergeant into an anteroom.

'Please wait here, my lord,' he said, 'and I will tell them you are here.'

Harold removed his cloak and placed it on a table before walking over to peer out of one of the windows. The view was of rolling, fertile hills dotted with healthy forests, all split by the shine of a lazy river meandering past the manor. It was an impressive place and exactly how he remembered it.

'Lord Harold,' said a voice from behind him, 'we were not expecting you.'

Aelfgar's second-in-command was standing in the doorway.

'Gerald Ericson,' he replied, 'no, I did not send messages as I had business in Gloucester and did not know if I would have the time, but when I found out the seriousness of the situation, I came as soon as I could. How is he?'

'Not good,' said Gerald, 'he deteriorates by the day. Would you like to see him?'

'Is that possible?'

'For you, yes,' said Gerald. 'Come with me.'

Harold followed the huscarl along the corridor and up a stairway until they reached a closed doorway.

'I will warn you,' said Gerald, 'it is not a good place to be.'

'However bad it is, I expect I have seen worse,' said Harold. 'Lead on.'

Gerald opened the door and led Harold into Aelfgar's bedchamber. The first thing to hit Harold was the heat from the roaring fire, followed closely by the overwhelming stench of human filth. He gagged, and his hand went involuntarily to his nose to try to block the smell. He quickly composed himself and walked over to the bed, which was surrounded by Aelfgar's family and two physicians, all staring down at the once-proud man that had caused him so much trouble over the years.

Harold was shocked and barely recognised the emaciated man who now lay before him. Gone was the proud man full of arrogance and self-belief, and in his place lay a seemingly old man aged far beyond his years. His hair had all but gone, and the blotched skin hung from his chin like the folds of an empty sack. His eyes were encircled with black and seemed to have retreated into his skull.

The overall situation, combined with the stench and heat, was horrific, for even though it was no secret that Aelfgar often suffered from ill health, it was a shock to see how far the man had deteriorated since last they met several months earlier.

'Earl Aelfgar,' said Harold, searching for something appropriate to say, 'I came as soon as I heard you were ill. If there is anything you need of me, all you need to do is ask.'

'He cannot talk,' said Gerald. 'He lost the use of his voice several days ago. Now he is hardly able to breathe.'

'Is there any chance of a recovery?' asked Harold, staring at the semi-conscious earl.

'No,' said Gerald, 'the physicians have done everything they can, but I have seen this illness a thousand times. There is no cure, so all we can do now is numb the pain and make him as comfortable as we can until the Lord God decides to take him home.'

'Has his successor been agreed?'

'It has,' said Gerald. 'As soon as he knew his health was failing, Aelfgar sent messages to the king requesting that his son, Edwin, succeed him as Earl of Mercia, a request that was finally agreed just a few days ago. We have that document under royal seal ready to show the Witan.'

'Can he hear me?'

'Probably, but we do not know for sure. Do you want to speak to him?'

'If I could.'

Gerald led Harold to the side of the bed.

'My lord,' he said quietly, 'Earl Harold is here, and he would like to say something.'

The earl did not respond, but Harold sat on the side of the bed and took his hand.

'Earl Aelfgar,' he said quietly, 'I do not know what plan God has for you, but what I do know is this. You are and always have been a passionate man who put his family and country first. When we faced a great war with Gruffydd, it was you who helped to make him see common sense. That act alone helped prevent the death of thousands of men, and for that reason, I am sure the gates of heaven already swing open for your arrival, but if you can hear me, also know this. As long as I am alive, and as long as there is peace between our houses, your family, your heirs and descendants will want for nothing. This I swear in the sight of God himself.'

Although Aelfgar's expression did not change, Harold felt the slightest of squeezes on his hand. He smiled gently and stood up.

'Journey well, my friend,' he said and left the room, followed by Gerald Ericson. Once out in the corridor, Harold stopped and breathed in huge breaths of air from a nearby open window, desperate to clear his lungs of the stench of death and filth.

'I told you it was bad,' said Gerald.

'Aye, you did,' said Harold, 'worse than I expected.'

'Did you mean what you said in there,' asked Gerald, 'about his family, I mean?'

'Of course, I did,' said Harold. 'We may have had our differences, but together we kept far more men alive than we sent to their deaths, and that is always a good thing.'

'You are a good man, my lord,' said Gerald. 'You have my gratitude.'

'You are welcome,' said Harold. 'Edwin has much to learn if he is to become half the earl his father was, but he is worthy of your full support. Nevertheless, do not hesitate to reach out if you need anything.'

'I will do that,' said Gerald.

'One more thing,' said Harold. 'Have they said how long he is expected to survive?'

'Two days,' said Gerald, 'three at the most. We have already made the burial arrangements. Will you be coming?'

'Alas, I cannot,' said Harold, his mind racing, 'for there is something I need to do, something that will have an effect on the future of England itself.'

'Well, whatever it is, I wish you well,' said Gerald. 'Fare ye well.'

'Goodbye,' said Harold and walked towards the exit of the house. 'Owen of Hereford,' he called as he passed the kitchens, 'back to the horses.'

Several minutes later, Harold and his men were once more in the saddle and riding south towards Gloucester.

'Well,' said Owen as they rode, 'are you going to tell me what happened?'

'You were right,' said Harold, 'Aelfgar of Mercia will never leave that house alive.'

'How long have we got?'

'About three days,' said Harold, 'no more.'

'That's not enough time,' said Owen. 'Tostig's army will never get here in time to aid your campaign.'

'Then we must act alone,' said Harold, 'this is just too good an opportunity to miss.'

Two days later, Harold mounted his horse just before sunset. Throughout the camp, another five hundred men followed suit and formed up behind him. They were lightly armed and carried enough food for only two days. Harold turned towards them and waited until the noise stopped.

'Men of Wessex,' he said, 'God has seen fit to offer us an opportunity that may not come round again. Up until now, King Gruffydd of Wales has basked in the knowledge that we dare not attack him as long as he shared an alliance with Mercia. Now, with the imminent death of Earl Aelfgar, that alliance is about to come to an end, and it is my judgement that Gruffydd is still unaware of how ill Aelfgar is. Our spies report that Gruffydd has encamped at Rhuddlan in the north of Wales for the winter, and I believe if we act now, we have a good chance of killing the beast in his own lair before he has a chance to react.'

A murmur of approval rippled through the mounted men.

'We number only five hundred,' said Harold, 'but we cannot wait any longer. This is a rare chance, so this is what we will do. For the next few hours, during the hours of darkness, we will ride as fast as we dare along the mountain tracks towards Rhuddlan. Assuming we get there without the alarm being raised, we will form up and attack at dawn. If God is with us, we will catch them unawares and take the town without too much difficulty.'

'And if we see Gruffydd?' asked one of the men.

'It would be better to capture him alive to be taken to London,' said Harold, 'but if he is killed, then so be it. Just take his head as proof for the king.'

'What about the route?' asked another. 'It is foreign territory, so we do not know the way.'

'This man does,' said Harold, nodding towards Owen of Hereford, 'he travelled the roads throughout Gwynedd for many years.' He paused and looked around the men. 'This will be a short campaign,' he said, 'but make no mistake: once the alarm is raised, they will muster their men to take retribution, but by the time they do, I want us to be long gone. Is that clear?'

'Aye, my lord,' shouted the men.

'Good,' said Harold. 'In that case, there is no need to wait any further. The future of England could lie in your hands, my friends. Let us do what has to be done.'

To the sound of cheering men, Harold Godwinson turned his horse to ride southward, followed by Owen of Gwent and five hundred mounted men. The fightback against Gruffydd had begun.

Chapter Fourteen

Rhuddlan Castle, Wales, November, AD 1062

Gruffydd and Macsen emerged from the timber longhouse and headed for their horses. Another fifty mounted men waited for them, all armed to the teeth and wearing heavily oiled cloaks against the notoriously bad Welsh weather.

Behind him came Gruffydd's wife, Alditha, and the other women of the house, all heading towards the several wagons waiting in the courtyard.

'Aled,' said Macsen, seeing the manor steward standing to one side, 'once we are gone, arrange foraging parties to stock up the barns with firewood. We may not be back for a while, but I want daily fires lit to keep the dampness from the timbers. Understood?'

'Yes, my lord,' said the servant.

'Good,' said Macsen. 'Once we have taken the women to Anglesey, we will return with all haste and see if we can bring down a deer or two on the way.'

'That would be most welcome,' said the steward. 'Travel well, my lord.'

King Gruffydd mounted his horse and, as soon as all the tailgates on the covered wagons were secured, turned to face Macsen.

'We are ready, my friend,' he said, 'take us to Anglesey.'

The royal party and the bodyguards headed out through the gates of the wooden palisade and headed westwards towards the distant mountains.

'I still think this is unnecessary,' said Gruffydd as they rode. 'Aelfgar may be ill, but even so, Edward would never dare come over the border, lest he risks a backlash he will never recover from.'

'You may be right,' said Macsen, 'but our spies say there is great concern amongst the English over the earl's health, and he may die sooner than we think.'

'Even if he did,' said Gruffydd, 'it would take the English king months to raise an army capable of causing us any problems.'

'Better to have the women safe than take any risks,' said Macsen, 'and besides, we can be back here within a few days.'

The wagons rolled on westward, following the coastal road, stopping only when the afternoon was drawing to a close to make the one camp that would be necessary on their journey. As was usual, Macsen sent scouts out from the camp to check the area before he would stand down half of his men to rest, but they had been gone less than an hour when two of them came racing back from the nearby mountains.

'Your grace,' shouted Macsen over his shoulder, 'something is wrong.'

Gruffydd strode over to join Macsen and stared at the scouts riding hard towards them. A few moments later, they reined their horses to a halt and dismounted.

'What's the rush?' asked Macsen. 'Are we under threat?'

'I do not believe so,' said one of the scouts, 'but something is happening at Rhuddlan.'

'What do you mean?' asked the king.

'We climbed one of the peaks to get a better view,' said the scout, 'but when we looked eastward, there was a heavy black cloud hanging over the town.'

'What?' gasped Gruffydd. 'Are you sure?'

'As sure as we can be,' said the scout. 'It looks like it is on fire.'

Gruffydd turned to face Macsen.

'Muster the men,' he said, 'we need to go back.'

'No,' said Macsen, 'there is only one reason that the town would be ablaze, and that is if someone has already put it to the torch. We should break camp immediately and ride as hard as we dare to Anglesey.'

'Do you think Edward has attacked Rhuddlan?' asked Gruffydd.

'I know not,' said Macsen, 'but if I was in his shoes, then it would have been the first thing on my mind as soon as Mercia was cut free from our alliance. We have to get the women to safety and then muster the army as soon as we can. I think that the English have just gained an advantage.'

—

In Rhuddlan, the air was filled with screaming as men and women alike fled the storm of violence inflicted upon them by Harold and his men. The mounted army galloped through the streets, trampling anyone who dared to stand in their way.

The surprise had been complete, and the English riders had reached the town before a single horn had been sounded. Those guards still on duty raced out to face the attackers but were cut down with impunity as the momentum of the five hundred lancers carried them like a storm amongst the buildings.

'To the manor!' roared Harold, and led fifty of his men to the heart of the town, desperate to catch or kill the Welsh king.

Men at arms poured from the buildings to defend the town, but they were disorganised and fell in their droves to the attackers.

'Dismount and spread out,' commanded Harold in the courtyard of the royal manor. 'A sack of silver to any man who brings me his head.'

Out in the town, the commoners fared no better, and anyone caught in the open was run through with spear or sword. By now, most of the attackers were on foot, smashing their way through the locked doors of the many buildings and setting fire to anything that would burn. Only the women and small children were spared, and they ran from Rhuddlan in terror, making for the perceived safety of the distant forests.

'Let them go,' shouted Owen, seeing some of the men set out in pursuit, 'we are here to find the king.'

For the best part of an hour, Harold and his men scoured the town, and by the time the sounds of the battle had eased, it was clear that the king and his household were not present.

'My lord,' said Owen, walking over to Harold near the harbour. 'We have searched everywhere. Either he escaped, or he was never here in the first place.'

Harold did not respond. His attention was on something that could be just as valuable.

'My lord,' said Owen, following Harold's gaze towards the many ships in the harbour, 'what are you thinking?'

'Forget Gruffydd,' said Harold, 'he has long gone. But look, if I am not mistaken, those are his warships and must make up the majority of their fleet.'

'I agree,' said Owen, 'but we do not have the time or men to sail them out of here.'

'We are soldiers, not sailors,' said Harold, 'and I have no intention of using them, but neither am I leaving them here for Gruffydd to sail against our coastal towns. Tell the men to burn them, Owen. Send each and every one to the bottom of the harbour.'

Just under an hour later, Harold and his men formed up half a league way from Rhuddlan and looked back at the devastated town. As far as they could see, families lay scattered across the open fields, having fled the destruction, and the menfolk started to emerge from their hiding places, grateful that they had escaped the slaughter. Plumes of black smoke spewed upwards into the morning air, fuelled by hundreds of burning houses and the dozens of ships now ablaze in the harbour.

Harold had lost only a few men, and the victory was overwhelming, but despite the feeling of exhilaration, he knew that ultimately, the attack had failed. King Gruffydd was still at large, and now a war against the Welsh seemed inevitable.

'We have to get out of here, my lord,' said Owen, 'and warn our border towns to reinforce their defences. There is no way Gruffydd is going to let this go unavenged.'

'I agree,' said Harold. 'Get us out of here, Owen, but this time, go by the quickest routes. There is much work to be done.'

–

Two days later, Harold was back in the Palace of Westminster, giving a report of the attack to the king. At first, Edward had been shocked, but the more he learned, the more intrigued he became.

'So you scoured the town of Rhuddlan?' he asked.

'Aye, we did,' said Harold, 'that and many other towns and villages in the area. There are few left that can offer him food or succour if Gruffydd decides to come that way, so he will have to bring whatever he needs by cart. Added to that is the fact that we burned many of his ships in the harbour, which puts pressure on his supply lines, so by my reckoning, we have time.'

'For what?' asked the king.

'To go back and finish the job,' said Harold.

'Are you asking me to authorise a full-scale invasion of Wales?' asked Edward.

'Not necessarily,' said Harold, 'but if you make the funds available, I believe the House of Godwin can bring the Welsh to their knees.'

'On your own?'

'Aye, your grace,' said Harold. 'You have honoured our family with power and lands – now it is time for us to repay that trust. With enough men and ships, and the supplies needed to keep an army on the march, I swear that I can remove the threat from Gruffydd once and for all.'

'How much do you need?' asked the king.

'I will have my treasurers work out the cost,' said Harold, 'but it will not come cheap.'

'And if I agree,' said Edward, 'when do you intend to do this?'

'Only a fool would attack Wales in the grip of winter,' said Harold, 'so it would be in the spring before he has a chance to rally his men and rebuild his fleet. Just give the word, my lord, and I swear we will be rid of this menace for ever.'

'You shall have your men and your supplies,' said Edward eventually. 'Let my clerks know your needs, but this campaign has to succeed, Earl Harold. Failure cannot and will not be tolerated.'

'I understand,' said Harold, 'and I will not let you down. I swear this on the name and memory of my father, Godwin of Wessex.'

'So be it,' said the king. 'You are dismissed, Harold Godwinson. Go and bring me the head of Gruffydd ap Llewelyn.'

Chapter Fifteen

Bristol, May, AD 1063

Harold Godwinson walked along the quay, passing the fleet of ships he had assembled over the winter months. Each was packed with supplies and could take up to fifty foot-soldiers or ten cavalrymen, including their horses and equipment. Beside him walked Tostig, who had ridden down from Hereford to take part in the final briefing.

'This is very impressive,' said Tostig. 'How many do you have?'

'At the moment, fifty,' said Harold, 'but I hope more will join us over the next few weeks.'

'And Edward has financed it all?'

'He has,' replied Harold. 'Don't forget, it is Edward that will be the main beneficiary of all this, so it is a small price to pay.' The two men walked into one of the storehouses on the quayside to meet the many commanders who would lead the men into battle, standing around a table made from packing crates and covered with a large map of Wales.

'Gather round,' said Harold, 'and I will make this as quick as possible, for there is no time to waste.' Once the room fell quiet, Harold started the briefing. 'As you know,' he said, 'today we launch a campaign against Gruffydd ap Llewelyn. For too long, we have been cowed by his threats and forays into England with little or no response. Today that ends, and by the time this campaign is over, his head will be on a spike at the southern gates of London.' He drew his knife to use as a pointer. 'At high tide today,' he continued, 'the fleet will set sail for Anglesey in the north of Wales.' He pointed at the island to confirm the destination. 'Not only is Anglesey the breadbasket of the Welsh nation, but it is also a strong location from where we can campaign further inland. It has a good harbour and can be easily defended by dominating the bridge over the straits that separates it from the mainland. Our aim is to sail our fleet straight into the harbour and sweep across Anglesey as quickly as we can, denying the Welsh access to their main source of food. At the same time, Tostig will lead our land army into North-East Wales, again attacking Rhuddlan. From there, he will wage a campaign along the whole of the northern coastline, eventually joining up with my command here in Anglesey and denying Gruffydd access to any of the fishing ports on the northern coast.'

He looked up at the silent gathering. Every man was fully concentrated on the map, taking in everything they could before heading off to battle.

'Assuming this phase of the campaign is successful,' said Harold, 'and I see no reason why it will not be, we will consolidate our positions before foraying around the mountains of North Wales and further inland. At no point will we attempt to wrest them from the high ground, for to do so is to invite disaster. At the same time, our fleet will be redeployed up and down the coastline, attacking any target that presents itself. Those targets include fishing villages, coastal towns, and any boat they come across not bearing the colours of Edward. The aim is to put pressure on Gruffydd by denying his people any source of food, and by doing so, we believe that they will soon turn against him and he will sue for peace. Any questions?'

'Aye,' said a voice. 'If Anglesey is so easy to attack from the sea, what is to stop Gruffydd counter-attacking with his own ships as soon as we land?'

'Gruffydd has no ships,' said Harold, 'we sank them in Rhuddlan before Christmas.'

'My lord,' said another voice, 'you say we are going to avoid the mountains, but will not Gruffydd use them as a base to launch his counter-attacks?'

'Aye, he will,' said Harold, 'and we have to be prepared for that, but if he has any significant number of men, then his food supply will soon run out, and with our forces dominating the roads, it won't be long before they suffer the pains of hunger.'

'I have a question, my lord,' said another man. 'It seems that our targets are mainly civilians. Is this a just campaign in the eyes of God?'

'It has been blessed by the bishops,' said Harold, 'and hopefully, the pain will not last long. Better a few suffer now than many in a war that neither side can win.'

'When do we attack?'

'We need time to get the fleet and the land army in place,' said Harold, 'so we will launch the attacks at dawn two days hence. As well as the ships you see outside, we have prepared a second fleet carrying nothing but supplies. In addition, there are a hundred carts waiting near Hereford to follow Tostig's army westward into Wales. If God is with us, we can be back with our families before autumn. Any other questions?'

When nobody answered, Harold sheathed his knife and looked around the room. 'There has never been a better-equipped army to fight the Welsh,' he said, 'but make no mistake, Gruffydd is a popular king with a strong army. Every one of us needs to be on our mettle every single moment of every single day. Some of us will not return, but there is no other option. If we let Gruffydd continue the way he is going, then this time next year, his ships could be moored on the Thames as he burns down Westminster. We are here to stop him in his tracks. Gentlemen, do not let me down.'

Enthused and determined, all the officers and commanders left the warehouse and made their way back to their men. Those that had travelled down from Hereford waited for Tostig to join them while the others returned to the dock to oversee the loading of the ships. When they had gone, Harold turned to Tostig.

'Are your men ready?' he asked.

'They are more than ready,' said Tostig. 'We will not let you down.'

'I'm sure you won't,' said Harold. 'Just keep pushing westward along the northern coast, and you will be fine.' He held out his arm and took Tostig's wrist. 'Good luck, brother, and may God go with you.'

In the north of England, there was another meeting taking place, one held behind locked doors without the knowledge of any king or earl. Twenty thegns, comrades of Gamelbearn and Dunstan, had gathered in a tavern at the edge of one of the towns, each one sworn to secrecy about the meeting on pain of death. Outside, several foot-soldiers stood guard, turning away any uninvited men hoping to get a tankard of ale after a hard day's toil in the fields and forests.

'Comrades,' said Gamelbearn, getting to his feet, 'I think you know why I have asked you here.'

'Aye we do,' said one of the men, 'it is to discuss how to get rid of that bastard, Tostig Godwinson.'

The men in the room shouted out in agreement, but Gamelbearn held up his hand to call for silence.

'Be careful what you say, my friend,' he said, 'for there have been no suggestions made to that effect. We are here to discuss the situation and see if we can agree on a resolution.'

'What is to discuss?' said another voice. 'The man is bleeding us dry! Since he came up here, it seems all I am doing is taking taxes to his manor. It has never been so bad, and I have lived here all of my life.'

'Most of us have,' replied Gamelbearn, 'and if there is anything to be done, then it falls to us to be the instigators, but before we discuss such things further, we have to look at it from the king's point of view, for if we do something drastic and annoy the Crown, we could face the gallows for treason.'

'Tostig has done nothing for us,' said one of the men. 'Except relieve us of all our coin.'

'It has to be said,' interjected Dunstan, 'that the roads and bridleways are far safer these past few months. The man has hung more brigands than anyone before him.'

'Aye, whether they were guilty or not,' said one of the men. 'Tostig and his cronies are far too quick to judge, and I know of men that were no more brigands than those standing in this room, and in my eyes, that is murder.'

'Yet the roads are definitely safer, Gluniarn,' said Dunstan, 'and people are no longer worried about travelling alone. There is also a feeling that, for the first time in many years, the Scots are happy to stay north of the border, so that is also a benefit.'

'I'm not surprised,' said Gluniarn. 'Tostig is always sucking up to his Scottish friend and spends more time across the border drinking and womanising than he does taking care of business down here. There are no excuses, Dunstan. Tostig is a cruel man worried about nothing except how to fill his own treasuries with even more silver at our expense. Even now, when our people are hungry and worried about how they are going to buy seed for the planting, where is he? On some pretentious crusade against a king that has never set foot on any of our lands, nor is ever likely to. How much is that costing him, for however large the price, every penny would have been better spent on our own people.'

The men in the room roared their approval, and Gamelbearn had to wait until the noise died down before speaking again.

'So,' he said, 'it sounds like we are in agreement that some-thing has to be done, but just to be sure, let me see a show of hands. All those in favour of taking direct action against Tostig, raise your hand.'

A forest of arms shot towards the tavern ceiling.

'Those against,' said Gamelbearn, and looked around the room, but nobody stirred. 'Then it is clear,' he continued, 'we all agree that we will stand no more of Tostig's poisonous rule.'

'But what can we do?' asked Gluniarn. 'He commands a strong army, and let us not forget he can call on any of his brothers should we rise against him.'

'And that is why we must not act alone,' said Gamelbearn. 'To have any chance of toppling him, we need every thegn in Northumbria riding alongside us. If we do that and command an army of the people, then the king cannot help but sit up and take notice. Our location protecting England from the Scots is far too important, and he relies on us to keep our eyes on the border.'

'So, what do you want us to do?'

'First of all,' said Gamelbearn, 'we need more people on our side. Let us go from this place and spread the word, but share it only amongst those you trust. If he should get the slightest idea that there are men that talk against him, then there will not be enough gallows north of London to accommodate us all. Most of those loyal to him are with him in the south, so we have some time. Recruit whom you can, but tell them to be patient. I also suggest we all meet here at the same time next month to report how things have gone – agreed?'

'Agreed,' shouted the men.

'Good. In that case, let us settle down and work out the details. Northumbria is dying under the lordship of that man, and now it is time to do something about it.'

Chapter Sixteen

Anglesey, Wales, September, AD 1063

Harold slept face down on a straw-filled mattress, physically exhausted after the events of the past few weeks. Since leaving Bristol back in May, his army had seen both victories and setbacks and time to rest was in short supply for both him and his men. At any one time, half of his fleet sailed up and down the coast attacking the towns and villages while the rest of his men sallied south across the Menai to push inland, keeping the pressure on Gruffydd by denying him the roads needed to bring much-needed supplies from the south.

Men died on a daily basis on both sides, and it was becoming obvious that they could not continue the campaign of attrition for much longer. Tostig, in particular, had found it hard and, as was predicted in the briefing shed in Bristol, faced the wrath of Gruffydd almost on a daily basis as the Welsh king had swept down from the high mountains to constantly harass his forces.

Tostig had lost a lot of men, and if it hadn't been for the reinforcements sent by Edward, he would have withdrawn weeks earlier. Despite this, the area between the mountains and the northern shore was now completely in English hands, and both Tostig and Harold had made their base on Anglesey, sharing the same manor house as their headquarters.

Harold snored quietly and did not even flinch when Tostig walked into the damp-smelling hall, slamming the door behind him. Some of the other men, also trying to get some much-needed sleep, cursed at the intrusion, but most just turned away and pulled their blankets tighter around their shoulders.

'It stinks in here,' said Tostig, making his way over to the table to pour an ale from the dozens of half-empty jugs. He took a few mouthfuls before spitting it out and throwing the tankard across the room. 'And this tastes of piss,' he shouted, waking up most of the room. He turned to the nearby servant, grabbing him by the jerkin and pushing him up against the wall. 'Go and get me some fresh ale now,' he growled, 'and if I come in here again to find spoiled ale and half-empty jugs, I will take your hands, understood?'

'Tostig,' said a voice, 'let him be.'

Tostig glanced across to see Harold sitting up and staring at him. He paused before releasing the servant and shoving him to one side.

'I meant what I said,' he shouted as the terrified man scurried away. 'Do your job or face the consequences.' He peered into more of the jugs, looking for mead as Harold walked over to him with a blanket wrapped around his shoulders.

'What ails you, brother?' he asked, staring at Tostig. 'Your mood is as foul as the devil's breath.'

'We lost another three men last night,' said Tostig. 'Their throats were cut as they slept in their tents.'

'The Welsh got into your camp? Where were the guards?'

'We had sentries posted all along the perimeter,' said Tostig, 'but the assassins must have crawled between them in the darkest hours and were long gone before we discovered the bodies at dawn. We cannot fight such men, Harold. Give me an open battle, and I will face any army, but how do we fight those we cannot see?'

'I know it is a frustration,' said Harold, 'but we must be patient. Our strategy is paying off, and our spies report that many of the villages blame Gruffydd for their troubles. I think that if we increase the pressure, he will have to come to the negotiating table, and when he does, it is us that will dictate the terms.'

'I hope you are right,' said Tostig, 'for we cannot go on like this much longer.'

'Trust me,' said Harold, 'there is no foe a king fears more than that made up of his own people. We are almost there. Gruffydd is on his last legs. Now come, let us go and find some food.'

The two men left the building and headed over to a barn that housed the cooking fires, but on the way, a rider entered the camp and reined in his horse just in front of them.

'My lord,' he said, 'you are needed at the bridge. One of Gruffydd's men carries a flag of parley. He seeks an audience with you and refuses to talk to anyone else.'

'Why did you not bring him here?' asked Harold.

'I tried, my lord, but he said he will not step foot on Anglesey while it is still in English hands.'

'Then tell him to go to hell,' said Tostig.

'No,' interrupted Harold, 'tell him to wait. I will come to the bridge as soon as I can.'

'As you wish, my lord,' said the messenger, and rode away.

'Why do you dance to their tune?' said Tostig. 'If they want to talk, let it be on our terms, not theirs.'

'It is a small sacrifice,' said Harold, 'and it could be the opening gambit for the king's surrender. We will make him wait a while, but it is an opportunity we should not miss.'

'Even so,' said Tostig, 'these devils should be given no leeway. They have killed too many of our men.'

'Understood,' said Harold, 'now come, let's eat.'

—

Two hours later, Tostig and Harold rode their horses across the wooden bridge attaching Anglesey to the mainland and through the fortified palisades erected against any Welsh attack. A few hundred paces away, two men sat at a campfire, wrapped in their cloaks against the cold and damp air, surrounded by at least a dozen of Harold's men, their hands resting menacingly on the hilts of their swords.

As they approached, the two men looked up but stayed sitting, their attention returning to the pieces of rabbit they had roasting on a spit above the flames.

'Get to your feet,' barked one of the English sergeants, 'and show some respect.' The men glanced at the soldier but ignored his demand, more worried about burning their meal.

'I said get to your feet,' said the sergeant, drawing his sword.

'Sergeant,' said Harold. 'Take your men back to the camp. We will take it from here.'

The sergeant hesitated before heading back to get some well-earned rest. Harold turned back to the two seated Welshmen, recognising one of them from his negotiations at Archenfield a few years earlier.

'Macsen,' he said, 'good to see you again. This is my brother, Tostig.'

'We are aware of Tostig,' said Macsen, without looking up. He nodded towards his comrade. 'This is Cynan ab Iago, kinsman and trusted comrade. You can speak freely in front of him.' He pointed to a log on the opposite side of the fire. 'Sit.'

Harold and Tostig sat down, grateful for the warmth of the flames.

Macsen retrieved one of the rabbit-laden sticks and offered it across to the two Englishmen.

'Food?' he asked.

'We have eaten,' said Harold. 'Thank you.'

Macsen shrugged his shoulders and pulled off a chunk of charred meat with his teeth as Harold and Tostig waited patiently.

'So,' said Macsen eventually, 'you have been very busy these past few months. The blood of many stains your hands.'

'Such is the way of war,' said Tostig coldly.

'Ordinarily, I would agree,' said Macsen, 'but rarely does the body count of the innocents outnumber that of the soldiers. Your actions have devastated those who did not cause any of our argument.'

'It is an unavoidable consequence,' said Harold. 'The only way to get to Gruffydd is via his people. Unfortunately, that means that they suffer more than he, but that is the way it is.'

'In that case, you should congratulate yourself,' said Macsen, 'for your tactics have been successful, and many of our people starve because of your actions.'

'I take no pleasure in hearing such news,' said Harold, 'but as I said, we are here to win this war. England's security depends on it.'

'I disagree with your reasoning,' said Macsen, 'but that is none of my business. The reason I have come is to offer you something that may make you withdraw your forces and allow our people to eat.'

'If you have come to offer gold and silver,' said Harold, 'then save your breath. King Edward has more wealth than you can imagine, so we will not be bought.'

'Oh, I think we can offer you something far better than that,' said Macsen, lifting his head to stare directly into Harold's eyes. 'How about if we give you Gruffydd himself?'

Harold and Tostig stared at Macsen in shock. Never in their wildest dreams had they expected that, especially from Gruffydd's most notorious warlord.

'I do not understand,' said Harold eventually. 'Is he dead?'

'He is not,' said Macsen, 'but if you swear by all that is holy that you will leave Wales, then I will deliver him into your hands.'

'Why?' asked Tostig. 'What has happened?'

'The affairs of my people do not concern you,' snapped Macsen. 'Just content yourself in the knowledge that his reign has run its course and we have people ready to take his place.'

'I need more information,' said Harold, 'but based on what you have said so far, I see no reason not to make such an agreement.'

'Then it is agreed,' said Macsen, and threw a goatskin of wine across the fire into Harold's lap. 'Drink, my friend,' he said, 'and let the killing come to an end.'

142

A few days later, Harold was once more standing on the far side of the bridge, awaiting a delegation from the Welsh. Messengers had been sent to all his men and to the fleet to suspend operations for seven days, pending delivery of the Welsh king into his custody.

The previous night, a message had arrived saying that Gruffydd would be handed over at noon, and now, most of Harold's army had lined up to see the ultimate disgrace of the man who had caused them so much trouble.

'Here they come,' said Tostig, seeing two horses emerge from the forest. 'This is a momentous day.'

A few moments later, the mood soured as it became clear that one of the riders was a woman.

'I don't understand,' said Harold. 'Who is she, and where is Gruffydd?'

'We have been betrayed,' growled Tostig. 'We should have known better. I'll send word to all our men to resume hostilities.'

'Wait,' said Harold. 'We will see what they have to say.'

The two riders reined in their horses in front of the earl.

'Cynan ab Iago,' said Harold, recognising the man from the fireside meeting a few days earlier. 'Where is Macsen?'

'He is needed elsewhere,' said Cynan, 'but I have come to complete the deal.'

Harold looked up at the beautiful young woman. Not once had she acknowledged anything or anyone around her, but kept her head high to gaze over the heads of the English soldiers.

'We agreed that you would deliver Gruffydd himself,' said Harold, 'not some woman I have never met before.'

'This is Alditha,' said Cynan, 'Gruffydd's wife. She is also the daughter of Aelfgar of Mercia and, with Gruffydd's reign coming to an end, has no further place at his court.'

'What do you want me to do with her?'

'That is up to you,' said Cynan. 'Bed her, kill her, sell her, the choice is yours – she no longer belongs in Wales.'

'And what about Gruffydd?' asked Harold. 'The arrangement was that he was to be handed over to me as my prisoner. That was not negotiable.'

'There was a problem,' said Cynan. 'Gruffydd refused to come.'

'Then your journey has been a waste of time,' said Harold, 'and we are done here. Tell Macsen that I will never again trust his word.'

'You are not listening, Earl Harold,' said Cynan. 'I said he did not want to come. I did not say he was not here.'

Harold frowned in confusion and looked past Cynan to see if he could see anyone else.

'You are speaking in riddles, Cynan,' he said. 'If he is here, tell him to show himself.'

Cynan paused before turning to the woman's horse, and as Harold watched, he threw something to bounce on the ground at his feet. It was the head of Gruffydd ap Llewelyn.

'There he is, Harold of Wessex,' said Cynan, 'and now our transaction is complete. *Get out of our country.*'

Chapter Seventeen

For the first time in what seemed like an age, Harold enjoyed the comforts of his ancestral home in Bosham. Christmas had come and gone. Messages from the king had been unusually infrequent since Harold had returned from London a few weeks earlier, allowing him, at last, to spend some quality time with his family.

The country had been peaceful ever since the war with Gruffydd, and Wales had finally been shared between two separate monarchs, once more dividing the country in two, a political move designed to make it harder for the warlike nation to threaten the English.

The negotiations between all parties had been led by Harold himself, and it took many weeks to agree a solution, but eventually, the talks were over, and a welcome peace descended across the country.

For once, Harold and Edyth were absent from the communal meal held every evening in the manor hall, choosing instead to have their food sent up to their quarters. As Harold sat at the long table, sipping warm mead, Edyth served ladles of piping hot broth, heavy with meat and vegetables, into ornate silver bowls. Once done, she placed them next to the freshly baked bread and joined her husband at the table.

'It has been a long day,' said Harold, cutting a slab of butter and dropping it into his broth to melt. 'I am looking forward to my bed.'

'As am I,' said Edyth. 'What plans do you have for the morrow?'

'I have to settle a dispute in Dover,' said Harold, 'and then I am going to see a pair of falcons one of the local thegns has for sale, but after that, I will be back here and, God willing, spend time with you doing very little.'

'Good,' said Edyth, 'you are rarely here these days. It is just good to have you around.'

'There is a lot to do,' said Harold, 'such is the burden we all bear.'

'I know,' sighed Edyth, 'but Edward always piles so much upon you. I worry for your safety, and besides, there are matters of the family to consider and seldom do we have a chance to address those.' She blew gently on her soup before sipping it carefully.

'Like what?' asked Harold, stirring in the butter.

'Well,' said Edyth, breaking a hand of bread from the loaf, 'I know that seldom a day passes without you wondering what happened to Wulfnorth and Hakon. Yet every time you try to make arrangements to find them, Edward finds you something else to do. If it's not dealing with some dispute, it's fighting the Welsh or travelling heaven knows where to find him an heir. It is never-ending, Harold, and surely there has to be some give.'

'You make a good point, Edyth,' said Harold, 'for though the responsibilities of my position are a burden I welcome, it has been far too long without word of the boys. I will speak to the king and request time to try and find them.'

'Good,' said Edyth, 'for if nothing else, it will ease your mind.'

'In what way?'

'In that at least you have tried something, and their memory has not been forgotten.'

Harold nodded and started to eat the soup, savouring the greasiness and flavour the heavily salted butter brought to the food.

'Tell me,' said Edyth, changing the subject, 'whatever happened to that girl you brought back from Wales? I have been meaning to ask, but as you are seldom here, I keep forgetting.'

'Alditha?' asked Harold.

'Yes, the one that was married to the King of Wales. Did she get her family back?'

'Aye, she did,' said Harold, 'her children were returned to her as soon as the truce with Wales was settled, as well as a generous parcel of land from her father's estate. She is now a wealthy and, it has to be said, quite a powerful woman.'

'In what way?'

'She has a foot in both camps,' said Harold. 'She is a major landholder in Mercia, as well as being the mother of two boys who may yet have a claim to the kingship of Wales.'

'I thought that had already been settled?'

'Aye, it has,' said Harold, 'but bloodline is a powerful reason to challenge a king, and I fear that once they are older, they may embark on a route they regret.'

'She is very beautiful,' said Edyth, glancing at her husband.

'Is she?' asked Harold, avoiding her gaze. 'I had not noticed.'

Edyth laughed out loud and wiped her mouth with a napkin.

'Oh come on,' she said, 'what man worth his salt could not have noticed? I have rarely seen such a beauty, and I am jealous of her.'

'You have nothing to be jealous of,' said Harold. 'She has her own life to live, and we have ours. The house of Mercia will look after her.'

'So why do you go there to see her so often?' asked Edyth, putting down her spoon.

Harold looked up at his wife.

'You know why I go to her,' he said. 'She had been shunned by her people, and it took a while to get settled. I promised her father on his deathbed that I would do whatever I could to look after his family, and that is what I am doing.'

'As long as that is all you are doing,' said Edyth.

'What are you implying?' said Harold, putting down his own spoon.

'All I am saying,' said Edyth, 'is she is a very attractive woman who does not have a man at her side, and you are often in her company for long periods of time. Any wife facing such a situation would have concerns.'

'It is a duty I vowed to her father,' said Harold, 'nothing more. You are my wife, Edyth, not her.'

'We are wed in the handfast tradition only,' said Edyth, 'as well you know. Our vows have never been confirmed in a house of God.'

'You need to smother these feelings,' said Harold, 'for they will make you ill. I am away from this house nine days from ten, and if I was so inclined, could be bedding women from Scotland to Wales without your knowledge. Why does this situation cause you so much angst?'

'Because she is very beautiful,' said Edyth, 'and I noticed the way she looked at you when she thought neither of us was looking.'

'You have nothing to fear, Edyth,' said Harold, taking her hand. 'My place is by your side. It always has been and always will be.' He released her hand and picked up his spoon. 'Now, let us eat, for the food is getting cold.'

Edyth smiled at her husband and picked up her own spoon. Her demeanour was calm, for Harold's words were reassuring, but her insides were in turmoil, for not once during the entire conversation had he denied sleeping with the woman. Trying desperately not to cry, she resumed her own meal in silence, knowing that if her suspicions were true, then her life was about to change for ever.

–

In the north, Tostig was facing challenges of his own. Since returning from Wales, he had faced deposition after deposition from aldermen and thegns from all across Northumbria. Hardly a day passed without someone asking for an audience to request help for their villages or a reduction in the taxes, but with every request, Tostig's heart hardened, and he rejected them all, investing instead in strengthening the ranks of those that protected him from danger. The cost was prohibitive, and the more people he hired, the more money he had to raise, a self-fuelling monster that was way out of control.

A lot of the time he spent across the border as a guest of King Malcolm, knowing that he was beyond the reach of those who saw fit to interrupt his love of hunting and womanising with their constant requests for audience, but the relief that those visits brought was just temporary, for Malcolm too had affairs to look after and the time passed all too quickly before Tostig had to return home to face his troubles.

More and more, he relied on paying his sheriffs and constables to control the growing anger across the earldom, but even though such dissent was dealt with quickly and violently, the feeling amongst the people grew stronger with every day that passed.

'You look worried,' said his wife, Judith of Flanders, at their evening meal. 'Is it something you wish to share?'

'Nothing you can help with,' said Tostig, staring at his half-eaten plate of venison.

'Is the food not good?'

'The food is fine,' said Tostig, 'I'm just not hungry.'

'Perhaps if we talked—' said Judith, but before she could finish her sentence, Tostig grabbed his platter and threw it across the hall to smash against the wall.

'Will you shut up, woman?' he shouted. 'I said there is nothing you can help with, so just leave me alone.' He threw his chair to one side and stormed over to where his cloak was hanging on a hook in the wall.

'Where are you going?' asked Judith. 'The hour is late.'

'To seek more favourable company,' he said as his two body-guards retrieved their own cloaks to follow him. 'Do not wait up for me, as I expect the sun will appear before I do.'

The three men left the hall, and Judith's heart sank, knowing full well that he was probably going to the one place in Northumbria where he could always expect a warm welcome: the tavern in the village at the end of his estate.

Even before he had returned from Wales, she knew that any support he once enjoyed was withering away, but now he was back, it was getting worse, and she knew that if he didn't do something soon, he risked losing everything.

—

In London, King Edward dined with the son of the now-deceased Edward Ætheling. The twelve-year-old boy, Edgar, had a joyful demeanour, and Edward enjoyed his company.

'How is your mother?' asked Edward, sitting back to allow a servant to put a whole pigeon on his plate.

'She is well,' said Edgar, doing the same, 'and sends her best regards.'

'I am pleased,' said Edward. 'Be sure to tell her that she is welcome to dine with me at any time. Just let my stewards know, and they will make the arrangements.'

'I will,' said Edgar, but he knew that such a request had been made on several occasions without any response from the steward. Whether that was by design or by simple oversight, he did not know, but his mother was far too proud to seek clarification.

'And your sisters?' asked the king.

'Both Margaret and Cristina are well,' said Edgar, 'and are studying at the abbey at Romsey. They say it is a place of extreme beauty that breathes the very essence of Christ himself.'

'It is indeed beautiful,' said the king, 'and I take great pleasure in sponsoring such a godly place.'

'You are very kind,' said Edgar.

'Such things are expected of a king,' said Edward, 'as you will no doubt find out one day.'

Edgar paused and looked down at his food as an awkward silence filled the room.

'What is the matter?' asked Edward. 'You know full well that the death of your father made you the next in line for the throne of England. Does that thought bother you?'

'No, your grace,' said Edgar, 'it's just…'

'Well?' said the king. 'Speak up, for to hesitate is to lose the moment, whether in battle or politics. What worries you so?'

'Your grace,' said Edgar, looking up, 'I am grateful for the trust you place in me, I truly am, but I often wonder why these conversations are kept between ourselves. At no time have you ever proclaimed me heir in public or indeed, as far as I am aware, in any court meeting or audience. As such, I often wonder if me being your heir is an idea rather than a commitment.'

Edward pushed away his plate and stared at the boy.

'Edgar,' he said, 'from the northern borders to the southernmost point of England, whenever you are mentioned, you are referred to as Edgar Ætheling, and that in itself is a powerful message. You are my heir, and that is common knowledge across the land. You need no ceremony to confirm your position.'

'I know,' said Edgar, 'but I do not attend royal functions, whether formal or otherwise and am certainly not allowed outside the walls of Westminster. Instead, I am forced to study from dawn till dusk, sometimes never seeing the light of day or breathing in God's clean air.'

'It is important you learn the ways of the court,' said Edward, 'especially as you were brought up in Hungary. We do things differently here, and there is a lot to learn. Just be patient and, in time, I promise you will be unveiled to the world with all the pomp and ceremony we can muster. Will that suit?'

'Aye, your grace,' said Edgar with a huge smile, 'it will.'

'Good,' said the king, retrieving his meal, 'now eat up, for as a future king, you will need all the strength you can get.'

Part Three

Chapter Eighteen

Bosham, May, AD 1065

Harold stood on the dock at Bosham with his wife, watching as his men loaded the last of the supplies onto the two ships that would accompany him to Normandy.

'The weather looks good,' said Edyth, gazing out to sea. 'It should be a good crossing.'

'No man worth his salt ever trusts the weather as a sign of a safe voyage,' said Harold. 'The sea has taken too many men from their families before their time.'

'Do not say that, Harold,' said Edyth, 'I am already consumed with worry.'

'God will do what God will do,' said Harold. 'All we can hope for is that he sees fit to deliver us safely, but if anything happens to me, you and the family will be well taken care of.'

'You just focus on staying alive,' said Edyth, 'and bring the boys home with you.'

'I will do everything in my power, Edyth. I promised my father on his deathbed, and it has been far too long without pursuing that vow.'

'My lord,' shouted a voice, and Harold turned to see Owen of Hereford standing in the bow of one of the ships. 'The captain says we have to make haste, else we will miss the tide.'

Harold turned back to Edyth.

'You take care, my love,' he said, 'and if God is with us, I will be back with the boys before autumn.'

'Travel safely, Harold Godwinson,' replied his wife. 'You will be in my prayers every night.'

Harold kissed Edyth on the cheek before walking away down the quayside.

'Is that the last of the stores?' he shouted, seeing a few men carrying sacks across their shoulders.

'Aye, my lord, it is,' said an overseer, following them out of the storage shed.

'Then get them aboard quickly,' said Harold, 'we are about to leave.' He walked across the gangplank to where Owen and the captain waited for him.

'So, are we ready?' he asked.

'We are,' said the captain. 'Give me a few moments to secure the gangplanks, and we can be on our way.'

'What about the horses?' asked Harold.

'All safely aboard the other ship,' said Owen, 'along with enough feed for a month.'

Harold paused and waited until the captain was out of earshot.

'What about the chests?' he asked quietly.

'Stowed amongst the crates of supplies,' said Owen. 'Nobody would ever guess their contents.'

'Good,' said Harold. 'There is nobody as dangerous as a covetous sailor. When we get to the other side, we will place the contents in several bags and share them amongst our men for easy carriage. That way, we will not have to find a cart and can move much easier.'

'Or we could find somewhere to hide them,' said Owen, 'and only retrieve them if and when we find the boys.'

'We could,' said Harold, 'but the thought of burying so much gold and silver beneath the earth sends shivers of fear down my spine.'

'As you wish,' said Owen. 'Just let me know what you desire when we reach Normandy, and I will make the arrangements.'

Harold nodded, and as he felt the ship move gently from the quay, he walked to the stern to see his wife still standing on the dock. He raised his hand in acknowledgement, but though he loved his wife very much, he could not prevent his mind from wondering what it would be like if it had been Alditha standing in her place.

As the ship headed gracefully towards the harbour entrance, Edyth, too, had Gruffydd's widow on her mind. She had spent many a sleepless night worrying about Alditha and the effect she had had on Harold, and the more she thought, the more worried she had become. Now, with Harold destined to be away from England for a couple of months at least, she could finally enact the only thing she could think of to put her mind at rest once and for all. She was going to Mercia to confront Alditha.

Several hours later, Harold stood in the bow of the lead ship, the wind and rain gusting around his face like an angry animal. The weather had taken a turn for the worse just an hour or so after leaving Bosham, but the captain had assured him that everything was under control. Consequently, they had decided to continue, and in the distance, they could see the shores of Normandy as a thin black line on the horizon.

'We seem to be getting no closer,' he yelled over his shoulder to Owen.

'I agree,' shouted Owen. 'I'll find out what is happening.' He staggered back to where the captain joined his men in wrestling with the rigging ropes, trying to find the right settings for the overburdened sail. 'What's going on?' asked Owen, wiping the rain from his face.

'The storm is getting stronger,' said the captain, 'and the wind stays in one direction for no more than a few moments at a time.'

'What does that mean?' replied Owen, struggling to be heard above the noise.

'It is difficult to get her to sail in one direction, and if we are not careful, we are at risk of losing the sail.'

'Should we resort to oars?'

'Not yet,' replied the captain, grimacing as another gust of wind placed enormous strain on the sail. 'I think we may just get away with it.'

Owen looked up at the sail, and even though he was no sailor, he could see that there was something wrong.

'Captain,' he shouted, 'enough is enough. Lower the sail, and we will all take to the oars.'

'This is my ship,' roared the captain, 'and I will sail her how I see fit.'

Owen felt his anger rise, but before he could respond, an almighty crack rang out over the noise of the storm, and the mast snapped clean in half, crashing into the boat and sending the sail over into the churning sea. Timber and bone smashed together as several men were caught under the falling mast, and several more got caught up in the tangle of rigging. The captain was sent flying across the deck but managed to get back to his feet relatively unharmed.

'*Cut the ropes!*' he screamed. '*Quickly!*'

Men ran over with knives and axes to sever the rigging, knowing full well that they only had moments before the sodden sails would capsize the already listing ship and send it plunging into the depths with everyone on board. Owen and Harold joined the frenzy, hacking at the ropes with their knives as the storm waves crashed over the side. Moments later, to everyone's relief, the sails finally broke away, taking the broken mast with them. The ship lurched back, but it lay very low in the water, allowing even more waves to crash over the side.

'Bail,' roared Harold over the storm, 'use what you can.'

Every man tried get the water out, working frantically to stop the ship from sinking. Some had buckets, some used their shields as scoops, while others just used their hands.

'Throw what you can overboard,' yelled the captain.

Some of the men threw the crates and sacks of supplies into the sea as well as anything else that had any weight. Even the bodies of the men who had died when the mast broke were discarded with no ceremony, until eventually, only two crates remained, the ones holding the gold and silver. Owen looked towards Harold, both men sodden and exhausted.

'My lord,' he shouted, 'what do you want to do?'

Harold stared at the two chests, knowing that the contents were intended to pay for all the costs on the campaign, not just for food and horses, but for any ransom demanded for the release of the boys. Without it, they would have nothing, but the ship was sinking, and they had to act fast.

'Do it,' he said, and as his heart filled with despair, Owen and another of his men threw the last of the crates overboard.

'Keep bailing,' he roared, turning his attention back on the crew, 'or tonight we will share a watery grave.'

The men turned back to their task, many with tears of fear mixing with the seawater on their faces. For many, death had never been so near, and to a man, they shared an uncontrollable fear of drowning. Together they increased the frenzied work rate, knowing that their chances of dying were overwhelming, but as long as there was any hope at all, then they would do everything in their power to live.

Chapter Nineteen

Ponthieu, France, May, AD 1065

Two days later, in the small county of Ponthieu to the south of Normandy, Count Guy of Ponthieu stood behind a table in one of the village squares, watching as the farmers and vassals of the county lined up to pay their taxes to his treasurer. A few paid with coins, but by far, the majority paid their dues with goods and chattels ranging from livestock to freshly forged weapons, always a welcome addition to the count's armoury. By the end of the day, the cart was full and headed back to his manor, drawn by two oxen. It had been a surprisingly good haul from the village, and one that he hoped would be matched by the many other villages his treasurers would visit over the coming weeks.

'It has been a good day,' he said to one of his nobles at his side, 'let us hope for more of the same on the morrow.'

'I see no reason why not,' said Phillipe of Charny, 'the winter was milder than we all feared, and many did not have to slaughter their pigs, so there is no reason not to pay the tithe.'

'Come,' said Guy, 'let us separate the tavern master from a flagon of his best wine and retire somewhere where the smell is not quite as bad.' As they walked away, they saw a small crowd standing around a man trying to sell a knife near the edge of the square. Guy paused and turned his head to hear a little clearer.

'My lord,' said Phillipe, 'is there a problem?'

'A moment,' said Guy, 'let me hear what this man has to say.' They both walked a bit closer, though stayed out of the seller's eye line, so as not to scare him away – a regular occurrence when a rogue saw the approach of any man of noble station.

'I am telling you,' said the man, his voice rising in frustration, 'this knife is absolutely genuine, for I took it from the Englishman myself.'

'I doubt that any English knight would allow you to disarm him,' said an old man. 'I suspect that even if your story was true, then your body would now be feeding the flowers.'

'As God is my witness,' replied the man, 'these men were shipwrecked during the storm a few days ago and are lucky to be alive. There were twelve in all, and they were bereft of all things, including food and water. I gave them some bread and cheese, and in return, they gave me this knife to sell.'

'If this is true,' said a voice, 'should you not report them to the constable?'

'I will,' said the man, 'but first I want to sell the knife, for it will surely be taken from me the moment anyone sees it.'

'I will give you a piglet for it,' said one of the older men.

'A piglet is no good to me,' said the seller, 'I want coin. Just look at the artistry on the hilt. It was surely the blade of a nobleman.'

At the side of the square, Guy had heard enough and pushed through the crowd.

'Hold there,' he shouted as the seller saw him and turned to run.

The man stopped in his tracks as he saw Phillipe of Charny blocking his way. His shoulders slumped as he realised that the very thing he had dreaded was about to happen. Many of the crowd dispersed, keen not to get involved in any of the drama that was about to unfold.

'What is your name?' asked Guy.

'I am Jean, my lord,' mumbled the man, 'a humble fisherman from this very village.'

'Show me that knife,' demanded Guy, holding out his hand.

Jean handed it over and waited as the count examined it in detail.

'And you say you took this from a man who had been shipwrecked?'

'I did not steal it, my lord, it was a fair trade, for I gave him bread and cheese from my satchel. They were starving, and it was not enough, so they offered me the knife if I would go and get some more.'

'How many men?'

'I counted twelve, but there may have been more.'

'Why did you not just go straight to the constable?'

'Because they kept my dog, my lord, and said that if I did not go back with more food, they would cut off his head. The story is true, my lord, and the remains of the ship still lay upon the sand. I can take you to the wreck if that is your want.'

'The ship doesn't interest me – where are the men?'

'In the shepherd's hut a mile upstream of where the river reaches the shore.'

'And you think they will still be there?'

'Yes, my lord, for they are expecting me to return with more food.'

Guy looked over towards Phillipe of Charny.

'How quickly can you gather your men?'

'I have twenty camped outside the town,' said the knight. 'I will need a few hours to get more from the manor.'

'Twenty will be enough,' said Guy. 'Muster your men and get this man a horse.' He turned to the fisherman. 'I am assuming you can ride?'

'I can, my lord.'

'Good, then when we are ready, you will take us to the shepherd's hut.'

Ten minutes later, all of the count's men were mounted by the town walls.

'My lord,' said the fisherman nervously, 'I was wondering if perhaps I could have the knife back. I traded it fair and square.'

Guy turned to one of the knights.

'Give this man a silver penny.'

'My lord,' said Phillipe of Charny, 'pay him nothing and just take the knife. It is yours by right anyway.'

'Aye,' said Guy, 'it is, but I am in a generous mood.' He handed over the knife to Phillipe. 'Take a look at the hilt. Do you recognise the crest?'

'I do not,' said the knight.

'I do,' said Guy, 'and if I am not mistaken, a weapon of this quality could only have been carried by one man, Harold of Wessex. Let's go and find those men, Phillipe, for if this fisherman tells the truth, then God has just gifted us a very fortuitous opportunity.'

—

A few leagues away, Harold stood at the window, keeping watch for any approaching trouble. It had been almost three days since they had dragged themselves ashore from what remained of their ship, and those that had survived had spent a miserable first night huddled together amongst the rocks from the ravages of the weather.

The following morning the storm had eased enough to allow them to scour the rock pools and tideline for anything they could eat. Some of his men were keen to just head inland to seek a farmhouse or village, but Harold had ordered them to stay, at least until they knew exactly where they had landed. The appearance of a fisherman confirmed his worries when he said they were actually in the county of Ponthieu, not Normandy.

With no love lost between England and Ponthieu, Harold knew that even though they needed food and water, they could not risk being taken prisoner and somehow had to make their way northward. At least there, he would be able to approach William of Normandy, a fellow noble with whom he shared a mutual respect.

'Any sign of him?' asked Owen of Hereford, walking over to join Harold.

'Not yet,' said Harold. 'We will give him until dark, and if he is not back by then, we'll head north.'

'We need to find some food,' said Owen. 'The men are starving.' He glanced over to where his comrades were huddled together against the cold.

'We'll find something as we go,' said Harold. 'There must be fishing villages along the coast.' He looked at Owen's head. 'How is the wound?'

Owen's hand went up to feel the weal stretching across his forehead where he had smashed it against a rock when he was trying to get out of the sea.

'Nothing the affection of a good woman can't sort out,' said Owen.

'I fear it will be a while before you encounter one of those,' said Harold. 'Why don't you try to get some rest. I'll keep watch here and wake you up if anything happens.'

'Aye, I'll do that,' said Owen and returned to sit amongst his comrades.

'Where are you, fisherman?' said Harold quietly, gazing out of the window.

–

Although Harold was still standing at the window an hour or so later, his eyes were closed as his body desperately sought the sleep he so badly needed. Every few seconds, his head dropped, forcing him back awake before his knees buckled. Realising he could go on no longer, he was about to ask one of his men to relieve him when he saw movement at the top of the hill in front of the hut. It was the fisherman, carrying a sack over his shoulder.

Instantly alert, he waited a few moments to make sure the man was alone before turning to rouse the others.

'Wake up,' he said, 'he's back.'

Immediately the exhausted men got to their feet and gathered around the window.

'It looks like he has got food,' said one. 'Come on.'

He pulled open the door and headed outside, followed by his comrades. As soon as the door opened, the large dog that had been used as leverage against the fisherman made a bolt for freedom and ran across the field to his master.

Jean the fisherman stopped in his tracks and dropped the sack, desperate to greet his faithful companion.

'Bring the food,' demanded one of the Englishmen, but Jean ignored him, interested only in making a fuss of the creature.

'A curse upon him,' said one of the men. 'We'll have to go and get it ourselves.'

'Wait,' said Harold. 'We are safer if we stay here. One man will go in case we are all caught out in the open.'

'I will go,' said Owen, and pushed his way through his comrades.

'Be careful,' said Harold, 'and as soon as it is dark, we will get out of here before that fisherman tells someone where we are.'

Owen nodded and headed up the slope to where the man was waiting alongside his dog.

'We thought you were not returning,' he said. 'What's in the sack?'

'Take a look,' said the fisherman.

Owen dropped to one knee and undid the ties. Inside he could see several loaves of bread, a wheel of cheese, and a brace of rabbits, already skinned and ready for the pot.

'Treasures indeed,' he said, 'but we cannot make a fire. Do you have flint and tinder?'

When the man did not answer, Owen looked up to ask him again. 'I said, do you have a flint?'

The fisherman just stared back, a look of despair on his face.

'What's wrong?' asked Owen, standing up to look over the fisherman's shoulder. 'What's going on?'

The man started walking backwards away from Owen, worried for his safety.

'I had no choice,' he said, 'they made me do it.'

'Made you do what?' asked Owen. 'What have you done?'

The fisherman turned and started running towards the woods.

Owen looked around, confused, but the situation became all too clear when he saw twenty riders galloping towards him from his flank. He turned and shouted back towards his comrades standing outside the hut.

'It's a trap!' he roared. '*Run.*'

Down at the shepherd's hut, Harold stared in horror, having already realised the threat.

'We have to get out of here,' gasped one of the men and turned to run towards the river.

Harold thought furiously. Some of the riders carried crossbows, so there was no way they could get across alive, and even if they did, where would they go?

'Hold!' he shouted. 'Get back inside the hut.'

'Why?' shouted the man. 'We will be trapped in there.'

'We are dead men anyway,' said Harold, 'but if we can get them to talk, we may just have a chance.'

All his men retreated to the hut to peer through half-closed shutters. Harold stayed outside and watched with horror as one of the mounted knights ploughed into Owen, sending him crashing to the floor.

The rest continued onward, reining in their horses just ten paces from the hut. Two of them had crossbows aimed at Harold's chest, but he did not flinch and just waited until the commander of the patrol walked his horse down the hill to join his men. When he arrived, everyone fell quiet as Guy removed the knife he had obtained from the fisherman and held it up for Harold to see.

'Is this yours?' he asked.

'It was,' said Harold. 'I traded it for food with a rascal who broke his word.'

'Be not too harsh on him,' said Guy. 'Either he broke his word, or one of my men would have broken his neck. Who are you, stranger, and why do you trespass on my land?'

166

'My name is Harold Godwinson,' said Harold, 'Earl of Wessex and advisor to the King of England. To whom am I speaking?'

'I am Guy of Ponthieu, lord and master of this county. Have you come to rob us, Harold of Wessex?'

'We have not,' said Harold. 'We were shipwrecked here a few days ago and have lost a lot of men in the storm. We now seek aid and shelter in the name of the English king. If you were to offer such succour, then you would be well rewarded.'

'Oh, this situation cannot be anything else but profitable for me,' said Guy, 'especially if what you say is true. But what I am interested in is why you were here in the first place.'

'We had no intention of landing on these shores,' said Harold, 'and were headed for Normandy to try and find some family members who were taken there against their will a few years ago.'

'You were going to rescue someone?' asked Guy, surprised.

'No, we were going to negotiate for their release.'

'And pay a ransom?'

'If necessary.'

'Which means you would have carried the payment with you.'

'It does, but all was lost during the storm.'

'Yet I am told the ship lies on the shore just a league from here.'

'It does, but we threw everything we could overboard when the ship was damaged.'

'Even the money?'

'Some things are worth more than silver and gold,' said Harold. 'Men's lives being amongst them.'

'We may have to disagree on that,' said Guy. He fell silent and stared at Harold for a few moments.

'If you are telling me the truth,' he said eventually, 'I would imagine that some people would pay a hefty price for your return.'

'You are right,' said Harold. 'And if you provide me with a ship to get back to England, I will ensure you get paid as soon as we arrive safely.'

'Oh come on,' said Guy, 'if you are indeed Harold of Wessex, you know how this works. I will detain you and your men while allowing one man to return to England with my demands.'

'I am no trickster,' said Harold, 'I am a man of noble birth and standing. If I promise to pay, then pay I will. On that, you have my word.'

'Nevertheless,' said Guy, 'we will play this game my way. Tell your men to come out and stand before me.'

'Is it safe to do so?' asked Harold, looking at the arbalists. 'Your men already have their crossbows loaded and aimed.'

'If I wanted to kill you,' said Guy, 'then you know full well that hiding in this hovel would not prevent me from doing so.' He turned to his men. 'Lower your crossbows.'

The riders did as he asked and watched as Harold's men emerged to stand behind their leader.

'You are all now my prisoners,' announced Guy, 'and will be taken from here to be detained at my leisure. Soon I will send a message to England to demand payment for your release, and if met, you can be back with your families within weeks. But know this, if even one of you tries to escape or causes my men or me any problems, then all will be punished. Understood?'

The Englishmen looked towards Harold to follow his lead.

'You will have no problem from us,' said the earl. 'Just make sure you send that message as soon as possible.'

'You are in no position to demand what I do or when I do it,' said Guy. 'Now everyone, put your hands behind your back.' He turned to Phillipe of Charny. 'Tie their wrists and take them to the chateau. I have business elsewhere but will be back to make the necessary arrangements as soon as I can.'

'Shall I put them in one of the empty storerooms, my lord?'

'Oh no,' said Guy, 'find the most secure and uncomfortable room in the chateau and lock them inside. They are prisoners, Phillipe of Charny, and until I decide otherwise, they will be treated as such.'

Chapter Twenty

Mercia, England, May, AD 1065

Edyth Swanneck waited in a side room of an elegant manor house deep in the heart of Mercia. Alongside her was her lady-in-waiting, as well as one of the trusted huscarls from Bosham. Outside, twenty more fully armed men at arms waited alongside their horses for her to emerge.

The steward of the house stood at the door to the room as two servants brought in a tray of warmed wine and sweet pastries.

'My mistress will not be much longer, my lady,' he said. 'She sends her apologies.'

'There is no rush,' said Edyth. 'Tell her to take her time.' She smiled at the steward as he bowed his head and left, but inside she was seething. She had sent word the previous day that she would be visiting and suspected that the delay was a deliberate ploy to make her feel uneasy. She looked at the pastries and, as delicious as they looked, stubbornly refused to contemplate even the slightest of nibbles.

'My lady,' said her servant, 'it has been an age since we broke our fast. Will you not at least try one?'

'I am not hungry, Lefwen,' said Edyth, 'but please, you go ahead. I will eat later.'

Despite Edyth's invitation, Lefwen did not touch the food and just waited patiently alongside her mistress with her hands placed delicately in her lap. Eventually, the door opened and a servant walked in, carrying a spare chair to place before Edyth.

'At last,' mumbled Edyth and got to her feet. A few moments later, Alditha entered the room and walked across to greet the woman who had taken her in just after her husband had been killed.

'Lady Edyth,' she said with a warm smile, 'I am so sorry for the lateness – please forgive me.'

She took Edyth's shoulders in her hands and, to Edyth's surprise, kissed her on either cheek.

'Welcome to my new home,' she continued. 'Have you been looked after?'

'We have,' said Edyth, slightly taken aback by the warmth of the welcome. 'Thank you.'

'Please, sit,' said Alditha. 'Is there anything else I can get you? Wine perhaps?'

'I think not,' said Edyth, 'for in truth, we are only passing by and thought it would be pleasant to catch up and see how you are doing.'

'And a lovely visit it is,' said Alditha, turning to Edyth's servant. 'Lefwen, it is also good to see you again. You look well.'

'I enjoy excellent health, my lady,' said Lefwen, 'thank you.' Lefwen liked Alditha enormously, and during the short time she had stayed at Bosham, the two had become close, albeit unlikely, friends.

'That is great news,' said Alditha and leaned forward to take the servant's hands in hers. 'Tell me,' she whispered, with a playful smile, 'have you given any thought about running away and joining me here in Mercia?'

Lefwen's face burned bright red, and she looked over at Edyth before turning her attention back to Alditha. 'My lady,' she said, 'I am honoured, I really am, but I could never leave my mistress.'

Alditha burst out laughing and gave the servant an unexpected hug.

'Oh Lefwen,' she said, 'I am only jesting with you. You are one of the kindest and most loyal people I know, and never

171

for an instant would I think you capable of such a thing. Your mistress is very fortunate to have you.'

She turned back to face Edyth.

'So, Lady Edyth,' she said. 'It has been quite a while, and I still do not think that I have given you adequate thanks for taking me in as you did.'

'It was the least we could do,' said Edyth. 'And after all, Harold gave your father his word he would look after you.'

'He did, and he has,' said Alditha. 'I am very grateful.'

'So, how are you now?' asked Edyth. 'For when you left Bosham, you were not doing so well.'

'This is true,' said Alditha, 'but as you can see, my fortunes have taken a significant upturn, and I am now considered a wealthy person. My father bequeathed me lands in his will, and the new King of Deheubarth also awarded me an income as the mother of Gruffydd's children.'

'Good news indeed,' said Edyth. 'I suppose that you have such an estate, you can begin to think about moving on and perhaps finding a good man to marry.'

'I could,' said Alditha, 'but as I have the means to run my own affairs, there is no rush.'

'On the contrary,' said Edyth, 'I would have thought it would have been a priority. There are all sorts of ill-intentioned men out there, of both low and high station, who would seize the opportunity to do you ill. A partnership in the eyes of God would deter the worst of them.'

'Edyth,' said Alditha, 'your concern about my marital situation is touching, but I can assure you that being married to King Gruffydd for so long has made me more than able to manage my own affairs. Why do you pursue the subject so?'

Edyth paused and turned to her lady-servant. 'Lefwen, could you give us a moment alone, please?'

'Of course, my lady,' said Lefwen and left the room. Edyth turned back to Alditha.

'Alditha,' she said with a sigh, 'you are right, my interest in your personal life far exceeds that which would be normal, so

I will be blunt with my response. I worry that my husband, the Earl of Wessex, holds a fascination with you that borders on the unhealthy. Even when you lived with us, it seemed that he spent more time with you than with me, and now you have returned to Mercia, he spends just as much time here as in Wessex. Consequently, I have come here directly to ask you if you have designs on my husband that I should be worried about.'

'Designs?' asked Alditha, taken aback at the directness of the question. 'What do you mean?'

'Harold and I have been married for many years,' said Edyth, 'and are raising a family together. You are a very beautiful woman and could probably have the pick of all men. I just worry that it is mine that you have set your eyes upon.'

'Edyth,' said Alditha, 'you are an intelligent woman, and as such, you must surely know that there is not one amongst them who does not seek the comfort of another woman's embrace when they are away from their homes. Why do you credit Harold with being so different?'

'I am not naïve,' said Edyth, 'and I am sure that he probably does the same, but fleeting liaisons to satisfy their needs, as hurtful as they can be, do not cause me undue stress. It is women like you that give me sleepless nights.'

Alditha sat back in her chair, shocked at the accusation.

'Women like me. What is that supposed to mean?'

'It is no slight,' said Edyth, 'but a compliment. You are beautiful, graceful and intelligent. Everything that a man wants in a woman. But now that you are also rich, powerful and influential, you pose an even greater risk, for the temptations may be too much for him to resist. I need to know before I leave today, do you intend to take my husband from me?'

For a few moments, Alditha stared at Edyth, considering her reply.

'Edyth,' she said eventually, 'you have been brutally honest with me, and I admire your courage in coming all this way to confront the issue face to face. So, I will return the compliment by doing the same. If you are asking me if I have slept with your husband, then as much as the answer is bound to cause you hurt, the answer is yes. He has shared my bed on several occasions.'

Edyth's heart sank, and she felt sick to her stomach, but she tried desperately not to react.

'However,' said Alditha, 'if you are asking me if I intend to steal him away, then I can honestly say that I do not have, nor ever have had, any intention of taking him from you. If it helps, I can assure you that he loves you deeply, and my bed only offers him the passing comfort that all men crave.'

'Why?' asked Edyth, trying desperately not to cry. 'You could have the choice of any man. Why my husband?'

'I never intended it to happen,' said Alditha. 'He was just in the right place at the right time. My husband had been murdered right in front of me, and I was sent away from the place I had called home for many years, not even allowed to take my children with me. I felt worthless, and he was the man who was there to comfort me. After that, well, it just happened.'

'Did it ever happen when you were at Bosham?' asked Edyth quietly.

'Don't go there, Edyth,' said Alditha, 'for down that route only lies pain and heartache.'

'So it did,' said Edyth. 'While Lefwen nursed you back to health, you were bedding my husband under my own roof. How could you, Alditha? Do you not have a heart?'

'I never meant it to happen,' said Alditha. 'I am truly sorry. Please forgive me.'

'It is not me you should seek forgiveness from,' said Edyth, 'but God himself. You have committed the sin of coming between a man and his wife, and the law frowns upon such liaisons.'

'But have I really committed a sin?' asked Alditha quietly. 'As far as I am aware, you and Harold are not wed in the eyes of the Church.'

'*What?*' gasped Edyth. 'Of course we are married.'

'Not in the eyes of the Church,' said Alditha, 'for your ceremony was one of handfast only.'

'That is still recognised in the eyes of the law,' shouted Edyth, getting to her feet. 'How dare you suggest otherwise?'

'I do not question the legality,' said Alditha, 'only the recognition in the eyes of the Church. Despite everything, I have committed no sin before God, Edyth – neither has Harold.'

Edyth stared at the woman, lost for words.

'I will not let you have him, Alditha,' she said eventually, 'do you understand? As God is my witness, I swear I will fight you with every breath in my body. Shame on you.'

Before Alditha could answer, Edyth turned away and stormed out of the manor, slamming the door behind her.

Lefwen saw her run down the steps and over to the cart they had both travelled in from Bosham.

'My lady,' she said, climbing inside to sit alongside Edyth, 'you are distressed. What happened in there to cause you so much pain?'

'Nothing that concerns you, Lefwen,' said Edyth through her tears, 'but we are done around here. It's getting dark. Let's just get back to Bosham.'

–

Many leagues away, across the channel, William of Normandy sat at a campfire alongside some of his men, poking the embers of the fire with a stick. The act had become almost a routine over the last few days, and he reflected that no matter how much power a man had or how magnificent the building he called home, there was something strangely comforting about sitting around a fire with a fellow man of war.

Many of his officers shunned such activities, especially if there was a warm inn nearby, but William and a few others preferred to stay with the men as much as possible, especially when they were on campaign.

'Well,' he said, looking up at his second-in-command, 'Alan the Red, do you accept my wager?'

The lord of Richemont stared at the duke. They were close friends and had been comrades for a long time, but when it came to making a wager, they both took it seriously, even though the amounts involved were relatively small.

'So,' he replied, biting on an apple, 'you say, that if the manor is surrendered to us before dusk tomorrow, you will claim my horse, but if the castellan still holds firm by the time the sun sets, then the same payment will be due to me.'

'That about sums it up,' said William.

Alan thought hard. They had laid siege to the minor noble's manor for the last few days, and though they all knew that it would not last much longer, the owner was known to be as stubborn as a mule and most thought he still had a few days left in him yet.

'Do you know something I don't?' he asked.

'Like what?' asked William.

'Like you intend to storm the manor at first light and force him to submit.'

'I give my word,' said William, 'I have no such intentions, but something tells me that he has had enough and will take the knee while he still has a chance.'

'No,' said Alan, 'he is too stubborn for that. He will want to string his defiance out for as long as possible, especially in front of his own men. At least that way, he can say he was rebellious to the last.'

'So,' said William, 'do we have a wager?'

'We do,' said Alan and both men leaned forward to shake hands over the fire. But as Alan withdrew his grasp to sit back, he saw that William had placed a folded parchment into his hand.

'What's this?' asked Alan, unfolding the document.

'It is a note from our opponent offering his complete surrender at dawn tomorrow,' said William with a grin. 'It was delivered to me a few hours ago.'

'Aaargh,' shouted Alan, as the rest of the men around the fire burst into laughter, 'I swear you are the most deceitful man in Normandy.' He scrunched up the document and threw it into the flames before standing up and storming off into the darkness.

'Where are you going?' called one of the other officers.

'Leave him,' laughed William, 'I think he is going to say goodbye to his horse.'

The men burst out laughing again, and yet another skin of wine started making its way around the fire. It had been a hard few days, but the mood was lifting by the moment, especially as they now knew the siege was coming to an end. As the night wore on, one of William's soldiers walked into the clearing.

'My lord,' he said, 'I have news. Can I approach?'

'Aye,' said William, his mood relaxed. 'Sit with us and have a drink.'

'I cannot, my lord,' he said, 'for I am due to command the next watch, but one of my men told me something a short while ago, something I think you would want to know.'

'Go on,' said William, lowering the wineskin.

'My lord, he said that his brother arrived back from Rome this morning and recounted how he had stopped a few days ago in a village on the coast of Ponthieu. While there, he found out that the count has imprisoned a group of men who had their ship wrecked upon the shore and intends ransoming them to the highest bidder.'

'So,' said William, 'why does this concern me? Guy of Ponthieu is well within his rights to do whatever he pleases with men who enter his county uninvited.'

'I know, my lord, but one of those men is said to be Harold of Wessex.'

William paused, the wineskin halfway to his lips.

'Say that again,' he said.

'My lord, the man said that the prisoners were all English, and one of them is the Earl of Wessex himself.'

'Is he sure?' asked William.

'He did not see him himself,' said the officer, 'and would not have recognised him even if he did, but the tavern buzzed with the news, especially a fisherman who claimed to have played a part in their capture. My brother said the man drunk his bodyweight in ale that night, bought for him by suitably impressed comrades.'

'Drunken talk,' said one of the men sitting alongside William, 'nothing more.'

'Perhaps,' said the duke, 'but rarely is there smoke without fire.' He looked back up to the messenger. 'Go and find the Lord of Richemont,' he said, 'and tell him to attend me immediately.'

'Aye, my lord,' said the officer and turned away into the darkness.

'Surely you are not going to take that tale seriously?' said one of William's officers.

'Not yet,' said William.

'So you are not going to suddenly ride off to Ponthieu?'

'No,' said William, looking around as Alan the Red returned into the circle of light, 'but I know a man who is.'

'What's going on?' asked Alan, seeing all the upturned faces staring at him. 'Have I missed something?'

'Aye, you have,' said William, 'but the good news is you get to keep your horse for a few weeks longer.'

'And how may that be?' asked Alan the Red.

'Because you are going on a journey, my friend,' replied William, 'and you leave at dawn.'

Chapter Twenty-one

Beaurainville, France, June, AD 1065

Harold and his men sat in the cold and damp cellar beneath the fortified manor at Beaurainville. Unlike many of the manor houses in England that were still built of timber, this one was constructed entirely of stone, offering great defensive qualities against anyone wishing to attack. The construction was impressive, but the cold stone meant that, without a fire, the temporary prison was a miserable place, and there was little chance of escape.

They had been there for three weeks, and though Harold had been offered better quarters, he had refused, preferring to stay with his men, even though it meant he suffered the same problems as them.

'Do you think he is there yet?' asked Owen from his place in the corner of the room.

Harold looked over at the man who had become his trusted friend and advisor. He, like all the men, was wrapped in one of the blankets the count's jailer had provided and struck a forlorn figure. All the men were dirty, unshaven and cold, but more than that, they were constantly hungry and devoid of hope, having not been allowed out once since their incarceration.

'I expect so,' said Harold, realising that Owen was referring to the messenger Guy had sent to England. 'Just be patient, my friend – Edward will respond soon enough. There is no way he will let us rot here for any longer than he needs to.'

'That may be true of you,' said Owen, 'but the rest of us hold little value to the king. He may just pay a ransom for you and to hell with the rest of us.'

'I will not allow that to happen,' said Harold. 'Either we all go free, or we all stay here, together.'

'It is a bold pledge,' said a voice from the other side of the room, 'and one that I will be surprised to see come to fruition.'

'Even if the king refuses to pay,' said Harold, 'I have more than enough funds to pay all the ransoms. I suspect that even as we speak, either the king or my wife are gathering the monies to get us out of here. All we have to do is be patient and try to stay alive.'

Before anyone could answer, the door unbolted, and the jailer stepped inside.

'Harold Godwinson,' he said, 'you are wanted upstairs.'

'Perhaps he has returned with the ransom already,' said Owen sarcastically, 'and by tonight, we will be as free as the birds.'

'Stay strong, my friend,' said Harold, getting to his feet. 'We will see this through together.' He followed the jailer out of the cellar and up the stairs to a small, sumptuously furnished room with thick tapestries hanging from the walls. An inviting fire roared in the hearth, and a pot of hot broth sat on the table in the centre of the room, along with a bowl of hot water. On the chair to one side was a pair of leggings and a clean jerkin.

'Eat,' said the jailer, pointing at the pot, 'then wash and put on those clothes.'

Harold could smell the nutritious broth from where he stood, and his mouth watered in anticipation.

'Are my men getting the same?' he asked.

'Don't be stupid, Englishman,' said the jailer. 'Just eat the food and get changed. My master wants to see you in the main hall.'

'I will not eat such things while my men suffer,' said Harold, 'nor will I dress in finery just to ease the conscience of the man who causes such misery. I will see him as I am or else take me back to my men.'

The jailer looked troubled as he knew it was important that Harold looked as well as he could.

'You do not understand,' said the jailer. 'The master is expecting an important guest, so you have to get cleaned up.'

'All the more reason to stay as I am,' said Harold. 'I am the Earl of Wessex, and it is important for those in positions of power to see how your master treats nobility. This is of your doing, not mine.'

'He will not like this,' said the jailer, and turned to the guard at the door. 'Watch him. I will be back as soon as I can.' He walked out of the room, leaving Harold drooling at the smell of the meat-laden broth.

Several minutes later, the jailer returned.

'I have spoken to the count,' he said, 'and on this occasion only, he gives his word that if you do as I ask, the rest of the prisoners will get the same broth.'

'And can I trust him?'

'My master is many things,' said the jailer, 'but his word is good.'

Harold nodded his agreement.

'In that case,' he said, 'we have a deal.' He walked over to the table and pulled his chair closer until his whole face was bathed in the steam coming from the broth. He broke off a chunk of bread and dipped it into the juice before placing it slowly in his mouth, savouring every moment and every flavour, knowing full well that it could be a long time before he again enjoyed such luxury.

Fifteen minutes later, he stood at the doorway as clean as he could get and with a stomach heavy with food. It was a feeling he had not enjoyed since leaving England.

One of the count's servants entered and looked Harold up and down.

'Is this him?' he asked. 'He looks like a beggar.'

'It is the best we could do in the time,' said the jailer.

'It will have to do. Tell him to follow me.'

'I can understand you well enough,' said Harold.

The servant nodded. 'Well, that is a start,' he said. 'Come with me.' He led the way out of the room and up the stairs to where two men were waiting for him before a roaring fire in another magnificent room.

'Ah, he's here,' said Guy of Ponthieu as Harold entered. 'Please, come closer. Harold of Wessex, please meet the Lord of Richemont, also known as Alan the Red.'

'A good day to you,' said Alan the Red and held out his hand.

'And to you,' said Harold, but his hand stayed firmly at his side, not willing to offer friendship to any man whose purpose was not clear.

Alan withdrew his arm and looked towards Guy.

'Harold,' said Guy, quickly trying to retrieve the situation, 'I have just been telling Lord Richemont about your tale of woe. He is very interested and asked if you could back up your claims.'

'What claims?' asked Harold.

'Your claim to be the Earl of Wessex,' interrupted Alan. 'For all we know, you could be anyone just claiming the name to save your neck.'

'I could be,' said Harold, 'but unfortunately, I fail to see how that can be proven either way. Everything I brought with me that may have been able to prove my name went down with the ship.'

'Yes, I can see how that could be a problem,' said Alan.

'My men have told me,' interjected Guy, 'that they have often overheard his men referring to him as an earl, so I have no doubt that he is telling the truth.'

'A suspicious man may suggest that it would be in your interests to substantiate his claim,' said Alan.

'To what end?' asked Guy.

'To increase the price you demand for transferring custody to the duke.'

'I have not said I am willing to part with him yet,' said Guy. 'He is worth a hefty ransom, and it would be far more lucrative to sell him back to the English king.'

'He is going nowhere until the duke says so,' said Alan, 'but first we have to establish his identity. If you are so sure he is an earl, why do you keep him locked away with common men when he is of noble birth?'

'Because he refuses to leave them,' said Guy. 'I have made the offer several times, but he has refused on each occasion.' He turned to Harold. 'Is that not the truth?'

'My place is with my men,' said Harold, who had been following the conversation with mild amusement.

'So,' said Alan, 'what are we to do?'

'About what?' asked Harold.

'If you are who you say you are,' said Alan, 'I will arrange for you to be taken to my master in Normandy.'

'And my men?'

'Perhaps,' said Alan.

'Then there is a way to prove who I am,' said Harold.

'And that is?'

'Get me in front of Robert of Jumièges. He has met me on many occasions and will vouch for my identity.'

'This is possible,' said Alan.

'Wait a moment,' said Guy, 'we have not yet agreed on a price, or even if I am willing to let them go.'

'The decision to let them go is not yours,' said Alan, 'for if you say no, we will take them anyway, over the bodies of your men, if necessary. However, we are not brigands and are willing to pay a fair price. Tell me what you want for all of them together.'

'This is nothing less than robbery,' said Guy, knowing that whatever he got would be nowhere near the ransom he had demanded. 'And I demand an audience with the duke.'

'William is far too busy to meet with someone as trivial as you,' said Alan, 'now name your price.'

Guy was furious, but he knew he had no other option. He had already lost one battle against William years earlier and was now only allowed to run Ponthieu as his vassal.

'I have already demanded two thousand pounds of silver from the English king,' he said eventually, 'so will accept half of that.'

'That is not true,' said Harold, staring at Guy. 'You asked for one thousand pounds of silver, not two, so half of that would be five hundred. I was present in the room when you gave the messenger the instructions, remember?'

Guy could feel himself filling with rage. He was being backed into a corner but knew he had to be careful, Alan the Red was known as a man of temper.

'Of course,' he said with a smile, 'how forgetful of me. Five hundred pounds will be acceptable.'

'We will give you fifty pounds of silver and not a penny more,' said Alan.

'*What?*' gasped Guy. 'That is a stupid amount for so many men, especially when one of them is an earl.'

'We have not proved that yet,' said Alan, 'and you can keep his men.'

'No,' said Harold immediately. 'Either they come with me, or I am not going.'

'That is not your decision,' said Alan. 'We will have you bound and thrown into the cart like a trussed pig.'

'And what do you think the King of England will do when he finds out that his most trusted advisor has been treated as such? Be careful, Alan of Richemont. You are navigating dangerous waters here.'

Alan stared at Harold, knowing he was correct. The last thing they needed at the moment was any sort of conflict with England.

'I will tell you what I will do,' he said, turning back to face Guy. 'We will give you fifty pounds of silver for this man, but leave the others here. If he is proven to be who he says he is, I will send my men to gather the rest with another fifty pounds of silver. That is my final offer.'

Guy knew he had no other option but to accept.

'Agreed,' he said, 'but I want them gone within the month. Without this one, they are worth nothing more than slaves, and they cost me a fortune to feed. If you have not sent for them within the next twenty-one days, I will sell them off to the highest bidder.'

'So be it,' said Alan, and turned to one of his men guarding the doorway.

'Tell the men to make ready – we leave before dark.'

As the guard left the room, Alan turned to face Harold.

'You have a manner about you,' he said, 'that suggests nobility, so I will treat you as such until your station is proved otherwise. On the journey north, you will not be bound, but this is how it will work: if you run, I will kill you; if you cause any problems, I will kill you; and if you are not who you say you are, I will kill you. Understood?'

'That seems straightforward enough to me,' said Harold, 'but if I speak truly, then I will be reunited with my men?'

'I can only promise to bring them to Normandy. What William decides to do with them after that is up to him.'

'Understood,' said Harold.

'This man will need riding clothes and a cloak,' said Alan, turning to Guy, 'and let it be known that if anything happens to any of his men before the agreed date, then I will hold you personally responsible. Is that clear?'

'It is,' said Guy. 'Now, if you will excuse me, I have other business to attend to.' He left the room and headed into the upper floors of the manor house, where, just under an hour later, he watched as Harold of Wessex was escorted northward.

Chapter Twenty-two

Rouen, Normandy, July, AD 1065

Duke William sat at one end of a table in the dining room of one of his chateaus in Rouen. On the opposite end, partly obscured by the silver decorations and mountains of food laid out for the feast, sat Harold Godwinson, looking far cleaner and healthier than he had when he had arrived almost two weeks earlier.

Despite having been in Bayeux almost all that time, this was only the second time Harold had met with the duke and the first time they had actually shared a meal, as William had been delayed elsewhere. On each side of the table sat some of William's nobles, including Alan the Red, but there were several empty chairs, and Harold was hesitant to start eating, unsure of the protocol this side of the sea.

'Please,' said William, 'our guests have been delayed, so feel free to begin.'

All the men around the table leaned forward with their knives and helped themselves to the abundance of meat on offer. Harold did the same, for though he was being treated extremely well, he found himself constantly hungry after the deprivations he had endured in Ponthieu.

'So,' said William, after a few mouthfuls of food, 'how are you enjoying our hospitality, Harold Godwinson? Are we treating you well?'

'You are,' said Harold, 'but I have to admit that I was getting impatient for your return. There are many things to discuss, not least the fate of my men in Ponthieu.'

'I would have thought that the fate of Hakon and Wulfnorth would be to the forefront of your mind,' said William. 'Is that not the case?'

Harold paused with a slice of pork halfway to his mouth. It was the first time anyone had explicitly named the two boys who had been held hostage for so many years.

'They are always in my thoughts,' said Harold, 'and are the reason I sailed from England. Do you know where they are?'

'I do,' said William, sipping from a goblet of wine. 'In fact, they are not far from this very place.'

'Are they well?'

'They are,' said William, 'and it has to be said, they have adjusted to life this side of the sea very well.'

'Can I see them?'

'Not yet,' said William, 'though perhaps the next few weeks may pave the way for such a visit to occur.'

'What do you mean?'

William was about to reply when the door opened, and two men of the Church walked into the hall.

'Ah,' said William, getting to his feet, 'two of our guests have arrived. Harold Godwinson, this is Bishop Florentine, and of course, the archbishop you have already met.'

Harold stared at the second man, Robert of Jumièges, his stomach knotted with hate. An uncontrollable rage rose in his stomach, and he got to his feet, his hand reaching for his meat knife, but as he threw back his chair, two of William's guards stepped in front of him to block his way. Most of the other guests looked on in shock at the terrible assault upon the rules of hospitality, but Duke William looked amused, having anticipated the reaction.

'Oh come, Harold,' he said lightly, 'surely you would not want to shed blood at such an auspicious occasion, especially that of a man of the Church?'

'I would spill the blood of no such man,' growled Harold, 'but this one is a servant of the devil himself, interested only in clearing his own path to importance and filling his own coffers with the pennies of the poor. Many men now rot in their graves because of the decisions he made.'

'Perhaps so,' said William, 'but can it be said that many of us are also guilty of such things?' His voice lowered to a more serious tone. 'Including you?'

All eyes turned to Harold, and though he did not break the stare aimed at the archbishop, he discarded the knife and picked up the chair from the floor.

'Consider yourself lucky that I will not insult my host by doing what should be done,' he said towards the archbishop, 'but I advise you strongly that you keep your distance, lest the ale removes my self-control and you find my blade between your ribs.'

'I can assure you,' said the archbishop, 'that I hold you in similar esteem, yet my manners and upbringing ensure that I keep such thoughts to myself. Alas, it is such a shame that you were not also raised learning similar courtesies.' He turned to face William. 'My lord,' he said, 'thank you for your invitation and please forgive the lateness. I was praying at the deathbed of a very good man.'

'You are here now,' said William, 'so please, take your seats and feel free to help yourselves. We need suffer no more cere-mony than is needed.'

The two clergymen sat, and for ten minutes or so, the room filled with idle chatter. Harold's gaze seldom left the archbishop across the hall, who, in turn, did everything he could to pretend the earl did not exist until, eventually, William looked up and called out across the table.

'Earl Harold,' he said, 'please join me.' He indicated the nearest chair to him. 'We have much to discuss.'

Harold pushed away his platter and, picking up his goblet, walked over to sit near the duke.

'I think we were discussing a way in which you would get access to your brother and nephew, were we not?'

'Aye,' said Harold, 'we were.'

'I have been giving the matter some thought these past few days,' said William, 'and I have come to the conclusion that I need to get to know you better. To that end, I have a proposal.'

'Continue,' said Harold.

'There is a situation that I need to take care of in Brittany,' said William, 'something that will go a long way to securing Normandy's borders. I intend to ride there within a few days and provide aid to a man called Rhiwallon of Dor, a vassal who has rebelled against Duke Conan.'

'I take it the duke is your enemy?' asked Harold.

'He is certainly a threat to Normandy,' said William, 'and by supporting this uprising, I believe it will focus Conan's attention inward.'

'So, what do you want from me?'

'You will join me on the campaign,' said William. 'You will be given command of a group of my men who will be ordered to follow your orders to the letter.'

'You know it doesn't work like that,' said Harold. 'A leader needs trust and at least some officers who know how he thinks and the standards he expects. Perhaps if you were to return my men, then it would be something I might consider.'

'I thought you might say that,' said William, and nodded to one of the servants at the far end of the hall. The servant turned and opened the doors, and Harold's men filed into the room, looking nervously around at those who witnessed their arrival with undisguised amusement.

As the servants showed them to the empty seats around the table, each one looked up and acknowledged Harold, some with a wave of the hand, others with no more than a slight nod of the head.

'What are you waiting for?' roared William with great delight. 'Fill your bellies, Englishmen, you are amongst friends.'

All the ex-prisoners stared at the piles of food in front of them, wondering if it was a trick. They had bathed and wore clean clothes, but their hair and beards were still uncut and made them stand out against the finery of the other guests.

Seeing their reluctance, Alan the Red stood up and walked around the table, picking on small pieces of food from in front of the men to prove that nothing was poisoned. Realising it was safe and losing all sense of self-control, the starving men launched themselves at the feast, thanking God for their delivery from captivity.

As they ate, Alan the Red walked over to join William and Harold.

'They are very suspicious, your men,' he said.

'Can you blame them?' asked Harold. 'They have gone from starvation in a freezing dungeon to a feast at a duke's chateau in less than a few days. It is a lot to take in.'

'They are here now,' said William, 'and as long as you agree to join us on this small quest, then they will be treated as well as any of my men. On that, you have my word.'

'And if I say no?' asked Harold.

'You are not going to say no,' said William. 'You are far too clever a man to even contemplate such an action.'

Harold stared at William, knowing he was right. Despite being framed as an invitation, he knew it was no such thing. It was a thinly veiled ultimatum.

—

Later that night, Harold walked across to the barracks above the stable where his men had been quartered. Inside he was surprised to find actual bunks with mattresses and blankets, far from the straw pallets his men were used to back in England. Most of his comrades were fast asleep, their gentle snoring stating the level of contentment each sleeper now enjoyed. One man was still awake, and Harold walked over to where he was sitting at a table, looking out over the dark fields outside the chateau.

'Can you not sleep?' asked Harold, placing a flask of ale on the table.

'I will,' said Owen, 'it's just a bit much to take in at the moment.'

'These are strange days,' said Harold, producing a leather jack from beneath his jerkin and filling it up before handing it to Owen.

'So, who is this man we are going to fight?' asked Owen, taking the jack.

'I have no idea,' said Harold. 'All I know is William sees him as a risk and wants his wings clipped.'

'And you are happy about this?'

'We don't have a choice,' said Harold. 'It may seem like we are his guests, but we are no more than well-fed prisoners until such time as he says otherwise, and besides, he has hinted that if we do this, he may give me access to the boys.'

'Do you believe him?'

'Again, how can I not? The dice are loaded in his favour, my friend, and all we can do is see which way they fall.' He looked around the room at the sleeping men. 'How are they?'

'Nothing a few hot meals and a good night's sleep won't sort out,' said Owen. 'We had almost given up on you back there. What took you so long?'

'William was elsewhere,' said Harold, 'and there was nothing I could do but wait.'

Owen sighed. 'Well, we are here now, so all we can do is see what God has laid out before us.'

'Aye,' said Harold, 'but we could also finish this flask of ale together.'

'That sounds like a plan,' said Owen, standing up. 'I'll see if I can find another jack.'

-

For the next ten days, Harold and his men integrated with a troop of French cavalry, learning new tactics and formations until they became second nature. Each of Harold's men were given ten men each, with Owen being given the position of Harold's second-in-command.

During these sessions, William and his officers often came to the training fields to watch with interest as Harold drilled his new unit. His ways were certainly different, and for a while, the Norman cavalry struggled to adapt, but as the days wore on, they slowly formed into a well-drilled and cohesive unit.

Towards the end of the training, Alan the Red walked over to join William as the lancers were once again put through their paces.

'I see no point in this,' he said. 'Harold is undoing everything our men have learned, and they suffer for the experience. Our own cavalry are far superior, and if it comes to a charge, they will put these to shame. It is a waste of time.'

'On the contrary,' said William, 'I think it is one of the most important lessons we can learn, especially for our officers who come here to watch.'

'Do not tell me that you think these are superior tactics, my lord,' said Alan, 'for even a child could see the difference.'

'I did not say the tactics were superior,' said William, 'only that there are valuable lessons to be learned.'

'What do you mean?'

'Alan,' said William, 'as you know, King Edward has already promised me the throne of England after he dies, an offer I am more than willing to accept, but the English ways are far different to ours and the more we learn from them, the better.'

'With respect, my lord,' said Alan, 'you only have that offer from the mouth of Robert of Jumièges. I know he is a close friend of yours, but I would be careful of such proclamations, for the man is only interested in his own self-enrichment.'

'No,' said William, watching as the horsemen galloped past his position yet again, 'he is adamant that the offer is real and that I am considered the next heir to England's throne.'

'If this were so,' said Alan, 'why have you not had any correspondence stating such an important thing? Do you not think that their Witan would have been in touch to recognise you formally as heir?'

'I do not know how their politics work,' said William, 'but Robert of Jumièges swears before God that this discussion took place and whether the nobles of England agree with it or not, the promises of a king are as good as any written word.'

'Even if this is true,' said Alan eventually, 'and I still have my doubts, what can you possibly hope to learn about leading the English just by watching how Harold trains a hundred of our men?'

'Oh, I am well aware that we will not learn much from Harold,' said William, turning to face Alan, 'but look with fresh eyes, my friend. We are not learning their tactics to learn how to lead them, but how to fight them.'

Chapter Twenty-three

Rouen, Normandy, August, AD 1065

Harold sat upon his horse alongside Owen of Hereford. Behind them were the rest of their comrades as well as the hundred Norman lancers. It had been almost a month since they had all arrived in Rouen, and now, after rebuilding their strength and training hard, William had finally announced that they were moving against Conan of Brittany.

As they waited, Harold and Owen talked quietly between themselves.

'So,' said Owen eventually, 'this is it. I hope we haven't come all this way and suffered so many trials to die in a battle that has nothing to do with us.'

'Only time will tell,' said Harold, 'but I have noticed that William has not mustered any of his foot-soldiers. That means that there is not going to be any sort of pitched battle, which can only be a good thing.'

'A cavalry battle can be no less bloody,' said Owen, 'and I am willing to wager that it will be us in the vanguard.'

'Probably,' said Harold, 'but we have prepared as well as we can, so must pray God will guide us through.'

A few minutes later, Alan the Red appeared from further down the road, leading a column of almost five hundred knights, each heavily armoured and heavily armed.

Harold glanced across at his own unit. Although they also wore helmets and chainmail, it was obvious that they were of far lower standing than the men now riding towards them with banners flying.

'Impressive,' said Owen, looking at the heavy knights. 'I suspect they are men of the noble houses. I wonder why we were not given these to command?'

Harold threw him a sardonic look, recognising the sarcasm in Owen's voice.

'They would never have accepted it,' said Harold, 'and anyway, I am happy with those we have. We may not have the banners and the heavier shields, but that will only make us faster and more mobile.'

The column of riders came to a halt in the courtyard and waited for William of Normandy to appear.

'So,' said Alan the Red, 'are you ready for this, Harold of Wessex?'

'Worry not about us,' said Harold, 'we can take care of ourselves.'

'I am more worried about you taking care of those lancers,' said Alan. 'It angers me that the lives of my countrymen lie in your hands.'

'And yet,' said Harold, 'within a few days, I could be killing other men from these lands with your blessing. Make your mind up, Alan the Red, for you seem to be confused in your reasoning.'

Alan stared at Harold, annoyed that he had allowed himself to be bettered in an argument, but before he could respond, William and a dozen of his officers rode from around the back of the chateau and approached their small group.

'Are we all ready?' he asked.

'Aye, my lord,' said Alan.

William turned to Harold.

'And what of you, Harold of Wessex – do you think you will make a difference?'

'We will not let you down,' said Harold.

'Good,' said William, 'in that case, you and your men will lead the column. Take us to Brittany.'

'With the greatest of respect, Duke William, I do not know Normandy well and will need direction.'

'Just head south-west,' said Alan, 'and we will correct you as you go. Do you think you can manage that, Englishman?'

Harold did not respond and just kept looking at the duke.

'Our destination is about seven days' ride from here,' said William, 'assuming we cover ten leagues a day. Have you heard of the Abbey of Mont Saint-Michel in the estuary of the River Couesnon?'

'I have,' said Harold, 'my father took me there when I was a boy.'

'Good,' said William. 'The river itself is the cause of an argument I have with Duke Conan, for he claims it as part of Brittany, while I know it belongs to Normandy. One day there will have to be a settlement of this argument, but for now, it is agreed that it forms the boundary between Conan's lands and my own.'

'What about the abbey itself?'

'It was my grandfather who was responsible for building much of what stands today, so my claim is beyond reproach, but Conan sees it differently, so again, there will have to be a reckoning, but that is for another day. For now, we will set up a camp this side of the estuary where we will make our plans. While we are there, my scouts will venture across the border to find Conan, and once we know where he is, I will decide how we are to proceed.'

'As you wish,' said Harold and turned his horse to face his men.

'You heard the duke,' he said. 'Let's go to Brittany.'

-

Over the next week, Harold led the column south-west without incident and on the last day, they crested a hill to see the impressive, fortified Abbey of Mont Saint-Michel rising proudly from an island at the mouth of the River Couesnon.

The island lay several hundred paces out into the estuary and for much of the time was inaccessible to anyone on foot or horseback. But, for a few hours each day, the low tide revealed a relatively safe causeway over to the abbey, allowing the arrival of all sorts of visitors, including pilgrims and supplies of food for the occupying monks. Anyone deviating from the causeway risked being trapped in the treacherous sands and then swallowed up by the tide as it turned.

Any attacks from the sea could be easily repelled as there were no places to land, while anyone attacking on foot via the causeway only had to be held at bay for a few hours before the rising tide forced them to retreat. It was a magnificent monument, and Harold could well understand why it was coveted by both William and Conan.

'It never fails to take my breath away,' said William, riding up to join Harold as he stared out over the estuary.

'It is truly an amazing place,' said Harold. 'I remember, as if it were yesterday, the day my father took us there. I would love to pray again in the monastery.' He looked over at the duke. 'Do we have enough time?'

'Perhaps on the return journey,' said William. 'Let us first deal with Conan before we allow ourselves such distractions.'

'As you wish,' said Harold, and turned away to join the rest of his men seeking a suitable place to set up the tents.

Chapter Twenty-four

Normandy, August, AD 1065

Several days later, William summoned Harold to his campaign tent, where Alan and several of the other officers were already present.

'Earl Harold,' said the duke as Harold entered, 'we have news. Two of my scouts returned this morning and reported that a number of Conan's men are laying siege to a chateau a few leagues south from here. This is the opportunity we have been waiting for. Muster your men; we head out at noon.'

'Why the rush?' asked Harold. 'Would it not be better to have a fresh start at dawn on the morrow?'

'We need to take advantage of the tide,' said William. 'The nearest ford is several leagues upstream, but down here, when the river is at its lowest, it is crossable and will save us two days' travelling time. Meet us on the banks at the river.'

'So be it,' said Harold, and left the campaign tent.

A few hours later, he and the rest of the column waited on the riverbank as the water receded. With them was one of the fishermen from the village who knew the river and estuary well.

'I think that is as low as it is going to get,' said the man. 'It will be as deep as your waist in the centre, and the current will be strong, but it is crossable.' He pointed towards a boulder sticking up out of the water. The best route is just upstream of that rock, so make it your target. If you should fall, I fear you will be swept out into the estuary, and the ground is far too treacherous to attempt any rescue.'

'Understood,' said William, and turned to Harold. 'You command the vanguard, Earl Harold; show the rest of us how it should be done.'

Harold paused but knew he had no choice in the matter. If anyone was to be swept away, then William was making sure it would be one of the Englishmen, not one of his own. He turned away and rode his horse down to the edge of the estuary.

'My lord,' said the fisherman, walking beside him, 'I suggest you lead your mount rather than ride. The sand is not so treacherous this far up, but the combined weight of you and your horse will make it heavy going. Also, I suggest you move as quickly as you can, for there was heavy rain last night, and that often affects the flow when the water from the mountains reaches the river upstream.'

'My lord,' said Owen at his side, 'let me go first.'

'No,' said Harold, dismounting, 'William is testing me with this, and I will not give him the pleasure of seeing me stand back. If anything happens to me, just make sure that you do everything in your power to get the men back to England.' Without waiting for a reply, he stepped out into the river.

Unlike the estuary itself, the riverbed was quite firm, consisting of sand and gravel, and though there was some give, it was firm enough to provide a solid footing to both him and his horse.

Without pausing or looking back, he continued out into midstream, heading for the boulder. Within moments the water deepened, surprising him with the strength of the flow. Slowly and carefully, he led his horse onward before pausing briefly at the boulder to catch his breath. Moments later, he pushed onward, always fighting the current to stay on his feet, but at last, he felt himself rising out of the water, and he continued up onto the far riverbank before turning to face the column back on the other side.

'The flow is quite strong,' he called as his horse shook the water from its back, 'but once you reach the rock, it gets easier. Use your horses for stability.'

'You heard the man,' called Owen, turning to face his men. 'What are you waiting for?'

Owen led his horse forward into the river, followed by the rest of Harold's command. The going was slow, and by the time most of his men had crossed, the tide had already started to come back in, causing the water levels to rise.

'Quicker,' shouted Harold, but as he watched, the current knocked one of the soldiers off his feet, plunging him beneath the water before he emerged coughing and spluttering next to the rock.

One of his comrades tried to help him, but he, too, was overwhelmed in the current, and within moments, the two men were pinned against the rock, afraid to move in case they were washed away.

'Someone help them,' roared Harold, but it soon became clear that the incoming tide combined with the strong river current was causing everyone terrible problems. Another man lost his footing, and Harold watched in horror as both the soldier and his horse were washed further downstream into the estuary.

'Everyone back,' shouted Alan the Red, still on the other side with the rest of the column. 'This is not going to work.'

'What about those two?' shouted Owen from the other side, pointing at the two men clinging onto the rock. 'You can't just leave them there.'

'We will risk no more men,' shouted Alan, 'it is too treacherous.' He turned his attention to the two stranded men. 'Try to swim for it,' he shouted. 'We will wait downstream and try to fish you out.'

'*No*,' roared Harold, 'you will never get anywhere near them.' Without waiting for a reply, he removed his jerkin before striding down to the water's edge.

'My lord,' said Owen, 'do not be a fool. The current will wash you away.'

'I will not leave them there to die,' said Harold. 'They may be Normans, but while they are under my command, they are my responsibility.'

He waded out into the water, immediately realising that the current was far stronger than when he had crossed. Despite this, he ploughed on, fighting against the flow with every step.

'What does he think he is doing?' asked William, walking over to join Alan the Red on the far side of the river.

'He is signing his own death sentence,' said Alan. 'The man is an idiot.'

Everyone watched the drama unfold, and they were shocked when Harold finally reached the terrified men.

'Hold on,' he shouted at the two Normans, 'we are going to get you out of here.' He looked over at William and Alan on the far shore.

'Rope,' he roared, 'someone find us a rope.'

Alan the Red looked around his men, but their blank faces told him that there was none to be had.

'I have some in the village,' said the fisherman, 'but by the time I get back, that rock will be under water.'

Alan turned back to face Harold.

'There is not enough time,' he said, 'you have to try something now.'

Harold cursed and turned to the two terrified men.

'Can you swim?' he asked.

Both men shook their heads, their eyes wide with fear.

With the water now up to his shoulders, Harold knew they could wait no longer and turned to face the shore, where his own men were watching in horror.

'Put your hands around my neck,' he shouted over his shoulder, 'and hold on.'

The two Normans stared in disbelief, knowing there was no way Harold could drag them back to shore.

'Do it,' roared Harold, 'or we will all die right here. Do what you can to keep us steady.'

The two men did as they were ordered, and to the astonishment of everyone watching, Harold stepped away from the temporary safety of the rock back into the murderous current, dragging the two men behind him. Immediately, all three disappeared as a wave swept over their heads but emerged a few heartbeats later, fighting with all their strength to maintain their footing. Step by step, Harold made his way towards the shore, battling the current with everything he had, knowing that one misstep would send them out into the estuary and a watery grave.

Up on the shore, Owen and several of the men raced into the river and linked arms to form a human chain, desperate to help their comrades. At the end, Owen was already up to his chest, and he held out his hand to try and reach the earl.

'A few more steps,' he shouted as Harold once again emerged from beneath the water, 'come on.'

Harold grimaced in pain. The water beat against him like a hammer, and the grips of the two men were vicelike against his flesh. Water crashed over them time and again, as if desperate to drag them down, but still he kept going, gasping for breath each time he emerged from yet another soaking.

'*Come on*,' shouted Owen stretching as far as he could, 'one more step.' Harold looked up at the man who had become his close friend, but he knew that he was done. His strength was gone, and he felt himself lose his balance.

'No!' roared Owen, seeing what was happening, and just before the earl and the two men were washed away, he lunged forward, grabbing Harold's outstretched arm in his hand.

'Pull!' he bellowed, and as one, the human chain dragged Harold and the two men from the current and into the shallow water. All three knelt on the gravel, coughing and spluttering as they gasped for breath.

'Thank you,' said Harold eventually, looking up at Owen standing above him, 'you could have been swept away and drowned.'

'I realise that now,' said Owen. 'Perhaps it was not one of my better ideas.'

'I know a couple of folks who would disagree with you,' said Harold, and nodded towards the two rescued men now being helped to their feet.

As if in response, both Normans looked over and stared at Harold, not knowing what to say, such was their obvious gratitude. Finally, the first man formed a fist and, nodding towards Harold, thumped it on his chest right above his heart. The second man did the same before both were led away by their comrades.

'I can't be sure,' said Owen, 'but I think that meant thank you.'

'Aye,' laughed Harold, 'I think it did. Help me up.' He held up his hand, and Owen pulled him to his feet.

'*Harold*,' called a voice, and the earl turned to see William standing on the opposite bank. 'That was a very stupid thing to do, my friend,' continued William, 'stupid, but brave. You have my gratitude and my admiration.'

'I would have done the same for any man,' said Harold.

'Even me?'

'Especially you,' said Harold, 'for without you, I will never see my brother and nephew again.'

'Understood,' said William, and looked towards the river. The rock was already underwater, the flow strengthened by the rain from further inland. 'The crossing is too dangerous,' he continued, 'so we will use the ford upstream. Make a camp in the woods behind you, and we will be with you in two days.'

'As you wish,' said Harold, and watched as William turned away to organise the rest of the column.

'This could be an opportunity too good to miss,' said Owen.

'In what way?' asked Harold.

'All our own men are on this side of the river,' said Owen. 'We are strong and have horses. All we need to do is ride as far away from here as we can and find a boat. If God is with us, we can be home in days.'

203

'That is not going to happen,' said Harold.

'My lord,' said Owen, 'with the greatest of respect, I doubt that William has any intention of returning the boys to you, not even after this display of bravery. They are just too important as bargaining pieces.'

'You may be right,' said Harold, 'but there is another reason I will not run.'

'And that is?'

'I gave my word,' said Harold, 'and to break that would make me no better than Robert of Jumièges. Now let's find a place to set a camp, Owen, I need to sit next to a fire for the next few days.'

'As you wish, my lord,' said Owen, and together with their men, they headed for the forest to wait for the arrival of William of Normandy.

Chapter Twenty-five

Scotland, August, AD 1065

In Scotland, Tostig was once more hunting with his friend, King Malcolm. The pressure back in Northumbria was growing on an almost daily basis, and when he had received the invitation from Malcolm, he had seized it with both hands. Now, they were both standing high on a hill as they watched their falcons swooping majestically down to catch the prey flushed from the undergrowth by the dogs and beaters. Despite the relaxing nature of the activity, it hadn't been long before the conversation had turned to politics.

'So,' said Malcolm, as the falconer launched another bird into the air, 'what are your main concerns?'

'There are many,' said Tostig. 'The campaign in Wales took longer than expected, and though Edward financed the whole thing, it still fell short of the cost.'

'Did you not get any bounty from Gruffydd's lands?'

'Some,' said Tostig, 'but it was not that sort of battle. His men took it upon themselves to behead him rather than be defeated in open battle. That way, they kept hold of whatever riches remained.'

'So your coffers are empty?'

'Almost.'

'Then raise the taxes on the people of Northumbria.'

'I already have on several occasions,' said Tostig, 'and fear that to do so again invites even more rebellion. There are rumours that the thegns already plot against me.'

'Tostig,' said Malcolm, 'before I defeated Macbeth, I lived as a guest of Earl Siward in Northumbria for a long time. We became good friends and discussed many things, much the same as we are doing now. During that time, I found out that the level of taxation in Northumbria was far less than that in the rest of England.'

'This is true,' said Tostig, 'for the north of England is a far poorer place than the south.'

'I have never understood that argument,' said Malcolm. 'If you are talking about nobles, then perhaps so, but even then, the source of the wealth of such men always begins with the peasants. After all, a man is a man, and a cow is a cow no matter which part of the country you live in.'

'I do not follow,' said Tostig, looking at the king.

'Think on this,' said Malcolm. 'If over the course of a year, one man can raise one cow in the south, then the same must be true for a man in the north. If that is the case, why does the northern man pay less in taxes to his lord? Surely they should all pay the same?'

'Many believe that the southern taxes are too high and should be lowered,' said Tostig.

'Or,' said Malcolm, 'could it be that the taxes in the north are too low and should be raised?'

'I take your point,' said Tostig, 'but as I said, I am already under great pressure from the thegns of Northumbria and fear that any rise in taxes will tip them into open rebellion.'

'And what if it does?' said Malcolm. 'You have an army, do you not? And besides, apart from Mercia, your family controls every dukedom in England and could raise an army ten times that of any rebellious thegns. It is about time that you stamped your authority on Northumbria and showed them who is in charge. Raise the taxes, call their bluff, and if anyone tries to challenge your position, cut them down without mercy. That is the only way to deal with situations such as these.'

Tostig nodded quietly. Malcolm made a good point, and though he knew that he risked the ire of the people of Northumbria, he also knew that he couldn't go on as he was.

'You are right,' he said eventually, looking up at the soaring bird of prey. 'It is about time I showed everyone across England exactly who I am.'

–

Across the border, the thegns of Northumbria were also making their plans. Support for a campaign against Tostig was growing, but for many men, there was still nervousness about how well they would fare against the earl's forces, especially as they knew that Tostig could call on the support of all his brothers. Once again, the ringleaders met in a wayside tavern far away from any of the Northumbrian towns. The mood was one of frustration, and after several hours they were still at a loss as to how to proceed.

'It's no use,' said Dunstan eventually, 'no matter how many men we can recruit to the cause, we will always be seen as an uprising of commoners rebelling against the Crown, and once that thought is in the king's mind, he will crush us like ants. And with most of England under the control of the Godwin family, Tostig can call on as many men as he needs, no matter how just our argument.'

'Most,' said Gamelbearn quietly.

Dunstan turned to face his fellow thegn. 'What do you mean?'

'You said *most* of England is under the control of the Godwins, and you are correct, for Mercia still stands outside of their reach. It is second in strength only to Wessex, and there has never been any love lost between those two earldoms. Perhaps we can ask them to support our cause.'

'Earl Edwin would never risk Mercia by standing against Tostig,' said Dunstan. 'Harold has the ear of the king and, should it come to conflict, Edwin could have the title stripped from him, or worse.'

'What about his brother?' asked Gamelbearn. 'Morcar is a strong man, but since Aelfgar died, he has had to be content serving under Edwin. If we could get him to support our cause, not only would it give us a respected figurehead, but it is also highly unlikely that Mercia would ally with Harold should it come to a fight.'

'Again,' said Dunstan, 'why would someone like Morcar risk his life and station to support a fight not of his interest. We have nothing to offer.'

'Oh yes we do,' said Gamelbearn, the light of excitement rekindling in his eyes, 'we have something he would kill for.'

'And that is?'

'An earldom,' said Gamelbearn. 'If we can get Morcar to support our cause, he could become the next earl of Northumbria, and that, my friend, is an outcome he could not possibly resist.'

On the other side of the channel in Brittany, Harold and his men were once more reunited with the main column and riding hard inland.

'There they are,' said Alan the Red, several hours later, 'it looks like we may be in time.'

Down in the valley, the fortified chateau was surrounded by the trappings of war, including an encamped army, mobile palisades to protect archers and the usual camp followers that made their living by servicing the needs of the men on such campaigns. The chateau itself was heavily damaged, and one of the turrets had already lost its roof due to fire, but the many men facing the building indicated it was still holding out.

'How many men do you count?' asked William.

'Two hundred,' said Alan, 'three at the most, and most of them are foot-soldiers. I don't see much cavalry.'

'Me neither,' said William, 'but it does not mean they are not there.' He turned to Harold. 'Tell your men to don their chainmail,' he said, 'and prepare for an assault on the camp. I will send out scouts to make sure there are no hidden surprises in that forest, and if it is clear, you will lead the attack. The rest of us will cut off their escape routes.'

'Understood,' said Harold, and he turned away to brief his men.

–

Two hours later, Harold's cavalry lay hidden on the reverse side of a hill. Up on the crest, Harold and Owen hid amongst the undergrowth, waiting for William's signal. Since arriving, they had witnessed another assault on the chateau. While it lacked numbers, it still had an impact; several fire arrows had taken hold in the second tower. Smoke billowed upwards, and as some of the defenders ran along the parapets with buckets of water, the besiegers took the opportunity to attack the main doors across the temporary bridge they had already constructed across the chateau's moat.

Dozens of men pushed a cart-mounted ram as fast as they could towards the door, while others kept the defenders' heads down with volley after volley of arrows. Few men fell in the exchange, but it was evident that it was only a matter of time before the door would give way, allowing the foot-soldiers to pour through.

'If I was that castellan,' said Owen, 'I would offer terms. There is no way they can hold out much longer.'

'William tells me that Conan hates Rhiwallon with a vengeance,' said Harold. 'Even if they agreed terms, he would probably have the castellan's head on a spike before dark.'

'Then I guess he will be happy to see us,' said Owen.

'I'm sure he will,' said Harold.

'My lord,' said a voice behind him, 'we have had a message that William is in position. You are to charge down the hill.'

'When?' asked Harold.

'As soon as you are ready.'

'So be it,' said Harold and turned to face Owen. 'Tell the men to mount up. We wait no longer.'

—

Ten minutes later, Harold led his men over the hill, an eighty-man, wedge-shaped attack formation, backed up with another twenty riders in reserve, each tasked with picking off anyone lucky enough to survive the charge.

'Lancers ready,' shouted Harold, and every man couched his lance beneath his arm before bringing it parallel to the ground. Up in front, several of the besiegers had seen the threat and raised the alarm, and within moments, the shouts of men mingled with the echoing blasts of horns as they realised what was about to happen.

'Lancers,' roared Harold, 'for England and for Normandy, *chaaarge!*'

Every rider dug in their heels, sending their horses galloping towards the enemy camp.

—

The attackers up at the chateau heard the alarm and looked around in confusion. For a few moments, they could not work out what was going on, but as soon as Harold's cavalry thundered into view, their hearts raced with fear. If the camp fell, there would be no reinforcements to support their attack on the chateau.

'Fall back,' shouted the commander, 'get back to the camp.'

'My lord,' called back one of the sergeants, 'the gates are collapsing. A few more moments, and we will be through.'

'I said *withdraw*,' roared the commander, 'or they will roll us up from the rear.'

With their archers covering their retreat, Conan's men turned and raced back to aid their comrades.

—

Back in the camp, men raced from their tents to gather what weapons they could, but it was too little, too late, and before anyone could organise a defensive line, Harold's lancers smashed into them, finishing off many before they had a chance to raise a weapon in anger. Many of those who escaped the attentions of the first charge were cut down with the swords and maces of those following behind, but the job was not yet done.

Harold and his men continued through the camp, despatching anyone in their way and, when they emerged at the other side, wheeled their horses around for another sweep. Again they galloped into the enemy camp, and though there was still little in the way of organisation, the element of surprise was lost, and many men were waiting for them.

This time, the fighting did not go all Harold's way, and some of the horses were cut from beneath his men, sending them sprawling to the ground. Hand to hand battles spread out, and for a few moments, it looked like the men of Brittany might prevail, especially when those who had been attacking the chateau only a few moments earlier joined the fight, but just as Harold thought he would have to withdraw, Alan the Red and two hundred more cavalry rode to his aid, turning the tide of the battle.

With the fighting spread out and difficult to oversee, Harold and the Normans reorganised on the far side of the camp, joined by Alan the Red and his men. They quickly took stock and removed those who were injured before turning back for another attack.

'This time, we will go only halfway,' shouted Alan. 'There we will dismount and fight them hand to hand, step by step. Understood?'

'Aye,' shouted his men, but before he could give the order to advance, Owen of Hereford called out.

'My lords, look. They are escaping.'

Everyone stared to where dozens of riders were galloping away from the camp as fast as they could. Those without horses made for the relative safety of the nearby forest, and it was obvious that Conan's men had had enough.

'My men will go after them,' shouted Alan the Red. 'Harold, you go after the foot-soldiers.' He dug in his heels, and the Norman knights galloped after the fleeing horsemen.

Harold turned to his own command.

'Owen, take half of the men and head for the chateau – there are still some over there. The rest of us will get after the foot-soldiers.'

Owen turned his horse in the other direction and headed towards the chateau, but if he was expecting any resistance, that thought was soon driven from his mind when the gates burst open and Rhiwallon of Dol led his men out to attack what was left of the besiegers.

Trapped between the two armed forces, Conan's men stood no chance, and within a few minutes, more than fifty men, who only an hour earlier had envisaged a great victory, now knelt in a straight line with their hands behind their heads.

Rhiwallon of Dol walked over and looked up at the riders who had come to their aid.

'Who is in charge?' he asked.

'That is me,' said Owen, walking his horse over towards the castellan. His French was not as good as Harold's, but he knew enough to make himself understood. 'My name is Owen of Hereford, and I am here under my master, Harold of Wessex.'

Rhiwallon looked around, confused. Almost half of the riders were Norman, but this man was obviously English.

'An Englishman leading a Norman army,' he said cautiously, 'how can this be?'

'We both serve William of Normandy,' said Owen.

'Forgive me,' said Rhiwallon, the doubt registering on his face, 'but why would an English earl ally with the Duke of Normandy when it is common knowledge that William covets the English throne? It makes no sense.'

Owen struggled to find the right words to convey what had happened when one of the Norman riders urged his horse forward to stand beside him. Owen looked across and recognised one of the men Harold had pulled from the river.

'I am Phillipe of Normandy,' said the rider, 'knighted by William's own hand. William called upon these men to help send Conan back under whatever stone he crawled from beneath. That has yet to be done, but make no mistake, these Englishmen have played a great part in lifting this siege. The duke will expect you to treat them as his own and pay unto them the respect that they deserve. I vouch for this man and all his comrades.'

'Of course,' said Rhiwallon, 'but you can understand my confusion. I meant no insult.'

'None taken,' said Owen. 'What do you want us to do with these?' He nodded towards the prisoners.

'Leave them here,' said Rhiwallon. 'We will deal with them. Perhaps you would like to come inside and celebrate the victory? We do not have much, but what is left is yours to enjoy.'

Phillipe of Normandy was about to accept the invitation when Owen cut across him.

'No,' he said. 'You have our gratitude, but there is still work to be done. Before we go, is there anything you can tell us about the whereabouts of Duke Conan?'

'Only that he has a main camp a few leagues away to the west. If you are lucky, word of this battle may not have reached him yet, and you may catch him cold.'

'That is exactly what I was hoping to hear,' said Owen, and turned to his men. 'Water the horses; we ride after Harold as soon as they are ready.' He turned back to face Phillipe. 'I appreciate your support,' he said, 'thank you.'

'I am just grateful I am here to offer it,' said Phillipe. 'You and your men are good people. I hope you will be able to return to England soon.'

'Aye,' said Owen, 'so do I, but until that opportunity arises, there is work to be done. Gather your men, Phillipe of Normandy, let's see if we can catch us a duke.'

Chapter Twenty-six

Brittany, August, AD 1065

Over the next few days, William of Normandy fought Conan's men across the northern reaches of Brittany, from Dol-de-Bretagne to Rennes, and finally back again to the town of Dinan, just south of the coastal port of St Malo.

During the whole campaign, Conan himself was rarely seen, always seemingly one step ahead of them, but at last, they had finally managed to corner him at the Chateau de Dinan.

The Normans immediately surrounded the fortified chateau to make sure nobody escaped and set up a camp in full view of the walls, but well out of range of any arrow shot from bow or crossbow. Everyone took the opportunity to rest and to prepare their weapons, though always with a close watch kept on the chateau, until finally, William called his officers to his tent.

'Men of Normandy,' he said, 'it has been a well-fought campaign, and for that, you have my gratitude. From the outset, my aim was to support those who rise up against Duke Conan, causing instability in his duchy and drawing his covetous eyes away from our borders. All this has been achieved, but we also find ourselves in a position where we have the man himself cornered, an outcome that far exceeds my expectations. What we need to discuss now is what we do about it. Do we attack the chateau and risk losing even more men? Do we place it under siege and risk being attacked by one of his armies? Or do we head back home to Normandy knowing that we have done all that we can?' He looked around the room before settling his gaze upon Harold.

'What say you, my friend? What would you do in my position?'

Harold paused and looked around his fellow officers. All were exhausted, and they had suffered many losses, with only two-thirds of his original column still alive. He also knew that too many of the enemy had escaped and had no doubt managed to raise the alarm. It would only be a matter of time before the nobles of Brittany would muster their men and launch a counter-attack.

'My lord,' said Harold, 'it has been an honour and a privilege to serve under your command and to lead the men that you placed with me. If this were a war of occupation and we were supported by a greater army, I would say to continue and finish what we started. However, I know this not to be the case, and whether we kill this man or not, we will soon be returning to Normandy.' He turned and faced William. 'Too many men have already died, my lord, and I am concerned that as yet, we have only faced a relatively small force. There can be no doubt that even as we speak, those that have escaped so far have spread the word and I suspect he has reinforcements mustering. I fear no man, but the longer we stay in the lands of your enemy, the more likely it is that we will soon face a far superior force. It is for that reason that I would advise we turn away. You have achieved far more than you had hoped; it is time to go home.'

William nodded and turned to Alan the Red.

'My friend,' he said, 'I can always rely on you to provide blunt but honest counsel. What say you?'

'I disagree with Earl Harold,' said Alan. 'Over the past few months, he has gained the respect of all of us, but in this decision, he is wrong. The deaths of our men are exactly the reason we should continue, for if we were to turn away now, just as we have the prey cornered, then our comrades will surely have died in vain. My counsel is that we attack the chateau while we still have time. Attack it, hang the duke, and burn the place to the ground.'

'My lord,' said another officer, 'there is a third way. When we surrounded the chateau, we caught several people out in the fields. They were responsible for keeping the chateau's kitchens well stocked and have told us that our arrival caught everyone by surprise – they have very little food within those walls. If we lay siege to the chateau, we can starve them out very quickly.'

'I do not believe we have the time for such an action,' said Alan. 'I suspect his nobles are mustering their men right now.'

'Perhaps so,' said the officer, 'but if we post sentries out on all the roads, we can get plenty of warning about any approach. My counsel is to besiege the chateau and let them think that there is no escape.'

'We are only a few hundred men,' said Alan, 'and will not be able to sustain such a siege for long.'

'They do not know that,' said Harold. 'For all they know we are the vanguard of a much larger army. If we are not yet to return, then at least let us try to get them to surrender.'

'You have all spoken well,' said William eventually, 'and there is merit in all your counsel. My mind is now clear, and I have a way forward. Gather closer, my friends, for this is what we will do.'

–

The following morning, every man in William's column assembled in front of the chateau. Despite the dwindling number, it was still an impressive sight, but the defenders in the chateau were more focused on the archers standing to the fore with fire pots at their feet than the ranks of cavalry behind them. William rode forward to stand before the army and called out to the defenders at the windows.

'Conan of Brittany,' he shouted, 'show yourself.'

For a while, nothing happened, but eventually, a man appeared at one of the windows, knowing he was out of range of any arrows.

'I am here, William of Normandy,' he said. 'What do you want?'

'What I do *not* want,' said William, 'is to have to burn this place to the ground and slaughter every man, woman and child within it. However, for that not to happen, I need you to surrender. I give you my word that you will not be harmed, and your people will be freed. Do this, and I also swear that I will return to Normandy within days.'

'And what of me?' asked Conan.

'We will discuss terms of a treaty between us, and if acceptable to all parties, I will release you to live much as you do now.'

'I do not believe you,' said Conan. 'And warn you that if you do not leave immediately, my army will cut you down without mercy. Even as we speak, ten thousand and more are on their way to release me.'

'I have no time for such claims,' said William, 'for you know as well as I that it takes far longer to muster such a force. I also know that you have few supplies and will suffer hunger and thirst within days. Thirst is a terrible way to die, so perhaps my sword through your heart will be seen as a blessing.' He looked up at the manor. 'I have seen many fine stone buildings during my time here,' he continued. 'It is a shame that this one is made of mostly timber. Still, it will make a fitting funeral pyre for a duke.' He turned his gaze back on Conan. 'Make your choice, Conan, or face the consequences. You have until noon.'

For the next few hours, William's army stayed in place, keeping the pressure on the Duke of Brittany. Finally, as the sun rose to its zenith, William once more approached the chateau.

As he got closer, the doors opened, and a lone guard emerged holding a lance. The doors closed behind him, and he walked across to stand before William. All the archers took aim at the lone man in case of trickery, and finally, he stopped walking just a few paces away from William's horse.

'William of Normandy,' he said, 'I have been sent here on behalf of my lord, Conan of Brittany, to surrender the chateau.

By doing so, he urges you to fulfil your promise to spare all the occupants within.'

'I so swear,' said William, and watched as the man produced a large steel ring containing several keys. He placed them on the end of his lance and held them up to the duke. 'My lord, these are the keys.'

Everyone started at the transaction, knowing that if William leaned forward to accept the keys, he would be wide open to a thrust that would pierce his heart.

'My lord,' shouted Alan, but William held up his hand for silence, staring at the officer for any sign of treachery. Finally, determined not to show any fear, he reached forward to take the keys, his eyes never leaving those of the lance bearer.

'It is done,' said the man, as William took the keys, 'the chateau is yours.' He withdrew his spear and threw it to one side before stepping out of William's way. The duke and his men looked up at the chateau and saw dozens of weapons being thrown from the windows and parapets as proof of the surrender. At the base of the walls, the doors opened wide, and all the servants filed out to line the bridge over the small moat, ready to welcome their new master inside.

William waited as Harold and his men rode past to check that it was not a trap. They dismounted at the doors before marching inside with swords drawn. Ten minutes later, Harold emerged and walked over to William.

'The chateau is secured,' he said. 'The building is yours.'

William looked over Harold's shoulder.

'And where is Duke Conan? Do you have him in custody?'

'We do not,' said Harold, 'for he is not there.'

'Yes, he is,' said William, 'for I spoke to him this very morn. You saw him with your own eyes.'

'Aye, I did,' said Harold, 'but at the back of the building, we found a rope hanging from one of the windows. He and his officers made their escape, my lord. Conan has gone.'

Chapter Twenty-seven

Normandy, September, AD 1065

Harold waited outside one of the many side rooms in William's castle. The campaign in Brittany had been costly for the Norman duke, especially when it came to men. The final humiliation by Duke Conan had weighed heavily upon them all, but what was done was done, and at least they were back on friendly ground, and the wounded were recuperating amongst friends.

William had lost a third of his force and Harold, four of his own men, a heavy toll. Now, he waited to be summoned by William to discuss his future.

Finally, the doors opened, and two servants stood aside to let Harold into the room. Within, William stood next to a table near the fire, pouring two goblets of fine red wine. Harold walked in and waited as the two servants left the room and closed the door behind them.

'Harold,' said William, turning to offer the earl one of the goblets. 'Welcome. Please, have a drink.'

Harold took the goblet and sipped on the wine as William walked over to sit in a chair.

'Join me,' said William, and waited as Harold sat opposite. 'So,' he continued, 'what are your thoughts?'

'About what?' asked Harold.

'About your time here,' said William.

'There are too many to recount,' said Harold, 'but I feel that my men have made many comrades here, especially in the ranks. It was a surprising but welcome outcome.'

'One that was mainly caused by you,' said William.

'Not just me,' said Harold, 'many were involved.'

'Perhaps so, but your leadership throughout the campaign was the main factor. It inspired confidence amongst those you led, which quickly spread to the rest of the men. On top of that, consider the events at the river. If it were not for your actions that day, two more families would be without their husbands and fathers. For that alone, your name is already being spoken throughout Normandy, and for that, I intend to reward you.'

'I need no reward for saving another man's life,' said Harold.

'Perhaps not, but nevertheless, you will receive one. However, before that, there are matters to discuss, mainly the return of the two boys you came to seek.'

Harold's heart missed a beat.

'Before we went to Brittany,' said William, 'I promised that there could be a way of returning them to you, and I am a man of my word. I have made arrangements that one of them will be released immediately into your custody.'

Harold's face fell.

'Why just one?' he asked. 'Have I not done everything you asked of me?'

'You have,' said William, 'but there is one more thing I need from you.'

'Name it,' said Harold.

'A few years ago,' said William, 'I received a message from King Edward suggesting that I would become his heir to the throne of England. This is of great importance to me and an honour I fully intend to fulfil. However, there are those that doubt that pledge, and I anticipate that when the king dies, there will be certain people who may argue against my coronation.'

Harold stared at William. Since hearing the rumour from Archbishop Stigand, he had put it to the back of his mind, but here was William, confirming that conversation had actually taken place.

'Duke William,' he said eventually, 'King Edward already has an heir in Edgar Ætheling.'

William waved his hand in dismissal.

'The boy is a fool,' he said, 'and will never be the uniting monarch that your country needs. Besides, the position was promised to me and was witnessed before God by a man of the Church.'

'You talk of Robert of Jumièges?'

'I do.'

'Then forgive me for doubting the witnessing,' said Harold, 'for the man is a servant of the Devil himself.'

'Careful what you say, Earl Harold,' said William, 'for though I know there is no love lost between him and your family, he is still very much part of this court, and by insulting him, you insult me.'

Harold fell quiet for a moment, knowing that to raise William's ire risked everything he had achieved so far.

'What do you want me to do?' he asked eventually.

'My proposal is this,' said William. 'I will return one of the boys to you, along with a ship and many gifts as a sign of appreciation. In return, all I need is a vow that in the event of Edward's death, you will do everything in your power to convince the Witan of my argument.'

'And that is it?' asked Harold.

'Yes,' said William, 'and as an added incentive, should these things come to pass, on the day of my coronation, the second boy will be released into your care.'

Again Harold fell silent. It was a huge ask, but if that was all that was on the table, he knew he had little choice. Eventually, he nodded.

'So be it,' he said. 'Draw up the documents, and I will sign a pledge.'

'There is no need for that,' said William. 'I have arranged something far more enjoyable. Wait here.' William got up and left the room, leaving Harold alone with the wine. Ten minutes later, one of the servants entered through the doors and spoke to Harold.

'My lord,' he said, 'your presence is required.'

Harold finished his wine and followed the servant through a series of corridors before stopping before a set of double doors manned by two knights in full ceremonial chainmail. At his approach, each took a handle and pulled the door open wide, revealing a hall on the other side, full of people. At the far end stood William dressed in the full regalia of his duchy.

'My lords and ladies,' announced the steward at the side of the dais, 'please welcome Earl Harold of Wessex.'

Immediately the room broke into cheering, and Harold could see that amongst them stood his comrades from England, each smiling with the knowledge of what was about to happen.

'I don't understand,' said Harold, turning to the knight at his side. 'What is happening?'

'Keep walking, my lord,' said the knight. 'All will be revealed.'

Harold continued through the cheering crowd until he arrived before William. The duke looked down and smiled at him as the noise eased away.

'Earl Harold,' announced William, 'despite the questionable circumstances of your arrival on these shores, you have proved time and time again that you are a man of honour. Your leadership and bravery have saved the lives of many men these past few months, and it would be remiss of me to let you go home without just reward.' He turned to the man at his side, who handed him a ceremonial sword. 'To you, Earl Harold of Wessex,' said the duke turning back to face Harold, 'I, William, Duke of Normandy, hereby bestow upon you the title of revered Knight of Normandy, as witnessed by all these good people and under the eyes of God Almighty.' He touched the sword onto both of Harold's shoulders before handing the sword back to the man at his side. 'In addition,' he announced as the noise abated, 'I bestow upon you and your men a ship and a hold full of silver as payment for your services. Take it back to England and tell your king that it is with great respect that we recognise his authority and grace.'

Again the room burst into cheering, and Harold turned towards the duke.

'Thank you, Duke William,' he said. 'We are humbled by your generosity.'

'I have not finished yet,' said William, 'for look around you and see if you recognise any familiar faces.'

Harold turned around and looked along the front row of men. At first, there was nobody he wouldn't have expected, but then his attention was caught by a young man who looked like his dead older brother, Sweyn Godwinson. He stared at the young man and realised it could only be one person: his missing nephew, Hakon Sweynson.

Harold gasped with emotion. The last time he had seen Hakon, the boy had been nought but a child, and now he stood as tall as Owen.

'Hakon?' he said. 'Is it truly you?'

'It is,' said Hakon, 'and may God bless you for not forgetting me.' He stepped forward to embrace his uncle as once again the hall cheered their appreciation. Finally, William held up his hand to call for silence.

'This is a great day,' he said, 'and there is a fully laden ship waiting for our friends in the harbour, but before we send them home to England, there is one more ceremony to be carried out, one upon which Earl Harold and I have both agreed.' He nodded towards a group of servants standing to one side.

Quickly they brought a table and placed it between Harold and the duke before covering it with a rich red cloth. Harold watched, unsure about what was happening, and a few moments later, two monks walked into the room, carefully carrying between them an ornate box engraved with religious imagery. They placed the box on the table before withdrawing to stand behind the duke.

The room fell silent, watching as the events unfolded until a few seconds later, a door opened, and a man entered to take his place behind the box. It was Robert of Jumièges, the deposed archbishop, who had caused Harold's family so many problems.

For a few moments, the two men stared at each other, one with hatred and the other with amusement at the humiliation he was about to inflict. Eventually, Robert looked up at the enthralled crowd.

'People of Normandy,' he said, 'honoured English guests. You are about to bear witness to a ceremony agreed before God between these two men, Harold of Wessex and William of Normandy.' He turned his attention back to Harold. 'Earl Harold, please place one hand on either box.'

Harold's eyes narrowed with mistrust, but knowing that he had no choice, he did as he was asked.

'Earl Harold,' said Robert of Jumièges loudly, so everyone could hear him, 'do you solemnly swear in the eyes of God and these people here present, that upon the death of King Edward of England, you will support William of Normandy's claim to the English throne both in word and in deed?'

Harold swallowed hard. He had discussed the situation only a few minutes earlier, but this pledge stretched far beyond what was agreed. In addition, to make such a pledge in front of his own men meant that he could never go back on it lest he lose all reputation and honour. He glanced up at William, who had a slight smile of triumph on his face, knowing full well that Harold was in an impossible situation.

'Come, Earl Harold,' said Jumièges quietly, 'everyone is waiting, not least your nephew, Hakon Sweynson. He is so looking forward to seeing England again.' His tone lowered as he voiced the obvious threat. 'Or not, as the case may be.'

Again Harold hesitated as the gravity of the vow sunk in. If he agreed, then should William ever come to England to claim the throne, he was sworn to fight on his behalf. If he did not agree, then there was no way William would ever let any of them leave Normandy alive, including Hakon.

With an aching heart, he knew he had no other option. His men's lives depended on him, as did Hakon's and Wulfnorth's, his still-missing brother. He took a deep breath and looked up to return William's amused gaze.

'I so swear,' he said, and for the last time, the hall burst into cheering as everyone celebrated the unlikely alliance. All, that is, except seven very angry Englishmen.

Part Four

Chapter Twenty-eight

Dunstan and Gamelbearn waited nervously in a village hall north of York. The locals were known to hate Tostig, but nevertheless, the meeting had been kept as secret as possible in case news reached the earl's ears. Some of their trusted men kept watch outside, and eventually, in the early hours of the morning, two riders arrived by horseback and were ushered into the hall.

The two thegns stood up and stared at the newcomers as they divested themselves of their wet riding cloaks. Finally, they turned around and faced the men who had invited them.

'Who between you is Gamelbearn?' said the first man.

'I am he,' said Gamelbearn, stepping forward. 'And you are?'

'I am the man you seek,' said the visitor, 'Morcar of Mercia.' He walked forward and held out his hand. 'I think you know why we are here.'

Gamelbearn breathed a sigh of relief. This meeting had been a long time coming, but at last, he felt that they were making progress.

'This is Eardwulf,' said Morcar, 'my second-in-command. In my absence, he will speak for me.'

'Understood,' said Gamelbearn. 'This is Dunstan, son of Aethelnoth; he too is a trusted man.'

'Good,' said Morcar, walking over to sit at the table. 'Let us get this done, for we need to be far away from here by dawn.'

Dunstan walked over to the fire and retrieved a pot of hot ale before placing it on the table along with four wooden tankards.

'Help yourself,' he said. 'It will warm your bones after the ride.'

Each of the men dipped his tankard into the bowl before staring at each other across the table.

'So,' said Morcar, 'I am in receipt of several messages asking for my support. Tell me exactly what you want.'

'My lord,' said Gamelbearn, 'you must know of the mess Earl Tostig is making in Northumbria. The taxes are unsustainable, and the people struggle to eat, such is the burden.'

'Tostig is an earl and as such can do whatever he likes within his own borders.'

'Aye, he is, but no other earl in England treats their people as he does. He has declared that his word is law and sentences people to death on a daily basis.'

'Again, he is an earl and such things happen.'

'My lord,' said Gamelbearn, 'I do not think you understand. The people of Northumbria wake up each day knowing that their lives could depend on whether a man has a heavy head from too much ale or whether he has lost at dice. In both scenarios, we know that before noon there will be more citizens hanging from the gallows, whether they are guilty or not.'

'I can't believe that Tostig hangs innocent men,' said Morcar.

'Not only men,' interrupted Dunstan, 'but women and children. If anyone in his employ, and there are many, accuses anybody of a crime, whether proven or not, they distribute whatever justice they see fit. This usually means hanging, but we have witnessed much worse deaths administered by the hands of his men.'

'So he has not personally ordered the executions?'

'He does not have to. He knows that his men will do the deed for him, and he pays them well. He spends most of his time across the border getting drunk with the Scottish king.'

'Perhaps we should be holding his men responsible,' said Morcar, 'not him.'

'He knows what is happening,' said Dunstan, 'make no mistake. And he pays them a king's ransom for their loyalty.

230

What adds insult to injury is that he then passes those costs onto us in the way of taxes. Today we received a message from Tostig that has finally caused the bough to break.'

'And that is?'

'He is doubling the taxes of every man with immediate effect, payment being due in the spring. It is too much, my lord – the people can take no more. Either you help us, or they will rise against him with nought but pitchforks and scythes, and that way lies only death for every man, woman and child involved.'

Morcar fell silent and sat back in his chair as he digested the information.

'My lord,' said Dunstan, 'if there was anyone else to help us, we would turn to them, I swear, but if you were to lend us your name, I think the king will be forced to sit up and listen.'

'Why do you think that? For I am no earl.'

'No, but your brother is.'

'Do you expect Mercia to back this uprising?' asked Morcar.

'No,' said Dunstan, 'for if truth be told, I do not think there will be a single blow struck between the earldoms, but the possibility of that outcome will make the Crown take us seriously. The house of Wessex may be strong and have powerful allies, but not even they would risk a civil war with the House of Mercia.'

'Remind me of what is on offer?' said Morcar.

'It is very simple,' said Dunstan. 'Help us get rid of Tostig and his henchmen, and you will have the support of every thegn in Northumbria to make you the earl.'

'That will not be your decision,' said Morcar, 'nor will it be mine. An earldom is awarded at the king's discretion.'

'Aye, it is, but if all of Northumbria stands up and pledges loyalty to the king only on condition that you are appointed as such, then I see no other possible outcome.'

Again Morcar fell silent and stared at the two men. Finally, he turned to the man at his side.

'Eardwulf, you have remained quiet. What say you?'

'I think that your name alone will carry no weight,' said the huscarl, 'and it will have to be backed up with men and weapons. Despite what these men think, there will be killing to be done, and that means trained men, not a peasant army.'

'How many can we raise?' asked Morcar.

'About a thousand,' said Eardwulf, 'maybe two. Add to that a few hundred Irish and Welsh mercenaries, and we will have ourselves an army. However, if you really want to become the earl of Northumbria, I agree with these two men. We need the support of Mercia.'

Morcar nodded and turned back to face the two thegns.

'How long do you need to muster your comrades?'

'A week, two at most,' said Dunstan. 'But we should make our move as soon as possible while Tostig is in the south.'

'Do you know where he is exactly?'

'Aye, in Bosham. Harold just returned from Normandy, and they have gathered there to celebrate the return of Hakon Sweynson.'

'Then there is no time to lose,' said Morcar.

'So you will do it?'

'Aye, we will,' said Morcar. 'Muster your forces and meet us back here ten days from now, but I will warn you both, there may be many deaths before there is a solution.'

'We know the risks,' said Gamelbearn, and stood up to hold out his hand. 'Thank you, my lord, you will not regret this.'

'We will see,' said Morcar, taking the thegn's wrist before turning to his huscarl. 'Get us out of here, Eardwulf. There is much work to be done.'

—

In Bosham, Harold and Edyth sat next to each other at the large table in the main hall. With them were the family matriarch Gytha Thorkelsdóttir and Hakon Sweynson, enjoying the many benefits that came with being reunited with his family at last.

The aftermath of the previous night's feast had long gone, and they sat quietly, picking on a platter of dried fruits.

'It is so good to see you again,' said Gytha, looking at her grandson, 'but you have grown so big I hardly recognise you.'

'It has been a long time,' said Hakon.

'Did you think we had forgotten about you?' asked Edyth.

'In the beginning, yes,' said Hakon. 'Every day that passed, I expected to hear the sound of my father's men storming the castle where we were held captive, yet that day never came.'

'Did they treat you well?' asked Harold.

'At first, no. We were kept in a room without windows, devoid of heat and light. Once a day, they would open the door just to throw us some scraps and a jug of water. We were treated no better than dogs. I do not know how long we were there, but it must have been months. Eventually, they took us out and sent us to separate places. It was the last time I ever saw Wulfnorth.'

'Do you know if he is still alive?' asked Harold.

'I believe so, for there was talk of both of us being handed over to you, but that was dismissed by the bishop.'

'Robert of Jumièges,' growled Harold. 'I should have killed that man while I had the chance.'

'And if you had,' said Edyth, looking at her husband, 'neither of you would be here now, so strike that thought from your mind.'

'So what about the intervening years?' said Gytha. 'Did your treatment improve?'

'At first, no, but after a while, they allowed me to walk around the courtyard, watched by the guards. It wasn't much, but I was glad to see the sky and feel the sun on my face. As I grew older, they gave me more freedom, even allowing me to ride out on the occasional hunt, as long as I vowed not to try to escape.'

'Did you ever consider breaking that vow?' asked Harold.

'Not once,' said Hakon.

'Why not?'

'Because they said that if I ran, they would hang Wulfnorth.'

Gytha stifled a cry and reached out to touch Hakon's arm.

'We are so sorry,' she said, 'we did try, I swear we did, but no matter how many men we sent across, none returned with any positive information. We just could not find you.'

'Then you should have tried harder,' said Hakon quietly. 'My life so far has been for nothing. Sometimes I wonder if it was all worth it, and perhaps an arrow in the back would have been better than the living death we suffered. Now I feel guilty that I am here and Wulfnorth is not.'

'If there is anyone who should feel guilty,' said Harold, 'it is I. We thank God that you are alive and well, but Wulfnorth's continued captivity weighs like a stone upon my heart.'

'Let us just give thanks for what we have,' said Edyth, 'and then, when everyone is fully recovered, perhaps we can engage King Edward's help in negotiating your brother's release. At least we know that he is still alive, and that is far more than what we knew even a few months ago.'

'It is pointless,' said Harold.

'Why do you say that? If the reports are true, I believe William was very impressed with you. Why else would he have given you a knighthood?'

'It was no more than trickery,' said Harold, 'a ploy, no doubt thought up by Robert of Jumièges.'

'To what end?'

Harold looked up. 'To garner my support for William in the event that he comes here to claim the throne.'

'Why do you say that?' asked Gytha. 'Is he going to attack?'

'I know not,' said Harold. 'He claims that Edward has made him his heir and that when the king dies, he fully intends to come here and claim what is his.'

'The Witan would never allow that to happen,' replied Gytha.

'That is why he needs my support,' said Harold. 'To argue his case and, if necessary, fight alongside him.'

'And you agreed?'

'I did,' said Harold. 'I had no other option.'

'Of course you had an option,' said Edyth. 'You could have just said no.'

Harold looked at his wife. He felt mentally exhausted after everything that had happened and did not want to argue.

'Edyth,' he said, 'this is a conversation for another time, but just be assured that refusal was never an option. Now I have to live with that decision and decide what I am going to do about it.'

'Like what?'

'First of all,' said Harold, 'I have to go to London to report back to the king. While there, I intend to confront him about William's claim to find out if it is true.'

'And if it is?'

'Then I have no option but to honour my pledge.'

'And if the claim is false?'

'Then perhaps there may be something we can do about it, but until we know for certain, there is nothing more we can do. I leave for London in the morning.'

Chapter Twenty-nine

York, October, AD 1065

Dunstan sat on his horse on a hill overlooking the sprawling city of York. Behind him in the valley stood several hundred cavalry and over a thousand foot-soldiers. A league to the east, though invisible in the pre–dawn darkness, he knew that Eardwulf stood at the head of a similar army, sent on the orders of Morcar.

Their orders were clear. At the first light of dawn, both forces were to advance on York, taking up station before the city gates. Unless confronted by the forces of Tostig, there was to be no violence inflicted upon the people of York, for they were just as much victims of Tostig's tyranny as anyone out in the towns and villages of Northumbria.

'What do we do if the gates are slammed against us?' asked Gamelbearn.

'That will not happen,' said Dunstan. 'We already have men inside the city spreading dissent. If Tostig's men try to close the gates, they will be attacked from the rear, giving us time to get through. This should be an easy task, my friend, one of occupation, not conquest.'

'Let us hope you are right,' said Gamelbearn, 'for I am told by Eardwulf that Earl Edwin will only pledge Mercia's full support if we can rally the north under one banner.'

'Well,' said Dunstan, 'this is the place to start.' He looked up as the sky started to lighten in the east. 'This is it,' he said, 'there is no turning back. Give the signal to advance.'

A few seconds later, the sound of a horn echoed through the pre-dawn gloom and thousands of men and horses headed towards York. The rebellion had finally started.

—

In London, Harold had finally managed to get hold of Archbishop Stigand, knowing full well that if he was to question the king on the delicate subject of his promises to William of Normandy, then he would need the support of the bishop during the audience. After several days, Stigand arrived, and now they stood before the doors of the king's audience chamber.

'Are you sure you want to do this?' asked Stigand, 'for recently, his mood is changeable, and he has been known to be, perhaps, unjust in his decisions.'

'It is something we need to know,' said Harold, 'not just for my sake, but for England's.'

'If you are sure?' said Stigand.

'I am,' said Harold and turned away as the door opened to allow them through. Inside, several nobles stood at the front of the chamber, each waiting their turn to present their petitions to the king. Harold and Stigand knew they had no other option but to wait, and stood at the back of the line. A few moments later, Edward looked up and, seeing Harold and Stigand at the back of the room, dismissed the next man in line with a wave of his hand.

'Earl Harold,' he exclaimed, 'you are here at last. Please come forward.'

Harold walked through the rest of the waiting men, sensing their frustration as he passed.

'Your grace,' he said with a bow. 'It is good to see you again.'

'And you,' said Edward. 'I have heard great things about your time in Normandy and look forward to hearing a full account.'

'It will be my pleasure,' said Harold.

The king looked up and faced the rest of the men in the room.

'This audience is now over. We will resume at midday tomorrow.'

The men murmured their disappointment but, knowing there was little they could do, turned away and left the room.

'Come,' said Edward, standing up, 'let us retire to somewhere more comfortable. You too, Archbishop Stigand.' They walked through a doorway behind the dais and down a corridor to Edward's private audience room, one Harold had frequented many times before. 'Sit,' said Edward, indicating the chairs. 'It has been a while since we last conversed thus.' He turned to the steward standing at the door. 'Arrange refreshments,' he said, 'and have them brought in here.'

'Yes, your grace,' said the steward, and left the room as Edward lowered himself into his seat.

'So,' he said, 'you must tell me everything that happened to you and leave out not a moment.'

'Of course,' said Harold. For the next hour or so he recounted all the events he had experienced since leaving for Normandy many months earlier. Edward was fascinated, asking many questions as Harold spoke, especially interested in the ways of William's court, for despite being the king of England, he had spent over half of his life in Normandy, and it still held a special place in his heart.

'So you are now a Norman knight,' laughed the king, as Harold recalled the final ceremony. 'Should I be afraid for my safety?'

'Never,' said Harold, 'though it does bring me on to matters of concern, the discussion of which may cause you angst and perhaps anger.'

'Really?' said Edward, sitting back in his chair. 'What are these matters that concern you so?'

'Your grace,' said Harold. 'Duke William of Normandy is convinced that he is your rightful heir, having been promised the position by you several years ago. So convinced is he that he has made it as clear as the nose upon my face that when you die, he intends to come to England to claim the throne, a situation that can only end in war.'

Edward stared at the two men in turn, seeing the concern in their eyes.

'He must be mistaken,' he said eventually, 'for I have made no such promise.'

'Your grace,' said Stigand, 'forgive me, but when you were close to death a few years ago, you said many things in your delirium. Most were nonsense, and I dismissed them as such, but there was a recurring theme: you expressed regret about nominating William as your heir. Again, I dismissed it as the visions of fever, but in light of Earl Harold's report, I have to ask you if there is any grain of truth in this matter at all.'

At first, Edward's face darkened as he realised his honesty was being questioned by one of his subjects. His initial thought was to dismiss both men without answer, but the seriousness of the accusation meant that even if he did, the question would fester with anyone who heard the account. He took a deep breath, his previous good mood rapidly disappearing.

'There was talk of such a possibility,' he said, 'at a time when it seemed that there was nobody else available. However, it was a discussion only and was certainly never a declaration or even an offer.'

'Can I ask, your grace,' said Harold, 'did this discussion take place with Robert of Jumièges?'

'It did, why?'

Harold glanced at Stigand.

'Because, your grace, the archbishop at the time reported back to William that his succession to the throne of England had been agreed, and as far as the duke is concerned, he will be the next King of England.'

'This is preposterous!' exclaimed Edward. 'There was no such agreement ever made, and everyone knows that Edgar

Ætheling is now my heir. That is a fact, and nothing that Duke William or Robert of Jumièges may say can change it.'

'Your grace,' said Archbishop Stigand, 'I know this is an unpleasant conversation, but we have to be sure. Did you, at any time, give Robert of Jumièges any indication, no matter how slight, that William was to become your heir?'

'I did not,' growled Edward, 'and resent the accusation. Now, this audience is over, and I suggest you leave while you still can.'

'Thank you, your grace,' said Harold, and as Edward stormed from the room, he turned to Stigand. 'I'm not sure how I feel about that outcome,' he said. 'On the one hand, it is a relief that England is not to be handed over to the Normans, but on the other, it would suggest that there will be only one outcome from this situation, and that is war with Normandy.'

'Let us deal with one thing at a time,' said Stigand. 'Edward is still very much alive, and while that remains the case, we have time to make preparations. Come, there is much to discuss.'

—

In the north, the people's army descended upon York before the rising sun could reveal their approach. As they neared the gate, Dunstan turned to Gamelbearn at his side.

'Take the lead, my friend,' he said, 'and secure the heart of the city. I will follow up with the foot-soldiers.'

Without needing any more encouragement, Gamelbearn spurred his horse and led two hundred horsemen towards the city walls.

Up on the gate towers, one of the tired sentries heard the thunder of approaching hooves and turned to peer into the grey morning light.

'Utred,' he said, kicking his comrade who was stealing a snooze at the base of the parapet, 'wake up!'

Utred looked up and saw the concern on his comrade's face. He got to his feet and looked over the wall.

'It sounds like horses,' he said, 'hundreds of them.'

'Do you think we are being attacked?'

'By whom?' asked Utred. 'The Scots?'

'I do not know,' said the sentry, 'but whoever it is, we had better sound the alarm.' He turned away to ring the alarm bell, but it was already too late as, down below, several men were emerging from the shadows to overwhelm the guards. Within moments, the giant gates swung open, and Gamelbearn and his men thundered through the streets towards the city centre. Just behind them came Dunstan and his foot-soldiers, spreading out to either side to search for those loyal to Tostig.

'*Get inside!*' shouted Dunstan as people started to emerge from the buildings to see what was going on. 'We want Tostig's men, not you.'

'Head east,' shouted a voice in the dark. 'They have set up a barracks near the cattle market.'

Dunstan ordered his men to follow him and headed east. Within a few minutes, he saw armed men running towards him.

'Onward,' he roared and ploughed into the men with his sword in one hand and a knife in the other. His men followed him into the melee, aided by momentum and sheer numbers, and, within a few moments, they had broken through and continued down the street towards the barracks.

To the west of the city, Eardwulf did the same with his army, and they rampaged through the streets seeking Tostig's men. Realising they were heavily outnumbered, many discarded their weapons and tried to mingle with the rest of the population, but as the day grew lighter and the occupants of York realised what was happening, they were only too keen to point them out to the newcomers.

All across the city, the resolve of Tostig's men fell apart. For too many years, they had enjoyed unfettered power over the citizens of York and, short of an attack from the Scots, had never dreamed they would face such a ferocious and well-organised assault. Any fighting was sporadic and then only between Tostig's men and those of the uprising. People watched from windows as those who had lorded it over them so brutally for so long were chased down and slain in the street. Few were given mercy, for those administering the final blows knew full well that these people were the ones who had sent so many to the gallows on behalf of Tostig.

Finally, by midday, people began to emerge from their houses and headed towards the city centre.

On the gallows, in the middle of the square, the ropes where so many had died still hung. Standing on the platform were Dunstan and Gamelbearn, talking to the aldermen of York, explaining what was going to happen next.

'Fret not,' said Dunstan, 'for we mean no harm to you or the people of York. In fact, we have come to lift the burden from around your necks and free this great city from Tostig's foul embrace.'

'That is all very well,' said the alderman, 'but once news of this gets out, Tostig will rally his men and come back for us with his brothers' armies.'

'That is not going to happen,' said Dunstan, 'trust me.'

'How can you say such a thing?' said the alderman. 'You may have caught these men sleeping, but you are only a few thousand. The House of Godwin has twenty times that amount and will seek retribution.'

'No matter how many men Tostig can muster,' said Dunstan, 'they would not dare to risk a war with the house of Mercia.'

'You have the support of Mercia?' gasped the alderman.

Dunstan looked over the square to the main keep of the city. The flag of Tostig had already been removed and now, as the people cheered, was being replaced by the colours of Morcar, Earl Edwin's brother.

'We do now,' he said, and turned away to where some of Eardwulf's men were dragging two prisoners up onto the platform.

'Who do we have here?' he asked.

'Amund and Ravenswort,' said one of the captors. 'I believe you know them.'

'Oh, we know them,' said Dunstan. 'Without these men, Tostig could never have sustained his campaign of fear and brutality. The blood of many people stains their hands.'

'What do you want us to do with them?'

Dunstan looked up at the empty gallows. 'Well,' he said, 'I was going to let the people rip these down, but I suppose that can wait a few moments longer.' He looked back at the two despondent huscarls, hatred etched on his face. 'Do unto them that they have done unto others,' he growled. 'Hang them... *slowly.*'

Over the next few days, all the officials who had served Tostig were sought out and punished, with many being executed. All of Tostig's lands around York were attacked, and his treasuries raided to return the taxes he had taken to the people who had suffered the most.

Hearing of the occupation of York, support for the rebellion rose quickly, and soon there were far more supporters in and around York than any of the instigators had hoped for. Realising they had a real chance to do something significant, Gamelbearn, Dunstan, Eardwulf and Morcar met again to decide the way forward, though this time in the comfort of York's main hall instead of some hidden wayside inn.

'The mood of the city is inebriating,' said Dunstan. 'It has been a long time since I have witnessed such joy.'

'I am not surprised,' said Morcar, 'for you have achieved a great victory here, and I have heard that you are already causing concern in London.'

'Good,' said Dunstan. 'We cannot afford this wave of support to wane. Never have I seen the northern people so united, and it is truly a once-in-a-lifetime chance to make a change for the better.'

'You have already forced a change,' said Morcar. 'Tostig hides behind the king in London like a frightened child. Our people have much to be grateful for.'

'It is not enough,' said Dunstan. 'If we allow them time to reorganise, they will only come back bigger and stronger. We need to know your brother will support us further.'

'In what way?' asked Morcar. 'He has already declared support for the liberation of York, and nobody would dare attempt to take it from you without his agreement, not even Harold.'

'It is not enough,' said Dunstan again. 'Every single man, woman and child involved in this uprising is now a conspirator against the Crown and as such could be executed at any time. What we need is for the king not only to recognise that Tostig is no longer the Earl of Northumbria but to grant a pardon to all involved.'

'He would never do that,' said Morcar. 'To do so would invite rebellion from all quarters.'

'He would if we gave him no other choice,' said Dunstan.

'And how do we do that?'

'Easy,' said Dunstan, 'we march on London.'

Chapter Thirty

London, October, AD 1065

Earl Tostig and Copsi stood before the king. Tostig's second-in-command had managed to escape the attack on York and had ridden south as fast as he could to warn Tostig about what was happening. Realising the seriousness of the situation, Tostig had requested an audience with the king to seek help.

'Your grace,' said Tostig, 'what these rebels have done is nothing short of treason, and each and every one of them should be hanged from the nearest tree. Northumbria is in disarray, and if we do not do something quickly, the whole of the north will be left vulnerable to the Scots.'

'I thought Malcolm was a personal friend of yours,' said the king. 'Should we be worried about him?'

'No, your grace, but the clan chieftains are ambitious men and if they realise Northumbria is exposed, who knows where their ambition will take them?'

'So, where is your army now?'

'Many have dispersed, your grace,' said Copsi, 'faced by the overwhelming numbers of traitors Dunstan and Gamelbearn have whipped to their cause.'

'Do you have nobody steadfast?' asked the king.

'A few hundred,' said Tostig, 'but most of our men were mercenaries and only show loyalty at the sight of a full purse. We need your strength to drive these men back and reclaim what is mine.'

'Yours?' asked the king.

'Forgive me, your grace,' said Tostig, 'of course I only rule Northumbria in your name, but that is even more reason we need your support. These men are committing treason right in front of our eyes, and the situation demands immediate retribution.'

'Your concerns are noted,' said the king. 'I will send for your brother immediately. Where is Harold at the moment?'

'He is at Bosham, your grace, but why are you sending for him? Just give me an army, and I will lead them myself. I need no help from Harold or any other man.'

'Nevertheless,' said the king, 'he is the strongest of my earls, so we will consult with him before deciding the way forward. Besides, he commands the largest standing army and can muster men to his call even quicker than I. Go back to Southwark, Tostig, and wait there. As soon as I have any more information, I will send for you.'

'Your grace—' started Tostig, but Edward raised his hand, cutting the conversation short.

'I have made my decision,' he said, 'now do as I ask. We will deal with this, Earl Tostig, but it will be done with forethought and not in the spur of the moment. You are dismissed.'

Tostig stared at the king but knew there was no more he could do.

'Thank you, your grace,' he said and turned away to head back to the family home at Southwark.

–

Ten days later, Tostig was once more in the presence of the king, though this time along with his brother, Harold, and the Archbishop of Canterbury. Stigand had brought everyone up to date with what had happened, and the discussion centred around what was to be done, but not ten minutes after the audience had begun, the door opened, and one of the royal stewards walked across to whisper in the king's ear.

'Bring him in,' he said eventually, and the steward walked back out of the room.

'It seems that there have been developments,' said the king, 'and this problem may be more difficult than we thought.'

'What has happened?' asked Tostig. 'I warned that we were wasting time.'

'We are about to find out,' said the king, and turned to see one of his marshals enter, walking briskly over to join the group.

'Your grace,' said the marshal, 'I bear grave news. The army led by Dunstan and Gamelbearn has marched south, wreaking death and destruction upon anyone who stands in their way.' He turned to face Tostig. 'My lord, I am sorry to say that they targeted all your holdings and have burned everything you owned to the ground. Many men have died, and your livestock has been killed to feed their army.'

'They are not an army,' hissed Tostig, 'they are untrained rebels whipped into a frenzy by traitors.'

'Nevertheless,' said the marshal, 'my scouts tell me that they are well armed, organised and relentless. They are going from village to village, town to town, demanding support. Notting-hamshire has fallen, as has Lincolnshire and Northamptonshire. They are only a few days away from London.'

'I knew it,' gasped Tostig, turning to face the king, 'they aim to topple the throne, your grace, and install their own king.'

'That is preposterous,' interjected Harold, 'and such a claim is dangerous. All we know at the moment is that a people's army has mustered to protest against the Crown. It is not the first time, nor will it be the last.'

'Are you not listening?' asked Tostig. 'They have already taken two major towns and are heading for a third. That is not a protest, that is conquest.'

'He has a point,' said the king, 'and it worries me that they have made so much ground, so quickly.'

Harold turned to the marshal.

'What news do you have of any casualties?'

'As far as we know, there are surprisingly few,' said the marshal, 'and most seem to be those militias and officials that were loyal to my lord Tostig.'

Harold turned back to face the king.

'If this was an attempt to overthrow the Crown, your grace, I do not believe for one moment that the campaign would be so well supported, especially by the common folk. They know the penalty for treason, and few are brave enough to raise arms against a king. It seems to me that this is indeed a protest, and as much as it pains me to say it,' he looked over at Tostig, 'it looks like it is against my brother.'

The king also looked over at Tostig.

'Well,' he said, 'what say you?'

'I think the reason is irrelevant,' said Tostig. 'The fact remains: a large body of armed men are burning their way to London, murdering anyone who stands in their way. Their motive is not important, but the potential outcome is.'

'Has anyone talked to these men?' asked the king.

'We do not negotiate with traitors,' said Tostig.

'Then perhaps it is time we did,' said Harold. 'Why not send someone up to Northamptonshire before they get there and try to find out exactly what they want?'

'That is a waste of time,' shouted Tostig. 'What we need to do is attack them without mercy and send them to hell where they belong.'

All the men in the room stared at Tostig with shock. His face was red with rage, and it was all he could do to stop himself from launching at his brother. After a few moments' silence, the king turned back to Harold.

'What do you suggest?' he asked, as if the recent outburst had never happened.

'Your grace,' said Harold, 'I have my personal guards billeted in Southwark. Just give the word, and we will ride to Northamptonshire immediately and seek an audience with the ringleaders. Once we know what they want, we can decide what we need to do.'

'Fifty men against five thousand,' said the king, arching an eyebrow.

'I do not intend to fight, your grace,' said Harold, 'I intend to talk. If we march to battle without even knowing what the problem is, then we risk losing a lot of men in a civil war, and with William of Normandy setting his eyes on England, that could be a massive disadvantage.'

'What has this got to do with Normandy?' asked Tostig.

'The threat of Normandy is a matter to be discussed at another time,' said the king, 'but I agree with Harold. We will not shed any of our countrymen's blood unless it is absolutely necessary.' He turned back to Harold. 'You have my permission to parley on my behalf. Go north and return as quickly as you can with an update. In the meantime, I will arrange a council to discuss what actions, if any, we need to take. You will report to us when you return.'

'I will go with you,' said Tostig, turning to Harold.

'No,' said Harold quickly, 'your presence will only antagonise them. Wait for the council, brother, and you will have a full voice there.'

'So be it,' said the king. 'This audience is over.' He stood up and left the room, leaving the men behind him.

'I don't know what you are up to,' said Tostig, turning to his brother, 'but whatever it is, I won't let you get away with it.'

Before Harold could answer, Tostig stormed from the hall.

'What did he mean by that?' asked Stigand.

'I have no idea,' said Harold, 'but I have no time to worry about it now. I have to get to Northamptonshire.'

Chapter Thirty-one

Northampton, Late October, AD 1065

Harold stood on a hill alongside his men. Down below and stretching into the distance was the town of Northampton, but it was not the city that caught his eye: it was the hundreds upon hundreds of tents as far as the eye could see.

The northern army, under the command of Dunstan and Gamelbearn, had obviously moved far faster than he had anticipated and was certainly far larger than he had imagined. There were no signs of battle surrounding the town, no smoke from burning buildings and no flocks of crows picking at the eyes of those who had fallen. In fact, despite its size, the whole camp looked quite organised and peaceful, the air pierced only by shafts of smoke from the many campfires.

Despite this, Harold was concerned, for he knew that even though the masses were untrained, the sheer number meant that any fight would be costly to both sides.

'My lord,' said Owen at his side, 'I think they've noticed us.' He nodded towards a column of armed men galloping from the city towards them.

'Let them come,' said Harold, 'and under no circumstances does anyone draw a weapon unless I give the command.' He watched as the column reached the top of the hill and split into two to completely encircle them. One of the men rode up and reined in his horse before Harold.

'Who are you,' he demanded, 'and what do you want?'

'I am Harold of Wessex,' replied Harold, 'and I have come to talk to the man in charge, whosoever that may be.'

'That would be Morcar of Mercia,' said the officer. 'What business do you have with him?'

Harold was shocked. He had heard that Morcar might be involved, but nothing had been confirmed. Now it had been verified, it added a whole new dimension to the emerging picture.

'I have been sent here by the king to discuss his demands,' said Harold, 'and to see if there is a way to stop any more bloodshed.'

The officer stared at Harold.

'You can come,' he said, 'but your men will stay here.'

'No,' said Owen, but Harold put up his hand to cut him short.

'The requirement is to be expected,' he said. 'Make camp here. I will return as soon as I can.'

'And what if they take you hostage?' asked Owen.

'Then Edward will respond accordingly,' said Harold, and turned back to the lancer. 'Lead the way.'

Twenty minutes later, Harold was led through a series of side streets until they reached the town hall. Inside he was made to wait until, eventually, he was led through to a room where several men sat on one side of a table, waiting for him.

'Thank you,' said one of the men to the guards. 'Leave us.'

The guards bowed and left the room as the speaker turned back to face Harold.

'Earl Harold,' he said, 'good to see you again.'

'Hello Morcar,' said Harold, recognising the young man. 'You are looking well. How is your family?'

'They are well,' said Morcar. 'Please, take a seat. I believe you have met my huscarl, Eardwulf,' he added, nodding to one of the men.

'Eardwulf,' said Harold, acknowledging the man with a nod as he sat.

'These two,' continued Morcar, turning to two of the other attendees, 'may not be known to you. Please let me intro-duce Gamelbearn and Dunstan, both well-respected thegns of

Northumbria, and, I have to say, men of vision and no little bravery.'

'We have not met,' said Harold, 'but over the past few days, I have heard their names repeatedly. And if by the terms vision and bravery you mean traitorous and foolhardy, then I concur with your description.'

Both thegns scowled at the insult, but before they could respond, Morcar spoke again.

'Come now, Earl Harold, that sort of talk is beneath you.'

'Then how should I talk?' asked Harold. 'For the actions of these men means that my brother is temporarily deposed from his earldom, and many innocent men from here to the Scottish borders now lay dead.'

'It seems that your understanding of innocence and mine also differs greatly,' said Morcar, 'but enough of the wordplay. I'm sure you have not come here just to trade insults. What do you want?'

'I am here on behalf of the king,' said Harold. 'We have sat on our hands and watched as this situation has played out, but now it has gone too far, and he wants to know what exactly you are playing at, as, indeed, do I.'

'Oh, there are no games being played here,' said Morcar, 'we are deadly serious. We have certain demands, and if they are not fulfilled in their entirety, then it will be extremely difficult to stop the army you just rode through from marching on London.'

'You dare to threaten the king?' asked Harold. 'What sort of fools are you?'

'Fools that are fed up with their people starving to death and being slaughtered by a tyrant for no other reason than trying to live,' said Dunstan. 'Your brother is a monster, and unless he is stripped of his title and kept far away from Northumbria, then we may as well die in London as in the north.'

'You paint a stark picture, Dunstan,' said Harold, 'but they are just words. My brother assures me that his rule imposes only that which he is allowed under the law to do, and by challenging those rules, you are directly challenging the king.'

'He is one man,' interjected Gamelbearn. 'Take his word if you must, but outside of these walls, there are twenty thousand others who would attest otherwise. Your brother dances with the devil, Lord Harold, whether you like it or not.'

Harold looked around the men, seeing the intensity in their eyes.

'Even if the king were to accept your demands,' he said eventually, 'which he will not, what is to say that the next earl is not just as bad?'

'He is not,' said Dunstan, 'for he has already been chosen.'

'Has he?' laughed Harold. 'And who, may I ask, is this man that seeks to bypass the tradition and power of the throne. You?'

'No,' said Dunstan, 'not I.' He turned to stare at Morcar.

Harold followed his gaze and realised what was happening.

'Oh, Morcar,' he said, 'I thought you were a sensible man. Surely you know that this is a battle you cannot win?'

'Perhaps not on my own,' said Morcar, 'but with the forces of Mercia behind me, I feel we have a very strong argument.'

'Morcar,' said Harold, 'you may be brothers, but Edwin would never risk civil war just to settle an argument between a noble and some angry thegns. I know him too well, and he knows that it would be too high a price to pay.'

'Then you do not know him as well as you think,' said Morcar. 'I have the full backing of my brother and, by association, Mercia.'

'I do not believe you,' said Harold. 'There may have been discussion, but there is no way Edwin would mobilise Mercia against Edward.'

'If you do not believe me,' said Morcar, 'then ask him yourself.'

Harold's brow creased in confusion, but when he heard a door open behind him, he knew he had been toyed with as Earl Edwin of Mercia entered the room and walked over to sit next to his brother.

'Earl Harold,' he said, removing his riding gloves, 'my apologies for the lateness, I had hoped to be here sooner. My sister sends her regards. Has my brother been looking after you?'

Harold was shocked. The fact that Edwin had travelled so far and now sat amongst the rebels as an ally made his heart race, and he knew that the perceived threat from the uprising had just changed dramatically.

'Earl Edwin,' he said eventually, 'surely you are not in favour of this uprising? You of all people must know that a civil war has never done any man any good.'

'On the contrary,' said Edwin, 'some may say the occasional civil war is needed to stir the pot of royal expectation, especially if that pot has spoiled.'

'Edward is not perfect,' said Harold, 'and he took a long time to let go of his associations with Normandy, but those days are gone. He is a good king.'

'We have no concerns about Edward,' said Edwin, 'only those around him, and in particular, Tostig Godwinson.'

'I cannot believe he is as bad as these men report,' said Harold. 'Someone would have said something long before now.'

'Oh, we tried,' said Dunstan, 'but Tostig has his spies everywhere, and each time there was any hint of trouble, Tostig's men hanged the suspect and anyone associated with him. The people soon became too terrified to speak up, so here we are.'

'I know it is hard to believe,' said Edwin, accepting a tankard of wine from a servant, 'but I assure you, I have made my own enquiries, and these men speak the truth. He is a monster, Harold. Cut him loose.'

'I do not know what to say,' said Harold. 'Even if it is true – and I am not saying that I believe you – the king is more focused on the treachery of his subjects than the cruelty of one man. He would never bow to the demands of the people over one of his nobles, for that way lies even more trouble. His back will be against the wall in this situation, Edwin, and he will have no choice but to deny your petition.'

'In that case,' said Edwin, 'it is highly probable that you and I will meet again quite soon, though probably at the head of our respective armies.'

'That is no good to anyone,' said Harold.

'I agree, but only you can sort this out.'

'How?'

'By going back to the king and telling him that unless he deposes Tostig Godwinson immediately, these people will sacrifice themselves on the walls of London and, who knows, some may even make it through.'

'Some already have,' said Dunstan quietly.

Harold stared at the thegn.

'What do you mean?'

'London is a very welcoming city,' said Dunstan, looking up, 'and some of our people were keen to see the new palace in Westminster. They say it looks magnificent, though perhaps a bit, shall we say, flammable?'

Harold got to his feet and smashed his fist on the table.

'I came here in good faith to save lives and find solutions,' he shouted, 'not to be threatened by a man not fit to clean my boots.'

'Earl Harold,' said Edwin, 'please calm down. Thegn Dunstan spoke out of turn, and I would never condone such an act. Nevertheless, it illustrates the strength of feeling and what these people are willing to do. I would also suggest that with Mercia watching their backs, there is little room for negotiation. Now, please sit down and have another drink. Let's see if we can sort this out as comrades.'

–

Several hours later, Harold rode alone from the gates of Northampton and rejoined his men on the hill above the city. Owen saw him approach and walked out to meet him.

'My lord,' he said as Harold reined in his horse, 'how did it go?'

'Not good, Owen,' said Harold, 'in fact, the situation is far worse than I had feared.'

'What do you mean?'

'Put it this way,' said Harold. 'We have to get back to London as soon as we can. The king may have to prepare for a civil war.'

Chapter Thirty-two

Oxford, 28 October, AD 1065

Harold stood in the entrance hall of St George's Tower in Oxford, waiting to be summoned. Impatient for the meeting to start, he paced back and fore, knowing that there was no time to lose.

Inside, many important nobles of the Witan were already present, along with several notable bishops who had already taken their seats on either side of the room. At one end were two empty thrones ready for the arrival of the king and queen, and in the centre stood a lectern bearing a bible, reflecting the seriousness of the meeting.

Edward and his queen, Ealdgyth, finally arrived. The king looked ill and was helped from his carriage by two courtiers. But as he was helped inside, Ealdgyth took the opportunity to walk over and talk to her brother.

'Harold,' she said quietly, 'I am relieved you have returned safely. That was very brave of you to head into the bear's den like that.'

'I was at no risk,' said Harold, 'for if nothing else, at least the flag of parley is still recognised in this country.'

'Is it as bad as we have been told?' asked the queen. 'Do they intend to kill us all?'

'The rumours are exaggerated,' said Harold, 'but it is certainly not a good situation and needs settlement urgently.'

'Just remember,' said Ealdgyth, 'whatever happens in there, Tostig is still our brother, and we look after our own.'

'I understand,' said Harold, 'and will do whatever I can to protect him, but these are serious matters, Ealdgyth, and our hands may be tied.'

Ealdgyth looked worried but nodded her understanding.

'How is the king, anyway?' asked Harold. 'He looks ill.'

'He has good and bad days,' said Ealdgyth. 'These past few weeks, he has weakened further, and I worry for him.'

'All the more reason to settle these matters as soon as we can,' said Harold.

Before the queen could answer, one of the courtiers walked over to pass on a message.

'Your grace, the king is ready to go in and has requested your attendance.'

'Of course,' said Ealdgyth, and turned back to Harold. 'I have to go, but remember what I said. We are a family, Harold, and father would expect you to act accordingly.'

For the next ten minutes or so, Harold's mind raced, still trying to work out all the different scenarios that could happen, depending on the Witan's decision. Finally, the doors to the chamber opened, and a herald called him in. He walked into the centre of the room and bowed to the king and queen, now both seated on their ceremonial thrones.

'Harold of Wessex,' said Archbishop Stigand from the side of the royal dais, 'please take your place before the lectern and place your hand on the bible.' Harold did as he was asked before Stigand spoke again. 'Harold of Wessex, do you swear that the testimony you are about to give is the truth before God?'

'I do,' said Harold.

'In that case,' said Stigand, 'let the council begin.'

For the next hour, Harold recounted in detail what had happened in Northampton, much to the growing horror of all present. Everyone listened intensely, none as much as Tostig, and when Harold had finished, he was first to his feet to question his brother.

'Harold,' he said, 'thank you for your testimony. You have proven to all present that this is indeed a crisis that needs immediate attention. Therefore, let it be known that when this council agrees to muster their armies against this threat, I stand ready to take overall command and, if necessary, lay down my life to defend the king.'

Some of the audience murmured in approval, nodding towards each other at the bravery of the young earl. Another noble stood up and added his own view to that of Tostig's.

'I, too, am happy to ride against these traitors,' he said, 'and hereby pledge my men to the king's cause.'

Several more followed until finally, Archbishop Stigand stood up, and the room fell silent.

'My lords,' he said, 'all I have heard so far is a statement of facts and a move towards instant retribution. What I have not heard today are any suggestions to avoid the bloodshed that such a course of action will inevitably cause. Is there nobody in this hall that would prefer a peaceful outcome?'

'What peaceful outcome could there possibly be?' said Tostig, getting to his feet. 'You have heard from my brother exactly what was said at that meeting. Threatening to burn London is a hanging offence in itself! There is no possibility of peace, and I say we march against them now before it is too late.'

'I realise your frustration,' said Stigand, 'but as the leaders of men, it falls to us to explore every avenue before committing so many to die in our name. All I ask is that all views are considered.'

Tostig sneered and looked around the room.

'Look,' he said, his voice echoing, 'there is not a single man supporting such a stance. Go on, ask them yourself, or should I do it for you?' He turned to face the rest of the attendees. 'Gentlemen, you have heard the evidence with your own ears, and while it is overwhelming in its condemnation, the arch-bishop here seeks a peaceful resolution, so let me ask you this: is there any man here who supports that motion?' He looked around as the room remained silent. 'Just to make sure,' he said a few moments later, 'let me ask again. Does anyone here think that there is any possibility of a peaceful resolution?' Again nobody answered, but as he turned back to face the archbishop, a lone voice cut through the silence.

'Aye,' said Harold quietly, 'I do.'

All eyes turned to face the earl, shocked at the interjection.

'*What?*' gasped Tostig. 'You do not have a say in this matter, for you are the main witness, and your views may be clouded.'

'I disagree,' said Stigand from the side, 'in fact, I think quite the opposite. Of all of us, Earl Harold is uniquely placed to make a judgement. I believe it is essential that he gives his views, no matter how controversial they may be.'

'Your grace,' said Tostig, facing the king, 'this is a disgraceful abuse of protocol.'

Edward lifted his hand for silence and looked at Harold. 'You are under no obligation to talk,' he said, 'but if you believe you can make our decision any easier, then you are free to do so. What say you?'

'My testimony has been full and truthful,' said Harold, 'and in light of the facts, it seems there is no other option but to face the rebels across the battlefield. However, there are other matters that this council should also take into consideration, things that you and most in this room may not be aware of.'

King Edward stared at Harold with annoyance.

'If there is more to consider, why was I not informed prior to this meeting?'

'My apologies, your grace. I did seek audience as soon as I returned but was denied by your steward as you were indisposed, having suffered a bout of illness. However, there are things to discuss that could affect the whole country, so if I may continue?'

'I do not like being ill-informed, Earl Harold,' replied the king, 'but these are exceptional circumstances, so please proceed.'

'Thank you, your grace,' said Harold, and turned to face the room. 'My lords,' he said, 'the facts dictate that we should quash this rebellion with every man we can muster, but to do so would mean a civil war between the Godwin earldoms and an alliance between Northumbria and Mercia. The numbers would be evenly matched, and the fighting could go on for years before a resolution is reached. That alone is a good enough reason to seek a peaceful route. However, there is a yet more pressing reason, and I ask you this. If we allow our men to spill the blood of their own countrymen, who do we turn to when the time comes to defend England?'

For a few seconds, there was silence until Tostig once again spoke up.

'This is scaremongering,' he said. 'England is under threat from nobody except those who march on London.'

'Yes, we are,' said Harold. 'In fact, I would say we are facing an even bigger threat than the rebels: the possibility of attack and conquest.'

'From whom?' demanded Tostig, his voice rising in exasperation.

'From William of Normandy,' said Harold, 'and before you dismiss my claim, I swear upon this holy bible that I heard this ambition from the mouth of William himself. He sees himself as the next King of England and waits only for King Edward to die before sailing here to claim the throne.'

'That is ridiculous,' shouted a voice, 'and he should be resisted at all costs.'

'I agree,' said Harold, 'but if our fighting men are decimated by civil war, who will be left to resist?'

Tostig stared at his brother, realising Harold had just gained a huge advantage in the argument. Rebellion from within was one thing, but the threat of conquest by a foreign power was far more serious.

'No,' he said, 'you are lying.'

'Why would I do that?' asked Harold.

'Who knows?' said Tostig. 'But I am beginning to wonder whether you actually support this rebellion.'

'Tostig,' said Harold, 'you know that is not true.'

'Is it not?' asked Tostig, his eyes widening as he identified a fresh argument. 'Not one man on this council was with you at this meeting with Edwin. How do we know that you did not collude with him for personal gain?'

'Tostig,' said Harold, 'I have more than any man could ever want. What could I possibly gain from such an unholy alliance?'

'There is one thing you do not have,' said Tostig, his glare almost manic in its intensity, 'something I know you covet.'

'And that is?'

'The one thing you can never have,' said Tostig, 'the Crown of England.'

For a few moments, the room fell silent at the shocking accusation, and Harold stared at his brother in horror.

'What are you saying?' he growled. 'I covet no such thing. Retract that accusation, Tostig, or I swear I will not be responsible for my actions.'

'It's true, isn't it?' shouted Tostig. 'You have organised this whole rebellion to get rid of me and kill the king before claiming the throne for yourself. It is all clear now.' He turned to face Edward. 'Your grace, don't you see? The answer was before us all the time. You should arrest this man and make me commander of your armies. Only by doing this will you and the throne be protected.'

He looked around the room, noticing that all eyes were upon him, some with anger, some with pity.

'You may doubt me,' he said, 'but I know Harold better than any man here. He is a dangerous and ambitious man.' He turned to face the back of the room. 'Guards, arrest this man and take him away.'

Nobody moved, and Tostig looked around in desperation.

'What's the matter with you?' he shouted. 'Are you all blind? It is all his fault. The loss of my lands, the rebellion, all the unnecessary deaths, it was down to him all this time.'

'Tostig,' started Harold, his tone soothing, 'that is enough.'

'No!' shouted Tostig. 'This is all your fault, and you should be punished.'

Before Harold could answer, King Edward raised his hand for silence.

'Quiet,' he said calmly. 'Your argument shames this place, but an accusation has been made that needs resolution. Earl Harold, you stand accused by a fellow earl of treason before this council. You have the right to respond.'

'What's the point?' shouted Tostig. 'He will only lie.'

'Guards,' shouted the king, losing his patience, 'restrain Earl Tostig until this matter is resolved.'

'What?' said Tostig as two guards walked over to grab his arms. 'You have got this wrong; he is the traitor, arrest him.'

'Earl Harold,' said the king again, 'I am waiting for your answer.'

Harold knew that whatever he said next would only cloud the issue, for the accusation was already in the minds of all the men watching. He looked down at the bible before him and knew there was only one thing he could do. He reached down and placed both hands on the book before looking up to stare at the king.

'Your grace,' he said, 'I know not why my beloved brother has brought these accusations, but I hereby swear upon this holy bible and before the sight of all these good men, my monarch and God himself, that I have not, nor will I ever plot against the throne of this country.'

'That is good enough for me,' said the king. 'Guards, remove Earl Tostig from this council and detain him.'

'*No!*' screamed Tostig as they dragged him out. 'You do not understand. It is he who is the traitor, not I.'

Harold remained facing forward, his eyes closed as he listened to the sounds of his brother being dragged away.

'That was a very unfortunate situation,' said Edward eventually, 'and one that must never be allowed to happen again, but it leaves us no further forward in how to deal with this threat.' He looked around the room, sensing the confusion and upset amongst all present, and knew he had to come to a swift decision. 'We have heard a lot of argument and counter-argument this day,' he continued, 'but the fact remains that we are facing a rebellion from the combined forces of Northumbria and Mercia. This is of real concern and threatens the throne of England. However, to raise an army capable of defeating this threat, I must turn to my remaining earls, all of whom are the sons of Godwin.' He turned to face Harold. 'Earl Harold, before I ask you your final advice, I need to know one thing. If it comes to war, whose battle lines will you occupy?'

'Yours, your grace,' said Harold, 'even unto death.'

'Earl Leofwine,' said Edward, turning to one of Harold's brothers, 'I ask you the same question. With whom will you stand?'

'Your grace,' said Leofwine, 'I stand alongside you and Harold.'

Edward nodded, and all eyes turned to the youngest Godwin brother.

'Earl Gyrth,' said Edward, 'where will your men fight?'

'Under your banner, your grace,' said Gyrth. 'I pledge my life to your command.'

Edward turned back to face Harold.

'So,' he said, 'it seems we can raise the forces necessary to bring this debacle to an end, so my final question goes to you, Earl Harold. Will you lead my army to quash this rebellion?'

Everyone stared at Harold, realising the importance of the occasion. They were but a moment away from civil war. Harold looked around the room and then back at the king. He took a deep breath and finally announced his decision.

'No, your grace,' he said, 'I will not.'

Everyone in the council stared at Harold, shocked to the core at his response. Without the men of Wessex, there would be little chance of defeating the northern alliance. King Edward, in particular, was obviously trying to control his rage, having expected an entirely different answer.

'Earl Harold,' he said eventually, his stare piercing through Harold like the sharpest of knives. 'I do not understand. Just a few heartbeats ago, you committed your life to me and this crown, but now you are going back on that pledge. Please help this house understand your stance, for I can assure you, at the moment, my intention is to march our army northward at the earliest opportunity.'

'Your grace,' said Harold, 'my pledge remains true, for if it comes to war, then I will fight under your banner, but only if you command me to do so. However, for many years you have asked my advice on such things and on this matter, I feel that to fight Mercia and Northumbria is the wrong path to take. Instead, and in the light of the threat from Normandy, we should be building the alliances between the earldoms, not destroying them. Let us carry the olive branch between all those involved and seek a peace that can only make us stronger.'

'Those men have threatened the Crown,' said Edward, 'and need to be punished.'

'Why?' asked Harold. 'All they are doing is standing up against corruption carried out in your name, albeit without your knowledge. If you turn against them now, exactly at the moment when their voice has been heard, then you will only be condoning the acts carried out by my brother. Why not show them the just and thoughtful king I know you to be, and all this can be over within a few days, with not a single drop more blood being spilt. Deny them their voice, and thousands will die irrespective of who commands your armies.'

'That sounds like capitulation to me,' said Edward.

'To me, it sounds like kingship, your grace.'

Edward fell quiet but still stared at Harold, knowing he had been cleverly manoeuvred into a corner.

'So,' he said eventually, 'tell me what you think we should do.'

'Your grace,' said Harold, 'in reality, their demands are quite small, and with the removal of Tostig from this council, I suspect they have already been half-met. There are three requirements in all. The first is that you replace Tostig with Morcar of Mercia as the new Earl of Northumbria. The second is that the severe tax imposition across Northumbria is returned to its former level, and the last is that everyone involved in the uprising will not be punished. If you can meet those demands, then the problem will disappear like the morning mist, and we can concentrate on the threat from Normandy.'

'So, you think that I should cave in to all their demands?'

'I think that you will be demonstrating that nobody in this country, not even an earl, can be allowed to be the cause of such insurrection. These people are sheep, my lord, not wolves, and will gladly return home given the opportunity.'

'And what of your brother?' asked the king. 'What should we do with him?'

Harold looked over towards his sister sitting at the side of the king. Her face looked sad, and he could see that she was struggling not to cry. Tostig and Ealdgyth had been particularly close, and Harold knew that she was hurting. As he watched, her lips silently formed two words.

'Help him.'

Harold swallowed hard and turned to face the king.

'Your grace,' he said, 'Tostig is my brother, and that creates unbreakable blood alliances, but I would be a hypocrite if I asked something of you that I am not prepared to do myself. It is a sacrifice for my family and me, but my recommendation is that Tostig Godwinson is immediately deposed from the position of Earl of Northumbria and exiled for his role in causing the uprising against you and the Crown.'

Everyone gasped in astonishment, shocked to the core at the severity of the punishment. They all turned to look at the king, whose face was red with anger. Slowly Edward got to his feet and waited as the room fell silent.

'This day will go down as a crucial moment in history,' he said, 'for today we all stand witness to a king who was ruled by his people. However, let it not be said that I put myself before my country, so to all you good men here today, I say this.' He paused and stared at Harold. 'I hereby accept your recommendations in full. This audience is over.'

As the room burst into clamour and activity, King Edward left the meeting, closely followed by his queen and courtiers. Back in the hall, the noise was deafening as men from both sides celebrated or criticised the outcome. Harold just stayed where he was, staring at the two empty thrones.

'Harold,' said a voice, and he turned to see Archbishop Stigand standing close behind him.

'Your grace,' said Harold, 'I hesitate to ask your opinion on these matters.'

'Yet I will give it anyway,' said Stigand. 'It was a brave move to defy the king, and the day may come that you will regret humiliating him so, but for what it is worth, I agree with what you did. You just saved the lives of thousands of men.'

'Perhaps,' said Harold, 'but now the task is done, I am unsure how to proceed.'

'Well,' said Stigand, 'first of all, you need to convey the good news to Northumbria, and after that, I would have thought that there is only one direction to take.'

'And that is?'

'To build alliances,' said Stigand. 'For if you are correct, and the day is coming that we need to face William of Normandy, then we have to be ready, and that task, Earl Harold, falls directly at your feet.'

Chapter Thirty-three

Northumbria, November, AD 1065

Harold and his huscarls sat at a table in a roadside tavern deep in the heart of Northumbria. It had been over a week since the meeting in Oxford, but as Edward had suffered another bout of illness just after the council, it had taken several days before he was well enough to sign the edicts that Harold needed to placate the rebels. Now, at last, Harold was in possession of the documents, and he was on his way to stop the rebellion and agree the alliances the country so desperately needed.

Opposite him sat Owen, who stared at the earl with growing concern. The success of Harold's statesmanship at the meeting in Oxford had paved the way to save many lives, but it seemed the earl was in a sombre mood, his mind elsewhere.

'You are very quiet, my lord,' said Owen eventually, 'and your tankard is still half full. What ails you?'

'My mind spins like a cart's wheel,' said Harold, 'and sleep is hard to find these past few days.'

'I suspect that once this meeting with the rebels has concluded,' replied Owen, 'perhaps your thoughts will be at greater ease.'

'I do not know,' said Harold. 'Recently, there is no respite from the worry. First, it was my time in Normandy, then the rebellion; now it is the health of the king. It is just one thing after the other, and if the king does not get well, then we may have an invasion to face. On top of all that, there is still the fate of Wulfnorth to worry about. There is just no respite, it seems.'

'You can only deal with one thing at a time,' said Owen, 'but I agree the current events are indeed burdensome. What you need is a place to relax and to forget your worries for a few days.'

'Ha, if only that was possible,' said Harold.

'I think it is.'

'In what way?'

'You do realise that Alditha's lands are only a few leagues from here?' said Owen. 'A good horse could get a man there within a few hours if the rider was so inclined.'

Harold stared at Owen. He had spent many nights with Alditha before going to Normandy but had not seen her since he had returned, having been so busy with the matters of state. To be welcomed into her arms again would certainly be a distraction.

'I cannot,' he said eventually. 'This business will not wait.'

'Why not?' asked Owen. 'We have already been delayed by the king's illness, so what is a day or so more? Edwin and Morcar know that a response is on its way, so are highly unlikely to march south just yet, and even if they do, our spies will make sure we know the moment they decide to mobilise their army.'

Harold fell quiet, considering the option. Eventually, he nodded in agreement.

'You are right,' he said. 'A day or so either way will make no difference, and I suspect there will be little time for such things in the weeks ahead.'

'In that case,' said Owen, 'there is no time to lose. You finish your drink, and I'll get someone to saddle a horse. The men and I will wait here until you return, and if anyone asks where you are, I will tell them you had to return to Oxford to pick up another document.'

'So be it,' said Harold. 'Thank you, my friend.'

Owen stared at Harold in mild surprise.

'Why do you stare like that?' asked Harold eventually.

'You just called me friend,' said Owen. 'And that is the first time since you held a knife to my throat in Bosham.'

'Is it?' asked Harold. 'If that is true, then I have been remiss. For that is what you have become to me, Owen, a true and loyal friend.' He lifted his tankard and, watched by Owen, drained the last of the contents. 'Two days,' said Harold, banging his empty tankard onto the table, 'and then our focus turns to more serious matters. Agreed?'

'Agreed,' said Owen, and as Harold headed to his rented room to get his cloak, Owen left the tavern to head for the stables.

—

Several hours later, at her home further east, Alditha felt someone shaking her gently in her bed.

'My lady,' said a voice quietly, 'wake up.'

Alditha opened her eyes and saw Elspeth standing beside her bed in the light of a candle.

'Elspeth,' said Alditha, 'what is it?'

'My lady, I am sorry to wake you, but you have a visitor.'

'A visitor?' said Alditha. 'But it is not yet dawn. Who comes calling in the dead of night?'

'My lady,' said Elspeth, 'it is Earl Harold of Wessex. He said he needs to see you urgently.'

Alditha's heart missed a beat. She had not seen the earl for a long time, and she thought that perhaps his time in Normandy had weakened his feelings for her.

'Does he have his men with him?' she asked.

'No, my lady. He is alone.'

Alditha thought quickly. If he was on his own, it could only mean that this was a personal visit and not one of courtly business. She pulled back the covers and swung her legs out of bed before heading over to a mirror and picking up a brush from a table.

'I take it you intend to see him?' asked Elspeth, with a knowing smile.

'Of course,' said Alditha, 'why would I not? He is an important man.'

'It would seem so,' mused Elspeth. 'Will you be seeing him in the hall or...' She left the question unfinished as her mistress turned to face her. Alditha's eyes sparkled with excitement, and her face was red from the exertions of the hard brushing she had inflicted on her own hair.

'Do I look fair?' asked Alditha.

'You look beautiful,' said Elspeth. 'There is a clean night-gown and shawl hanging on the door, so I suggest you get changed. In the meantime, I will entertain the earl with a warmed wine and keep him talking to give you more time. Would that suit?'

'Indeed it would,' said Alditha, 'but not too long, lest he changes his mind.'

'Something tells me that nothing you or I say or do will make him change his mind, my lady. Now you get ready and leave the rest to me.'

The servant left the room, leaving Alditha alone. She hadn't seen her mistress so giddy for a long time, and it made her heart sing to see her so happy.

-

Three days later, Harold and Owen led their men through a tented camp set up in the fields before a country manor house. Again they were stared at by man and woman alike, though this time with less menace, as the word of a potential truce had spread like wildfire throughout the rebel army.

'Good luck, your grace,' shouted a lone voice as they neared the house, for though he was amongst potential adversaries, nobody wanted a war.

Moments later, Harold and Owen entered the manor, leaving their horses with their men outside, and were shown through to an audience chamber where a dozen men stood in small groups near to a roaring fire. As they entered, all eyes turned to watch them approach.

'Earl Harold,' said one of the men walking forward, 'welcome. We have been waiting for you.'

'Earl Edwin,' said Harold, grabbing his fellow earl's proffered arm, 'my apologies for the lateness; I had some other business to attend en route.'

'So I understand,' said Edwin, staring into Harold's eyes. 'Some matters are more important than the avoidance of war, are they not?'

'What matters could possibly outweigh the importance of this meeting?' asked Edwin's brother, walking over to join them.

For a few moments there was an awkward silence, and Harold's gaze did not leave that of Edwin's as he wondered if he already knew he had just come back from his sister's house. If he did, this meeting could get seriously awkward. He turned to face Edwin's brother.

'Morcar of Mercia,' he said, 'we meet again. Perhaps talk of such matters is for a different time, but for now, let us just thank God that he has guided our footsteps here this day, and with goodwill on all sides, the lives of countless men may be saved.'

'That remains to be seen,' said Edwin. 'Do you require refreshment?'

'Thank you but no,' said Harold. 'We would like to conclude our business here and to report back to the king as soon as possible.'

'Of course,' said Edwin. 'I understand he suffers ill health?'

'Indeed he does,' said Harold.

'Then send him our best wishes,' said Edwin, before looking around the room at the rest of his nobles. 'So,' he said, returning his attention to Harold. 'What news do you have for us?'

'If I recall correctly,' said Harold, 'your demands are as follows. The first is that the king removes Tostig as the Earl of Northumbria and replaces him with your brother, Morcar of Mercia. Is that correct?'

'It is,' said Edwin.

'The second demand is that all those involved in the uprising against the king so far are granted amnesty with immediate effect.'

'Again, you are correct,' said Edwin, as the men in the room looked on in silence.

'And the last demand is that all excess taxes demanded in Northumbria, over and above those that would have been normally expected prior to the arrival of Tostig, are returned immediately, to be redistributed by the new earl. In return, you stated that if all three requirements were met in full, then you would all return whence you came and disband all armies mustered to threaten the Crown. Is that correct?'

'Our demands have not changed,' said Edwin, 'so what is the king's answer?'

Harold turned to Owen, who gave him a satchel containing the signed documents. Delving inside, he retrieved the two rolled documents, each secured with the king's seal.

'These documents,' continued Harold, 'contain the king's response. The first is in regard to your demands and states that he agrees to your requirements in full.'

A huge cheer erupted in the room, but Edwin stayed quiet, knowing there was more to come.

'And the second document?' he said when the room fell quiet again.

'The second document,' said Harold, 'is for you to sign. In it, there is a pledge written on behalf of Mercia and Northumbria stating that in the event of a summons to war on behalf of the king, against any foe, domestic or foreign, that you will rally to his aid, as did your father before you.'

Again the room fell quiet, and Edwin looked across to his brother for a moment. Seeing nothing but excitement in Morcar's eyes at potentially becoming the next Earl of Northumbria, he knew there would be no argument from him. He turned back to Harold.

'This current unpleasantness aside,' he said, 'our family has always been loyal to Edward and see no reason for that to change. If the details on both documents match that which you have just stated, then I see no reason why there cannot be peace in our lands.' He held out his arm, and as Harold grabbed his wrist in friendship, the room erupted again.

'Actually,' shouted Harold over the din, 'I think I will have that drink.'

'Make that two,' shouted Owen at his side, 'for this is a great day and deserves celebration.'

'Aye,' said Edwin, 'that it does, Owen of Hereford, that it does.'

Part Five

Chapter Thirty-four

Harold walked through the corridors to the main chamber of the palace alongside the other four earls of England, each talking quietly amongst themselves as they made their way to the annual Christmas court.

Since he had conveyed Edward's decision to the rebels in Northumbria weeks earlier, the uprising had dispersed, and Morcar of Mercia had been confirmed as the new Earl of Northumbria. Tostig, following his outburst at the council of Oxford, had been declared an outlaw and had fled across the sea to Flanders, along with his family and many of his men. Now, as suspicion and the situation eased, things were beginning to return to some sort of normality.

Many of the other prominent nobles from across the country were also in attendance, as well as all the bishops and arch-bishops, not just because the annual gathering was so important, but because news had started to filter through that Edward had once again taken to his sickbed and the physicians held little hope of survival.

With the possibility of the death of the king and a potentially messy succession looming, everyone in power wanted to be a part of any process that selected the next king of England. The mood was sombre as they filed into the hall and took their places.

For the next few hours, they discussed matters of state before Archbishop Stigand finally turned to the subject that was preying on everybody's mind.

'My lords,' he said, 'I now turn to the terrible news about King Edward. As most of you are aware, his health deteriorates by the day, and I am told that there is very little chance of recovery. Obviously, we are all devastated by the struggle of such a great monarch, but we have to face reality and discuss the succession.'

'The king is still alive,' said a voice. 'Let us at least give him the courtesy of letting him die before we replace him on the throne.'

'I accept your concerns,' said Stigand, 'and there will be no coronation or even an agreement before that fateful day, but we need to discuss the options, so we all have time to consider before a decision has to be made.'

A murmur of approval rippled around the room.

'The king already has an heir,' said another voice, 'Edgar Ætheling. What is there to discuss?'

'Ordinarily, I would agree,' said Stigand, 'but the unfortunate fact remains that there is another claimant, William of Normandy.'

'Your grace,' said Earl Leofwine, 'I do not think there is one man in this room that supports William's claim.'

'I believe that is correct,' said Stigand, 'but it is only right that we give any supporters a chance to voice their opinion.' He turned to face the hall. 'It is probably easier to ask for a show of hands. Is there any man present who knows of a good reason why we should consider William of Normandy as the next king of England?'

He looked around the room, but not one man stirred.

'In that case,' said Stigand, 'it makes our decision much easier. As Edgar Ætheling is the nominated heir, we will take his name to the Witan upon the death of the king.'

'I have a question,' said Earl Leofwine. 'The boy is young, and some say, not yet ready for kingship. With the threat of the Normans hanging over us like a storm cloud, I wonder if he may not be quite ready to lead us into war.'

'The boy is indeed young,' said one of the nobles, 'but his veins are filled with royal blood. We are in no position to deny him what is his by right.'

'There was no suggestion of denying him the throne,' said Leofwine, 'only that perhaps an alliance of stronger men should take control of any attempt by William to impose his claim upon us. Once England is secured, he can be elevated to the throne.'

A murmur of concern rippled around the room. The problem was obvious, but to immediately curtail the powers of a newly crowned king would only create diversion and argument at a time when unity was crucial.

'And who would lead this alliance?' laughed another noble. 'You? For I will tell you this right now: my pledge is to whosoever wears that crown, not the privileged son of Godwin. If Edgar is crowned king, as he should be, then it is to him that we will look for guidance, irrespective of age. We are in no position to deny him that God-given right.'

Again the noise in the room rose with men on both sides of the argument trying to get their opinions heard. Finally, Archbishop Stigand banged on the wooden floor repeatedly with his staff for silence until the noise died away.

'This chaos is unseemly,' he said, 'for we are doing God's work, but the passion exhibited here today is exactly the reason why it was important to have this conversation. We have uncovered some concerns, and everyone here will have a voice, but with the king lying ill not far from here, today is not the time for argument or final decisions. I am now going to close this court on behalf of the king, but I invite you all to leave this room with these concerns at the forefront of your mind. We are all here for a few days, so take the opportunity to discuss everything between yourselves in a calm and thoughtful manner while still keeping the health of the king in your prayers. With God's will, he may make a full recovery, but if not, we will need to move quickly. My lords, this court is concluded.'

Stigand turned away, and as the rest of the participants rose to leave the chamber, Harold walked over to speak to him.

'Your grace,' said Harold, 'do you have a moment?'

'For you, always,' said Stigand. 'Let us go to my rooms.'

—

Fifteen minutes later, Harold stood at a window, looking out over London as two of the servants removed Stigand's ceremonial clothes before leaving the room.

'Wine?' asked Stigand, walking over to a table.

'Not for me,' said Harold, 'thank you.'

'So,' said Stigand, filling up a beautiful goblet, 'what concerns you?'

'I have a question,' said Harold, 'about Edgar Ætheling.'

'Why did you not voice it at the court?'

'Because to do so would have caused even more argument, and that is the last thing we need.'

'I agree,' said the archbishop. 'What is your question?'

'It is more of a request,' said Harold. 'The Ætheling is rarely seen, so none of us really know his true nature. Is it possible that I could have an audience with him?'

'To what end?'

'Just to see what he is like,' said Harold. 'For all we know, he could be well worthy of the crown and make a great leader, but without meeting him properly, how are we to make a decision?'

'He will be presented to the Witan upon Edward's death,' said Stigand.

'Aye, but by then, it may be too late.'

'Surely you have met him before?'

'I have,' said Harold, 'but on each occasion, he rarely talked, and the king often spoke for him. It was as if Edward was keen to keep the boy's personality hidden. Just an hour, that's all I ask.'

'I see no problem with that,' said Stigand. 'I will see what I can do.'

The following morning, Stigand met Harold and led him along one of the corridors. Finally, he stopped before a door and turned to the earl.

'We have less than an hour,' he said, 'but if truth be told, I fail to see what you are going to gain from this.'

'We will see,' said Harold and both men walked into the room to see Edgar Ætheling sat upon an ornate chair, looking down upon two servants kneeling on the floor before him.

'Ah, Archbishop Stigand,' said Edgar, looking up, 'there you are. What do you think of my throne? Of course, when I am king, it will be far more elegant, made of gold and covered with precious stones. Could you arrange that for me, please? But you will have to hurry, for Edward is dying, and I need to look my best.'

'Your grace,' said Stigand, 'I believe you have met Earl Harold.'

The boy looked at Harold as if seeing him for the first time.

'Of course,' he said, 'this is the man responsible for bringing us to England. At first, I was angry, but now I am happy for I am going to be a king. Isn't that so, Archbishop Stigand?'

'Yes, your grace,' said Stigand with a sigh.

Harold frowned. The boy's manner was strange, and he talked very fast, his strong accent making it difficult to understand much of what he said.

'Look,' said the boy, looking down at the kneeling men, 'I am already making my servants practise. It is important that on the day, everyone knows exactly what to do. Isn't that so, Archbishop Stigand?'

'Your grace,' said Stigand, 'Earl Harold is here to discuss some important matters with you. Perhaps we could dismiss the servants for a little while.'

'Of course,' said Edgar, his face becoming far more serious. He turned to the servants. 'Begone,' he said, 'and tell the kitchens that I want swan at my next meal. Two of them.'

'Yes, your grace,' said the servants, and hurried from the room.

Edgar turned back to face Harold and Stigand.

'So, what can I do for you?'

'Your grace,' said Harold, glancing at Stigand before continuing. 'As you know, the king is unwell, and it may soon fall to you to rule this country.'

'Yes,' said Edgar, 'and I want the biggest coronation that has ever been seen. Every noble in the land needs to be present on pain of— I don't know, death or something. And I want gifts, each one made of silver and gold, mainly gold.'

'Your grace,' interrupted Harold, 'we can discuss your coronation a different time, for there is a far more serious situation that needs your attention.'

'Good,' said Edgar, leaning forward. 'I like solving problems. What is it?'

'Your grace,' said Harold, 'there is a high probability that in the very near future, we may have to fight men who want to steal the crown from your head. How do you suggest we deal with that?'

'Ha,' said Edgar, sitting back in his chair. 'You speak of William the Bastard. I know of him, but worry not, Earl Harold, for I will look after you.'

'Um… how?' asked Harold, growing concerned at the boy's manner.

'By fighting William man to man,' said Edgar. 'We will meet at dawn, stripped to the waist, and fight until he lies dead upon England's soil. All my people will gather around to see me beat him.'

'Your grace,' said Harold, 'is that wise? The man is a seasoned soldier.'

'As am I,' said Edgar.

'Have you ever fought another man?' asked Harold.

'Of course I have. I receive lessons every morning in the armoury, and my tutor says I am highly skilled. I will fight this

William of Normandy and prove to all how great a king I will be.'

Harold's heart sank, and he knew it was pointless remaining any longer.

'Is there anything else?' asked Stigand.

'No,' said Harold, 'I am done. Let's get out of here.' Both men bowed and turned to leave the room.

'Thank you for coming to pay homage,' shouted Edgar as they walked down the corridor. 'Let me know when the preparations for my coronation are complete.'

The two men walked out into the courtyard and away from the main building.

'Well,' said Stigand, 'what do you think?'

'I think the boy is a complete imbecile,' said Harold, 'and there is no way he can ever sit upon the throne of England.'

'Sadly,' said Stigand, 'I agree. Edgar's lineage makes him the natural heir, but despite my initial enthusiasm as to his station, my support was wrong. I have since had chance to learn the true nature of the boy and now realise he is far from suitable. We have to do something.'

'Like what? You saw the reaction when Leofwine suggested sharing responsibility across the earldoms – it was dismissed out of hand. The country needs a strong king behind whom we can all rally. Only then do we stand even the slightest chance against William.'

'Edward left no stone unturned,' said Stigand. 'Edgar is the last of the royal bloodline.'

'Then we have to look elsewhere,' said Harold, 'and if that means elevating someone to the throne, then so be it. There must be a suitable candidate, but I need time to think.'

'Actually,' said Stigand, 'waste not a minute longer, because I know exactly the man we need.'

'And who may that be?' asked Harold.

'I'm looking at him,' said Stigand. 'Harold Godwinson, you should be the next King of England.'

Chapter Thirty-five

The following day, Harold and Archbishop Stigand met again, though this time in the Godwinson residence in Southwark.

Harold had suffered a sleepless night, with Stigand's shocking suggestion from the previous day going round and round his mind relentlessly. At first, he had dismissed the idea out of hand, but now, less than twenty-four hours later, his view was changing, and he had sent a message to Stigand to meet him to discuss the possibility further. Now, the archbishop sat in a chair, staring at Harold as he paced back and fore like a caged animal.

'Harold,' he said eventually, 'you are obviously vexed. Please sit so we can discuss this further.'

'I am waiting for someone,' replied Harold, and was about to explain, when the door opened, and Gytha Thorkelsdóttir entered the room.

'Mother,' he said with a smile, 'thank you for attending. Please have a seat.'

Gytha nodded and joined Archbishop Stigand at the table.

'I have invited my mother to join us in this discussion,' said Harold, 'as she is probably wiser than most men, and through her, I will draw on the wisdom of my father.'

'The presence of Gytha Thorkelsdóttir needs no explanation,' said Stigand with a smile, 'and will always be welcomed, no matter what the circumstances.'

'Thank you, your grace,' said Gytha. 'Harold has explained your proposal to me, and I have to say that while I am honoured that my son is considered in this way, it does carry a huge amount of risk.'

'It does,' said the archbishop, 'but not as great as the loss of England to the Normans.'

'The thing is,' said Harold, voicing his concerns, 'if I were to agree to this, everyone would think that Tostig was right all along and that I have always had designs on the throne, a situation that is simply not true.'

'I agree,' said Stigand. 'If we were just to announce it without warning, then it would look bad, but if we garner allies behind closed doors, explaining to them exactly why there is no other option, then we can grow enough support to shout down the naysayers.'

'But why me?' asked Harold.

'Because you are the only man who can do it,' said Stigand. 'You have served as the king's trusted right-hand man for many years, you are known for both your prowess in battle and for your diplomacy, and you alone have seen how William of Normandy operates.'

'Yet all of these traits can serve a different king,' said Gytha.

'Then whom do you suggest?' asked Stigand. 'With the greatest of respect, Earls Gyrth and Leofwine are just not strong enough. Earl Morcar is new to his position, and Earl Edwin is not trusted by the majority of the Witan, especially after supporting the rebels against the king.' He turned to face Harold. 'You saw the Ætheling for yourself. He is not capable of commanding a kitchen, let alone a country, so no matter what it takes, we have to find a way.'

Harold turned to stare at the archbishop, knowing he was right. He walked over and joined them at the table.

'Let us just imagine, for a moment, that I said yes,' he said. 'Who can we rely on to give their support?'

'Well, first of all,' said Stigand, 'I expect you can count on the queen and your brothers. At least Gyrth and Leofwine, anyway. Obviously Tostig is out of the question. I also believe you will have the support of most of the nobles in the south, especially in the light of the threat from William.'

'What about Earls Morcar and Edwin? For without their support, we would probably be in the same position we faced a few weeks ago.'

'They may be more difficult to persuade,' said Stigand, 'but I do not believe they are out of reach. If we can come up with some arrangement to tie them in, it will create a formidable argument, one that few nobles would dare to challenge.'

'So that just leaves the clergy,' said Gytha. 'Without their blessing and recognition, the whole thing is dead in the water.'

'Leave the clergy to me,' said Stigand. 'All I need is your son's agreement, and I will start this very day.'

'Edward is not dead yet,' said Harold.

'No, he is not,' said Stigand, 'but every man of note is still in Westminster for the Christmas court. If we seize the moment, we can rally as many of them as we can and present the case at the final sitting in a few days' time. After that, they will return to their lands all across the country. There is no time to lose, Harold; we need to strike while the iron is hot.'

Harold got to his feet and walked over to the window. 'I need more time,' he said eventually.

'There is no more time,' said Stigand, getting to his feet. 'You saw that boy with your own eyes and know he can never be crowned king. It is now or never, Harold. Either seize this moment and fulfil your destiny, or stand down and let others rip this country apart. The choice is yours, but it has to be made now.'

Harold stared at the archbishop. The decision was huge, and if he failed to secure enough support, he knew he would be deposed and exiled immediately, or worse. For a few moments, he thought of the differences between Edgar Ætheling and William of Normandy, a chasm almost too huge to grasp. One was an inexperienced child with no knowledge of leadership, while the other was a feared warrior with an army of thousands waiting to sail across the channel. The reality was frightening, and the more Harold thought, the more he realised there was only one thing he could do. He looked over at his mother, wondering what his father would do.

'What say you, mother?' he asked. 'For if I was to agree to this plan, our family would be forever changed, especially if the Witan vote against the idea.'

'I have no doubt you are more than capable of succeeding in the role,' said Gytha, 'but I do have one question that has yet to be resolved.'

'And that is?'

'The fate of your brother. Wulfnorth is still in William's custody, and while he may be safe for the time being, I fear that once you broke cover and revealed that you had not only broken your promise to the duke but now planned to oppose him, then that situation could change.'

Harold realised she was right. Amidst all the argument and counter-argument, he had forgotten about Wulfnorth, and there was no doubt that ploughing forward with Stigand's plan meant his brother's life would be at risk. He turned to the archbishop for comment.

'Lady Gytha,' said Stigand eventually. 'Your concerns are valid, and I wish I had the answers you want to hear. Alas, I do not and can only suggest that you trust in God's grace to do what is right. However, what I will say is this. As hard as it sounds, we have to face the fact that the fate of an entire country lies in our hands and that the needs of the many have to outweigh the needs of the few. England is at risk, and this has to be addressed. What I am proposing is indeed dangerous, but I honestly believe that Harold is the man to save our country, and if that means Wulfnorth remains in custody or worse, then alas, it is a price we have to pay.'

Gytha stared at the archbishop. She hadn't seen her youngest son for years but knew that some things in life had to take precedence, and the life of one child fell short of the fate of a country. Finally, she sighed, and though there was a tangible pain in her heart, she turned to Harold and nodded.

As soon as Harold saw the look in her eyes, he knew what he had to do and turned to face the archbishop.

'I take no personal pleasure in this, your grace,' he said, 'but I know you are correct, and if England is to survive the threat of William, then someone has to step up and be counted.'

'So you will do it?' asked Stigand.

'Aye,' said Harold, 'if I have the support of the council, then for the sake of our people and the future of our country, I, Harold Godwinson, will sit upon the throne of England.'

—

For the next few days, Stigand and Harold worked furiously in the shadows, cornering nobles wherever they could to explain their concerns about Edgar Ætheling and the risk from William. One by one, their support grew, and by the time the day came for the last meeting of the Christmas court, they were confident of at least half the votes needed if it came to a poll.

Once again, the nobles of England filed into the chamber, with most knowing that the future of England could be decided in the next few hours.

Harold was already inside, knowing that it would be the most important day of his life. He sat in silence, staring at the empty throne at the end of the room.

Outside, Archbishop Stigand waited nervously. The last few days had gone well, but he had hoped for more and knew the result could fall either way. Most of the clergy were on board, though some intended to abstain while others had voiced opposition. It was too close to call, but he knew that he had one more throw of the dice to swing the result. If he could swing earls Edwin and Morcar to his way of thinking, then the result would be a foregone conclusion, but he knew it was going to be a difficult conversation. A few minutes later, the brothers arrived and looked over at Stigand.

'Archbishop,' said Edwin as he removed his riding gloves, 'why are you not inside?'

'Because I wanted to speak to you,' said Stigand, 'both of you.'

'What is there to discuss?' asked Morcar, removing his cloak. 'We have already made our decision.'

'And can you share that decision with me?' asked Stigand.

'You will find out soon enough,' said Edwin. 'Shall we go inside?'

'Wait,' said Stigand. 'I appreciate we have discussed this over and over again, but there is one more thing to consider before the final decision is made.'

'And that is?'

Stigand stepped to one side and indicated an open door behind him.

'Let's go in here, it is far more private.'

'The council is already assembling, Archbishop,' said Morcar. 'We should not keep them waiting.'

'This day is bigger than all of us,' said Stigand. 'Let them wait.' He turned away and headed into the side room, followed by the two earls. Morcar shut the door behind them and turned to face Stigand.

'So,' he said, 'what new offer do you have to tempt us?'

'You know as well as I,' said Stigand, 'that the appointment of Harold as king is the only thing that can save this country if it comes to war. You are both good men, and your father was close to Harold. Your sister still is.'

'The fact that Harold beds Alditha does not add weight to your argument,' said Edwin, 'and do not forget that it was his campaign in Wales that caused Gruffydd's men to turn against him. Harold made Alditha a widow.'

'Perhaps so,' said Stigand, 'but it was also his diplomacy that delivered Northumbria into Morcar's hands.'

'Only when faced with an overwhelming army,' said Morcar. 'He had no other choice.'

'Oh, he had a choice,' said Stigand, 'and Edward himself favoured marching against you both with no delay. It was Harold that fought for a compromise, and he is the reason you are both here now.'

'What is your point, Stigand?' asked Edwin. 'Where are you going with this?'

'What if I was to say that there is a way to unite Mercia and Wessex together under one banner as well as giving you, Morcar, a guarantee that, if and when Harold becomes king, he will never see fit to restore Tostig to power?'

'I see no such route,' said Edwin, 'but I am interested. Go on.'

Archbishop Stigand took a deep breath. What he was about to propose was unethical and would cause hurt amongst those he loved the most, but England was at stake, and he knew it was a risk he had to take.

'You had better sit down,' he said eventually, 'this may take a while.'

Half an hour later, the two earls took their seats in the chamber as Archbishop Stigand stood before the empty throne to start the meeting. The mood was sombre yet intense, for everyone knew what was at stake. Harold Godwinson sat amongst them yet took little part in the debate, save to explain yet again the threat from William. Finally, when all the talking was done, Stigand once more stood up to address the court.

'My lords,' he said, 'it has been a long few days, and I know you are keen to get back to your homes, but we owe it to the king and to our own consciences to make a decision today, and we have an absolute duty to get it right. To that end, we will now adjourn to consider everything that has been said and reconvene at the sound of two bells. Then, we will decide the future of England.' He banged his mace on the floor, bringing to an end the session, and watched as everyone walked out, most deep in conversation.

'Earl Harold,' said Stigand as he passed, 'please wait. We have something we need to discuss.'

Both men waited until the chamber was empty before Harold turned to the archbishop.

'I feel the argument is getting away from us,' said Harold.

'It is not the argument that counts,' said Stigand, 'but the final vote.'

'It's the same thing,' said Harold. 'Earl Edwin was particularly scathing, and whatever direction he takes, Morcar will follow.'

'I agree,' said Stigand, 'we need their votes, and to that end, I have a suggestion that you may not agree with, but it is the only way to bring this to a conclusion.'

'What suggestion?' asked Harold.

'Harold,' said Stigand, 'you have to look at this through the eyes of Edwin and Morcar. Not only does the House of Godwin control most of England, but it also wields influence through the queen. From their perspective, if you become king, then it grants your house almost total power, and they fear for their future.'

'I am not interested in deposing Edwin or Morcar,' said Harold, 'quite the opposite. I need the strength of Mercia and Northumbria to fight at my side. If anything, we need to be closer, not arguing like children.'

'I agree,' said Stigand. 'I have an idea to do exactly that. There is a way to ally Wessex with Mercia permanently.'

'And how is that?' asked Harold.

'Through marriage,' said Stigand. 'If someone of import-ance from Mercia was to marry someone of importance from Wessex, the ties would be binding, and with Edwin on board, we can also count on Morcar's support.'

'I agree,' said Harold, 'but do you think that I have not already explored that option? Edwin is already married, as indeed is Morcar. There are no suitable candidates.'

'Yes, there is,' said Stigand, 'their sister.'

'Alditha?'

'Yes,' said Stigand. 'She has been widowed long enough and should be married. Her brothers have agreed and have said that if the marriage goes ahead, then we will have their support.'

'It matters not what the brothers say,' said Harold, 'I know Alditha well, and she is a stubborn woman with her own mind. There is no way she will marry just any man for the sake of convenience.'

'So I have been told,' said Stigand, 'but luckily, there is one man whom Edwin informs me that she is quite taken with, and he is sure she would agree to the union with little argument.'

'I know of no such man,' said Harold, 'so tell me, who is he?'

Stigand paused and stared at the earl.

'Remember, Earl Harold,' he said eventually, 'the future of England is at risk. If we want to carry this day, then it is *you* who has to marry Alditha.'

'What are you saying?' gasped Harold eventually. 'You know that is impossible. I am married to Edyth Swanneck, and if you think I am going to divorce her just to make an alliance with Mercia, then you are sorely wrong.'

'Nobody expects you to leave your wife,' said Stigand, 'and besides, you cannot seek a divorce if you are not married in the first place.'

Harold stared at Stigand as realisation dawned upon him. He and Edyth Swanneck were only married in the Danish custom of handfast, and the union had never been blessed in a church of God.

'No,' he said, 'I will not do it.'

'Listen to me,' said Stigand, 'it is a marriage of convenience only. Once the ceremony is over, the decision as to where you live or how often you see Edyth is yours, but the fact that the houses will be united clears so many obstacles out of the way. All you need to do is marry Alditha, consummate the marriage and then go about your life as usual.'

'And what do you think the mother of my children will say about this?' asked Harold. 'It will surely break her heart.'

'Harold,' said Stigand, 'it is common knowledge that you often share Alditha's bed, so do not claim the moral high ground. Without the support of Mercia and Northumbria, this proposal falls apart. I need you to do this. *England* needs you to do this.'

Harold stared at the bishop. The argument made sense, but he knew that if he agreed, despite Stigand's assurances that life could be the same as before, that was not true, for he would be king, and Alditha would be his queen. It was an impossible decision to make.

–

Two hours later, the court reconvened with Stigand once more presiding. Everyone fell silent, and he cleared his throat.

'My lords,' he said, 'the time for talking is over, so we will get straight to the point.' He reached out his hand, and one of the courtiers handed him a parchment.

'I have here,' he continued, 'the results of the vote. At the moment, the numbers are equal, but some of the earls have yet to decide. As he is an interested party, Harold will not cast a vote, so in the event of a tie, the status quo will remain, and Edgar Ætheling will become the new king.' He turned to face one side of the chamber. 'Earl Leofwine,' he said, 'what is your vote?'

Leofwine got to his feet. 'Your grace,' he said, 'we vote in favour of Harold becoming king.'

Stigand nodded and turned to Harold's other brother. 'Earl Gyrth, where do you stand on this matter?'

'Your grace,' said Gyrth getting to his feet. 'I think our country will only survive with Harold on the throne. I stand with my brother.'

Stigand turned and faced the opposite side of the room. Only Earls Edwin and Morcar remained, and everything depended on them. Since speaking to Harold an hour earlier, he had briefed the two earls about the outcome without receiving any response. Now, like all the others in the room, he had no idea which way they would vote.

'Earl Morcar,' he said, 'how speaks Northumbria?'

Morcar got to his feet. 'Your grace,' he said, 'there are many things to consider, and as I am already trying to undo the mess made by one Godwin brother in Northumbria, I am tempted to vote against the proposal. However, I agree that the Ætheling is not ready to claim the throne, so consequently, I cede my vote to a man who knows much more about such things than I: my own brother, Earl Edwin of Mercia. How he votes, then so shall I.'

He sat down as the court burst into conversation. It was an unprecedented decision, but one which had been highly anticipated.

Stigand turned to face Edwin and waited as the silence fell again. Edwin got to his feet, knowing that every man in the chamber was staring at him. The burden of responsibility weighed upon him like a sack of lead, for he knew that the next words that came out of his mouth would decide the future of England. However, the conversation he had shared with the archbishop only moments earlier had finally helped him make up his mind.

'Thank you, your grace,' he said eventually and turned to face the hall. 'Like my brother, my mind has been torn in two over this decision, as has my heart. However, this situation needs to come to an end, and in the light of a conversation conveyed to me by his holiness, the Archbishop of Canterbury, only moments ago, I have made my decision.' He looked around the room, lingering for a few moments upon Harold Godwinson, before returning to look at the archbishop. 'Your grace,' he continued, 'my lords, revered men of the church, Mercia hereby supports the motion that upon the death of King Edward, the next King of England should be Harold Godwinson.'

Chapter Thirty-six

Westminster Palace, January, AD 1066

Harold pushed his way through the many people filling the corridors of the palace. He had been asleep in the family manor in Southwark when a messenger arrived from Archbishop Stigand demanding he attend the king immediately. More than that, he did not know, but as he pushed his way through, he knew it could only mean one thing, Edward had taken a turn for the worse.

He reached the king's chambers and was ushered through by the guards at the door. Inside, the room was full of people, including those closest to the king in everyday life. The queen sat on the side of the bed, holding Edward's hand, while Edgar Ætheling sat near the fire, playing with one of the dogs as if nothing were wrong.

The other four earls were already there, as were several bishops and an army of physicians. Archbishop Stigand saw Harold enter and hurried over.

'Thank God,' said Stigand, 'I thought you had gone back to Bosham.'

'How is he?' asked Harold.

'Not good,' said the archbishop, 'and it is a miracle he has lasted this long. Come, he wants to see you.' Stigand led Harold over to the side of the bed.

Queen Ealdgyth looked up at her brother through teary eyes. Though she and the king had never had children, Edward had always treated her kindly, and they had a special bond.

'Harold,' she said, 'I am so glad you made it. He has been asking for you. Come, sit here.' She stood up, allowing Harold to take her place.

'Your grace,' said Stigand as the queen stepped aside. 'Harold Godwinson is here.'

Edward's eyes flickered open, and for a moment, he stared into space, struggling to focus. Eventually, he turned his head to face the man who had served him so well since the death of Godwin.

'Earl Harold,' he said, his voice no more than a whisper, 'you came.'

'I only regret that it was not sooner,' said Harold. 'Forgive me.'

'Nothing to forgive,' said Edward. 'They say I may recover, but I am no fool, Harold, they are just words to allay my fears.'

'And are you afraid?' asked Harold.

'I am not,' said Edward. 'I have spoken to the Lord in my prayers and believe that I could not have done anything differently. I am ready to go.'

'Then do so knowing that you were a good king,' said Harold, 'but more importantly, a good man.'

Edward started to cough, and the physicians ran forward to help him, but the king waved his hand towards them.

'Keep them away from me,' he said, 'there is nothing more they can do.'

Harold stared at the king. He was obviously fading fast. His skin was tight around his face and his eyes sunken into circles of darkness. The man who had once ruled such a strong kingdom was close to death.

'Harold,' said Edward, his voice weakening even further. 'Tell them to draw close.'

'Who?' asked Harold.

'The earls,' said Edward, 'and the bishops.'

Harold turned and summoned the men in. They all drew closer and fell silent, knowing they were about to hear the king's final statement.

'My friends,' said the king. 'The darkness closes in upon me fast, but there is one more thing to say. I know that my lack of an heir has caused angst between you all, but the time has come to put such things aside, so before I die, there is something you should know. At no time did I promise William of Normandy my crown – this I swear upon my deathbed and may God judge me if I speak false.'

'Your grace,' said Archbishop Stigand quietly, 'you will fly to heaven on the wings of angels, but until that moment, you are still our king, and I ask one more thing of you.'

'What is it?' asked Edward.

'Your grace, to help us guide this country forward throughout all that faces us, will you now, before all these good men, declare who is to lead us in your place.'

Edgar heard the question at the fireplace and jumped to his feet to join those at the foot of the bed with a smile of anticipation on his face.

King Edward closed his eyes and breathed deeply. For a few moments, nobody thought he was going to answer and everyone looked at each other with concern. Finally, he opened his eyes, and the room fell deathly silent.

'Men of England,' he said weakly, 'there is only one man capable of saving our country, and he stands amongst you.' He looked down to the smiling Ætheling for a moment before using the last of his strength to reach out to take Harold's hand.

'Earl Harold Godwinson,' he said, 'you have been a true and loyal friend to the throne. When I was right, you enforced my decisions. When I was wrong, it was you and you alone that pulled me back onto the right path. Let it be known across the land that I go to God knowing my legacy is in good hands, and to that end, I hereby declare that you, Harold Godwinson, Earl of Wessex, are my only heir, and therefore, upon my demise, the King of England.'

–

Several hours later, everyone gathered in the audience chamber of the palace, discussing the distressing events of the day. Soon after his declaration, Edward had passed away while holding the hand of his queen, and Archbishop Stigand had ordered the room cleared while he prayed over the body of the dead king.

The mood was sombre yet strangely focused. Yes, there were still many preparations to be made for Edward's funeral, but there was also a coronation to arrange, for, with the king's deathbed proclamation, any doubt about Harold becoming monarch had been swept away. As the ebb and flow of people in the chamber changed over the hours, many nobles, including those who had opposed Harold's nomination, now approached to pledge their unfettered support. Eventually, towards evening, Edwin of Mercia appeared and walked up to Harold.

'Well,' he said, 'you finally have what you wanted. I pray to God you are a strong enough man to deliver what is needed.'

'As do I,' said Harold.

'Just to make it clear,' said Edwin, 'I still hold you to your promise to wed Alditha.'

'I am a man of my word,' said Harold. 'Let us just get the coronation out of the way first.'

'Understood,' said Edwin, 'and after that?'

'After that,' said Harold with a sigh, 'we have to work out a way to defeat William of Normandy. And that, my friend, is a hill almost impossible to climb.'

Epilogue

Rouen, January, AD 1066

William of Normandy was sitting at a table enjoying a meal with his wife, Matilda of Flanders, when a servant entered with a worried look upon his face.

'My lord,' he said, 'Bishop Robert of Jumièges wishes an audience. He said it is urgent.'

'Send him in,' said William, 'we have finished here.'

The servant left the room as William's wife finished her wine and returned to her own chambers. A few moments later, the servant returned and showed the bishop in before stepping outside, closing the door.

'Your grace,' said the duke, 'welcome. Alas, you have just missed our meal, but I can have something sent up.'

'There is no need,' said Robert, 'for I have important news.'

'Go on,' said William.

'Duke William,' said Robert, 'my spies tell me that Edward died a few days ago, and yesterday, Harold Godwinson was crowned the King of England by their Witan.'

William stopped walking and stared at the bishop. '*What?*' he gasped. 'But he swore a holy oath that he would support my claim above all others. How could any man who so publicly breaks his word be worthy of kingship?'

'It seems he was absolved of that oath by the Archbishop of Canterbury before the coronation,' replied Robert, 'as it was agreed by their clergy that it was obviously made under duress. What is more, he has not only publicly denounced your claim but is actively rousing the people's opinions against you, assuring them that there needs to be unity lest you challenge his kingship.'

'Oh, I can assure you,' said William, 'there will be a challenge, of that there is no doubt. That crown belongs to me and me alone. Send word to my nobles and tell them to gather here ten days hence for a council of war. Also, arrange for every woodsman within a hundred leagues to start selecting trees for felling. If we are going to do something about this treachery, then we will need a fleet far larger than I have now.'

'My lord,' said Robert, 'it will take an age to build the number of ships we need for any sort of campaign against Harold.'

'Time is not the issue,' said William, 'England is going nowhere.'

'Understood,' said the bishop. 'But there is one more issue to discuss, something so unexpected that, at first, I refused to believe it.'

'And that is?'

'I have someone waiting outside who craves audience. He claims to have a plan that could bring Harold to his knees even before you have landed upon England's shores.'

'An unlikely claim,' said William, 'but I will hear him out. Bring him in.'

Robert of Jumièges turned and walked over to open the door, standing aside as a well-dressed man crossed the room to stand before the duke.

'Duke William,' said the man with a bow, 'I have travelled a long way to meet you and hope to be of service to you in any campaign you may launch against England.'

William looked at the strangely familiar stranger, instantly recognising the accent.

'And why should I believe you?' he asked. 'For all I know, you are here to spy on behalf of the English.'

The man stared right into the duke's eyes before responding.

'You should believe me,' he said, 'because I have knowledge that can be used to strike right at the heart of England itself. I am no spy, my lord. In fact, I am quite the opposite. I am Harold's brother, and my name is Tostig Godwinson.'

Author's Notes

In the telling of this tale, I have tried to maintain historical accuracy as much as possible, but as is usual in such novels, there has had to be some artistic licence to allow the story to flow. Any inaccuracies are mine alone, and I hope they did not distract from the fascinating story that led up to the Battle of Hastings.

Aelfgar – Earl of Mercia

In AD 1055, Tostig Godwinson's elevation to Earl of Northumbria caused anger amongst many nobles, not least of whom was Aelfgar, son of Earl Leofric, who coveted the earldom for himself. It is not clear if he caused his own exile by threatening the king, but his anger resulted in him fleeing England and raising a fleet of eighteen fully manned Viking ships from Ireland.

That same year, Aelfgar helped King Gruffydd of Gwynedd defeat his old rival, Rhydderch of Gwent, a victory that meant Gruffydd was, at last, the sole king of Wales. The victory meant that, for the first time, Wales was governed by a single monarch, resulting in several years of peace and prosperity. It is not clear if the Vikings took any part in the battle.

Once Rhydderch was defeated, Gruffydd and Aelfgar turned their attention onto Hereford, sacking the city and defeating Earl Ralf of Mantes, also known as Ralf the Timid. It is recorded that Ralf tried using cavalry in the fight against the Welsh, a tactic he was not used to, and his men paid the ultimate price.

Not long after the battle, Harold led his own men against Gruffydd and negotiated peace in the name of the king.

Aelfgar regained his earldom, albeit only of East Anglia. He was named Earl of Mercia when his father died in AD 1057.

Edward Ætheling

Edward the Exile (AD 1016 – 19 April AD 1057), also called Edward Ætheling, was the son of King Edmund Ironside. He spent most of his life in exile in the Kingdom of Hungary following the defeat of his father by Cnut the Great.

In 1054 King Edward sent Ealdred, Bishop of Worcester, to try and persuade Edward Ætheling to return to England to become his heir, but was unsuccessful.

A few years later, some records state that the same task fell to Harold Godwinson, who brought Edward Ætheling back to England, along with his family. Unfortunately, the new heir to the throne died soon after arriving in England, leaving his son Edgar as the nominal heir to the throne of England.

During his journey, Harold collected many artefacts from many places, including Ghent, Aachen, Cologne, Worms, St Omer, Regensburg, Metz, Rheims, Noyon and St Riquier. Eventually, he donated them to a non-royal collegiate church in Waltham.

The Battle of the Seven Sleepers

The Battle of the Seven Sleepers is another name for the Battle of Dunsinane, fought on 27 July 1054. It is believed that the location, although disputed in detail, was north of the Firth of Forth and likely close to Scone. Reports suggest that Siward of Northumbria led an army into Scotland to fight King Macbeth, but during the battle, his son was killed along with many of Siward's huscarls.

The exact date of Aelfgar's death is unknown, but it is highly probable that Harold took advantage of the situation to launch his lightning strike against Gruffydd at Rhuddlan. Many historians believe that his raid would have consisted mainly of mounted men to be able to strike and get out as soon as possible.

Gruffydd managed to escape the attack, so Harold and his men ravaged the surrounding area and burned his fleet before returning to England.

The surprise attack shocked Gruffydd and ensured that when Harold returned to the offensive a few months later, the Welsh king was in a far weaker position to offer much resistance.

The Second Attack on Gruffydd

On 26 May AD 1057, Gruffydd launched a combined attack on Wales from both the land and the sea. His brother, Tostig, commanded the land forces while Harold commanded the fleet and raided many towns and villages up and down the west coast. He also attacked the island of Anglesey in the north, ensuring that Gruffydd's armies struggled for food.

The campaign was well thought out and relentless. Harold and Tostig won many battles and took a lot of hostages until, eventually, the morale of the Welsh army broke, and they turned on their king, killing him themselves before turning his head over to Harold. Some records claim that he was killed by a man called Cynan ab Iago in retaliation for Gruffydd killing his own father many years earlier, but whoever was responsible, ultimately brought the war to an end.

Edyth and Alditha

Harold married Edyth Swanneck (or Edyth the Fair) in or around 1045, but it was only in the traditional ceremony called *more danico*, a form of marriage that was not blessed or sanctioned by the Church. It was, however, widely recognised as legitimate and accepted by most laypeople in England at the time. Edyth gave Harold at least five children, and it was she who identified his body at Hastings after it had been brutally mutilated.

Alditha (also known as Ealdgyth, a popular name at the time) was the daughter of Aelfgar of Mercia and was eventually married to King Gruffydd of Gwynedd.

Early in 1066, Harold married Alditha, uniting the houses of Wessex and Mercia. Some historians believe that the purpose of the marriage was purely to unite the two houses to face the growing threat from the Normans. As Alditha was the mother of Gruffydd's heirs, it also went some way to easing the tension with the Welsh, a people who once more were beginning to pose a threat to England. He went on to father one child with Alditha, a son who was born after Harold died in the battle of Hastings.

Harold in France

In or around 1064, Harold set sail for Normandy but was shipwrecked on the coast of Ponthieu to the south. Some records claim he had set out to find the two boys who had been taken prisoner by the Norman bishop, Robert of Jumièges, several years earlier.

When the local count, Guy of Ponthieu, discovered Harold and the survivors, he had them imprisoned with the intention of claiming a ransom for their release. However, William of Normandy found out and, with a combination of bribes and threats, convinced Guy to hand them over into his custody.

It seems that Harold then went on to fight alongside William in at least two campaigns, earning so much respect that the duke knighted him. During this time, Harold also rescued two of William's men from a river while crossing into Brittany (an image shown on the Bayeux tapestry), adding to his growing reputation.

During their campaign across Brittany, some reports say that William cornered Duke Conan in the Chateau de Dinan. After a brief battle, Conan surrendered the keys on the end of a lance, a scene that is again depicted on the Bayeux tapestry. Other reports claim that Conan made his escape via a rope out of a back window before rallying his men and marching to face William across the River Couesnon, a standoff that eventually came to nothing as both armies dispersed when their supplies ran out. Conan is said to have died in 1066 when he put on a pair of poisoned gauntlets. Some say it was a devious assassination organised by William himself.

Before Harold returned to England, William revealed his ambition to one day become the King of England and persuaded Harold to swear on a holy box that when that day came, he would support his claim. Harold swore an oath to that effect, and when the ceremony was done, it was revealed that the box contained holy relics, making the pledge even more significant.

The Northumbria Uprising

Tostig was not a popular earl, and in 1065, the region rose up against him, led by thegns Dunstan, Gamelbearn and Gluniarn. They took York, Nottinghamshire, Lincolnshire and Northamptonshire, eventually supported by Earl Edwin of Mercia and his brother, Morcar.

After meeting with the rebels in Northamptonshire, and keen to avoid a civil war, Harold recommended to the council of Oxford that the rebels' demands be met. Tostig accused him of colluding with the rebels, forcing Harold to swear an oath that this was not the case. Despite wanting to support Tostig, King Edward eventually backed Harold, and Tostig was outlawed. He fled to Flanders soon after. After the settlement, Morcar was made Earl of Northumbria and the rebels pardoned.

The Christmas Court

At the end of 1065, Harold realised that if the king did not survive, then England would be at severe risk from William of Normandy. With little other option, he understood, probably with the support of many of his allies, including some very senior clergy, that he was in a better position than most to claim the throne. Consequently, he started canvassing other noblemen for their approval, and in or around the time of the Christmas court in 1065, the nobles of England informally agreed to his claim.

More from the author

The Blood of Kings
A Land Divided
A Wounded Realm
Rebellion's Forge
Warrior Princess
The Blade Bearer

The Brotherhood
Templar Steel – The Battle of Montgisard
Templar Stone – The Siege of Jacob's Ford
Templar Blood – The Battle of Hattin
Templar Fury – The Siege of Acre
Templar Glory – The Road to Jerusalem
Templar Legacy – The Search for the Shroud

Other-Worlds
The Legacy Protocol
The Seventh God
The Last Citadel
Savage Eden
Vampire